RE: TELLING

An Anthology
of
Borrowed Premises,
Stolen Settings,
Purloined Plots,
and
Appropriated Characters

RE: TELLING

An Anthology
of
Borrowed Premises
Stolen Settings
Purloined Plots
and
Appropriated Characters

Edited by
William Walsh

AMPERSAND & BOOKS

Ampersand Books, LLC
St. Petersburg, FL
www.ampersand-books.com

Cover and book design by Christopher E. Katz, Pequod Book Design
PequodBookDesign@gmail.com

Cover contains elements of *Where There's Smoke There's Fire* by Russell Patterson, 1925

Printed in the United States of America

First Printing: February 2011

ISBN-13: 978-0-9841025-6-3

"Big Blue" originally appeared in *Camas: The Nature of the West*; "Borges in Indiana" originally appeared in *Del Sol Review*; "DesiLu Three Cameras" and "Law & Order: Viewers Like Us" originally appeared in *FriGG*; "Distractus Refractus Ontologicus: The Dissemination of Michael Martone" originally appeared in *Lamination Colony*; "Down at the Dinghy" and "Fire Walk With Me" originally appeared in *Titular*; "Go Ninja Go Ninja Go" appeared in *Pangur Ban Party*; "Mario's Three Lives" appeared in *Bound Off* and *Barrelhouse*; "My Secret Life as a Slasher" originally appeared in *Not What You Think*; "So Cold and Far Away" originally appeared in *Make*; "Why The Minotaur Remained A Virgin" originally appeared in *The Denver Syntax*; "Bartleby in Domesticity" originally appeared in *Handsome.*

TABLE OF

CONTENTS

EDITOR'S PROCLAMATION

...**Whereas** the Biblical; and
Whereas a redhead ruled a black & white world; and
Whereas the Borgesian and the Beckettian and the Musilian and the Updikian and the Martonian; and
Whereas the Godzilladelic and the Bunyanesque are both tales of dwarfing awe; and
Whereas the Abbaesque and the Madonnaish; and
Whereas the world's favorite plumber can buy a new life, again and again, with a mere one hundred coins; and
Whereas the Stonehenge remains, in essence, a dialogue; and
Whereas virginity has always been a bull market and sex is too often stolen; and
Whereas the Wolfian and the Abramsian and the Lynchian; and
Whereas the Humpert was one cracked egg; and
Whereas domesticity is a complex set of agreed upon preferences and preferences not to; and
Whereas the TMNT go and go and go; and
Whereas while the Devil can be found vacationing happily upstate, Odysseus is lost in hell; and
Whereas Jonathon Bender was *the* Burger King during the summer of 1975; and
Whereas the Milleresque and the Salingeresque; and
Whereas Jack and Jill were always quite fetching; and
Whereas Dickens was slashed but not done in by a self-confessed aca/fan; and
Whereas a stolen book is a liberated book; and
Whereas the Shakespeare has many tops but only one Bottom...

All thanks and honor to the retellers; and much appreciation to the per se publisher and good cook of this book.

William Walsh,
September 2010

MARIO'S THREE LIVES

Matt Bell

The plumber has three lives left, or else he is already dead.

Maybe he leaps across the gorge with ease, flying high through the air to land safely on the other side, the jump simple because he's been able to check the edge several times, waiting until he is sure of his footing, or else it's impossible, because on this world there's an invisible hand pushing him forward, speeding him along, forcing him to leap before he's ready. If that happens, then the plumber is going to die. Otherwise he continues his quest, sprinting and jumping to hit blocks with his head and turtles with his ass. The blocks contain either money or food, gold coins or else mushrooms and flowers he can devour to grow bigger or stronger. Sometimes, they make him fly or else shoot fireballs from his fingertips. Of course, he does not actually eat anything. The closest any of these flowers or mushrooms ever come to an orifice is when he jumps up and lands on them with his ass, just like he does to the turtles. He eats with his ass. He kills with his ass. His ass is a multi-purpose tool. Why do I have a mouth, he thinks, if I never speak or eat with it? He wonders if it's this way for everyone but there's nobody to ask. The only people he knows are the Princess, who's been abducted, and his brother, who is always missing but who the plumber knows would carry on his quest if he should fail.

The plumber always dies with the same surprised look on his face, his mouth hanging open as he flies upward through the air before being born again at the beginning of the world. He's tiny and frightened without his mushrooms and his fireballs, desperately banging his head against blocks, looking for more. Sometimes, between reincarnations, the plumber thinks he senses God trying to decide whether to give him another chance or to just bag the whole thing. He's scared then, but who wouldn't be? He prays for continuation and then God says Continue and the music plays that means the plumber will live again. Back in the real world, he realizes that the God he senses between deaths is there when he's alive too, guiding his motions. His triumphs are God's triumphs but so are his failures. It bothers him that God can fail but he doesn't show it. He is a stoic little plumber, looking for mushrooms and jumping on turtles, at least until after the Princess is safe and he has the time to think things through. Still, while he's alive and running or, heaven forbid, swimming, he sometimes realizes that the God Who Continues is possibly not the only god there is. Surely, that god isn't the one who put all the collapsing platforms and strange, angry wildlife everywhere. At first he thinks it's the Turtle King, the one who captured the Princess and started him on this whole adventure, but then he thinks, Who made the Turtle King? Not God, or at least not his God. Does this prove the existence of the Devil? He doesn't know.

The plumber stomps the tiny mushroom-headed foes who wobble towards him. They only kill him if he's completely careless, and he is not careless. He bounces from one head to another, crushing a whole troop of them without touching the ground once. He is an efficient weapon, and these lowliest of enemies are no more than an inconvenience. Later, crawling through a maze of green pipes, the plumber realizes that he doesn't believe the Devil made the turtles or their king, because that would mean the Devil also made the world and that he will not accept. He hopes he is on the side of good and decides that he must be. He is on a quest to save the Princess, and surely that is a good thing.

Now there is snow covering the land, and the plumber slips and slides precariously down hills toward open crevasses, his feet scrambling for purchase. He springs into the air and bounces off a winged turtle to reach a higher cliff, another slippery landscape. There is money everywhere, and although he picks up as much as he can, it never gets too heavy. His coins are constantly disappearing from his pockets, going who knows where, and all the plumber knows is that when he's found a lot of gold it makes it easier to come back after he falls down a pit or gets hit by some spiky creature thrown from the sky by a surprisingly anthropomorphic cloud. The more money he finds, the less he ends up in the Place Where One Waits Between Continues. He hates that place, with its tense anticipation, and so he looks everywhere for gold coins or else green mushrooms, which both make the same music and have the same life-giving effect.

Finally, he sees the castle in the distance. He's passed several fake ones on his way here, convincing replicas built on other worlds, but he knows that this is the real deal. The Princess is there and so is the Turtle King. He enters.

The plumber leaps across lava and disintegrating paths. He ducks under spikes falling from ceilings and kills every enemy in his path. His mouth, his stupid useless mouth, it is smiling. Soon he will save the Princess. He eats a red mushroom and turns into a giant. He eats a flower and breathes fire. The Turtle King must not defeat him. The music plays and the final fight begins, but the plumber cannot win. He dies until he runs out of lives and then he waits for God to say Continue. He waits for a long time and so he knows that God is frustrated with him. He wants to say, you're the one controlling me. It's your fault too. Give me one more chance, he prays, and I will do exactly as you say. I will jump when you say jump. I will run when you say run. I will hit anyone with my ass that you want me to hit. Please, just say the word and I shall be yours. God ponders and then says Continue, or else he doesn't. The plumber saves the Princess, or else the Turtle King conquers everything. There is no way of knowing what God will do until the moment he does it. He prays and prays. It's all any plumber can do.

Desilu, Three Cameras

Alicia Gifford

A new dancer is auditioning, stacked, bubble rumped, café con leche and legs like anacondas. Ricky imagines bending her over his conga, yanking that bushy dark ponytail like reins and ripping into her. He sits, watches, legs crossed, smoking a cigarette. He needs a dancer for the Jezebel number now that Connie is showing. This girl would make a fine Jezebel, he thinks, blowing perfect blue smoke rings.

Lucy can barely zip her capris. She balls up her face and wishes she hadn't had pancakes. Six of them! She's so damn *hungry* all the time. She peers into the mirror and squints. Crow's feet! How fleeting it all is. There's a knock on the door and it's Fred. He asks Lucy if Ethel's there. Lucy asks Fred if she looks fat and Fred rolls his eyes and says, yeah, I'm going to answer that. Where's Ethel?

Lucy tells Fred she has no idea where Ethel is; maybe she went to the store. But Lucy has a pretty good idea where Ethel is; Lucy's pretty sure Ethel's in 4B with that Mr. Ripley. Ethel's been like a cat in heat lately.

Well I'm *hungry,* Fred says, and he asks if Lucy has anything to eat and Lucy asks why everything always has to be about food, so Fred says, if you see Ethel, tell her I went to Mort's for pastrami, and it's coming out of her allowance. He leaves.

Pas*trami,* Lucy thinks. Visions of cured meats dance in her head.

Back at the club, Ricky takes the girl into his office. She says she's twenty-one but he doubts she's eighteen. The buttons of her blouse tug around her tumid breasts. She leans forward and warm moisture, the kind that fuels hurricanes, lifts up from her cleavage, filling Ricky's mouth. With narrowed eyes she tells him that she enjoys sucking on a good Cuban cigar. He asks for I.D. and she brings out a crumbled New Jersey license with a photo that may or may not be her. The March, 1931 birthday makes her exactly twenty-one years and one month. And she can dance.

She's still wearing the little calypso skirt she was shaking with an ass like maracas. He imagines sliding his hand up her sweaty thigh, finding her with his fingers. That's when she opens her legs and he sees the whole thing laid out like Sunday dinner. *Aye dios mío,* he says. *Estoy fregado.*

Someone pounds on the door and Lucy yanks it open. It's Ethel and she says she's in an awful mess.

Well at least you're not fat, Lucy says. She looks Ethel up and down. Never mind, she says. Ethel folds her arms and grimaces at Lucy, but then becomes distressed again, telling Lucy she did something awful, so Lucy says, I'll say, you're acting like an alley cat and leaving me ahem and a-humming to your husband.

I killed him, Ethel says, wringing her hands. Mr. Ripley. Bertram. Bert. He's dead.

You *killed* him? What do you mean you killed him?

I went to see Dr. Gottlieb this morning because of a female problem, and he told me, he said—Ethel hangs her head—I have gonorrhea.

Gono*rrhea!* Lucy says, her eyes big as ping-pong balls, and she asks again what Ethel means about killing Mr. Ripley and

Ethel says she went to his apartment in a rage over him giving her the clap and she smacked him hard across the face. She says that he lost his balance, back-flipped over the Chinese modern coffee table, and his head hit the brick hearth like an asteroid. Ethel starts crying. Oh Lucy, she says, it was just awful, like a broken egg.

So what'd you *do?* Lucy joins Ethel in the hand wringing.

I went to check his pulse but his eyes, both pupils black and huge. And his brain.

His *brain!* Lucy says.

Yeah, Ethel says. A bloody, gray blob poking out the hole in his head like the stuffing in Fred's chair. So I left and came here.

Fred goes to Mort's and orders a pastrami sandwich on rye with Swiss cheese, coleslaw and Russian dressing, with fries, and coffee. The waitress is a strapping blonde woman with ruddy cheeks and skin like a bowl of milk. Fred's always had a weakness for big blondes. He thinks back to the days when all he could think about was climbing onto Ethel. Man that was good sex. No place he'd rather be than buried in Ethel's big, warm muff. Fred takes a bite of his messy sandwich, Russian dressing oozes down onto his shirt and coats his lips. He watches the waitress. What he wouldn't give to have it all back again. When he started having trouble, he and Ethel never talked about it. The best part of them just stopped.

Ricky zips his pants and tells the girl she has to go. Here, he says, fishing out his wallet, take a cab. He hands her twenty dollars, and she takes it. Then she says, what about the job? I need to work, she says, and Ricky says that he's married and after this afternoon it wouldn't be a good idea for her to work with him at the club. He never wants to see her again. I'll call you next week, he says.

And she says, oh I know you're married, Mr. Ricardo. I've met your wife. See, to make ends meet, to pay my rent—*until I get a decent paying dance job*—I'm working as a shampoo girl where your wife gets her hair done. She talks about you all the time: Ricky this, Ricky that. Ricky, Ricky, Ricky.

Ethel takes Lucy into 4B where Bertram "Bert" Ripley lies with his feet in the air over the coffee table and his head in a small, black pool of blood at the edge of the brick hearth. The women wrap their arms around each other and then take quick, bitty steps toward the body. They brace themselves—then look down. One eye looks east, the other one west—same as they looked when he was alive. His dentures loosened on impact and are half out of his mouth. Lucy couldn't see what Ethel found attractive in this guy—she would've guessed him to be the "confirmed bachelor" type.

I didn't know he wore dentures, Ethel says glumly.

You didn't know he had the clap, either.

Oh Lucy, I was so embarrassed. I wanted to die when the doctor said gonorrhea. He thinks it's Fred.

Lucy looks sharply at Ethel—then they're bent over, snorting, squeezing their legs.

Oh honey, oh honey, Ethel gasps, *he thinks I got the clap from Fred.*

Lucy's face contracts into a wordless, squint-eyed, open-mouthed grimace. She shakes her hands. Ethel wipes her eyes on her sleeve and says she doesn't know why she's laughing; it's more tragedy than comedy.

There's a knock on the door then, and they recognize the voice of Mrs. Trumbull from 4D. Bertie, she warbles, I have a bowl of gumbo for you. Homemade and spicy—just like you like it.

Mrs. Trumbull! Lucy whispers. Just *listen* to her.

Ethel frowns, folds her arms. Bertie? Bertie?

Oh Bertie dear—spicy rich gumbo and cornbread for your supper. I brought the honey pot, too. Mrs. Trumbull giggles like a girl and Lucy's mouth stretches into a long oval, her arched brows knit together.

Ethel blinks and blinks, rubs her arms. *Bertie? Bertie?*

Then there's a jiggling in the lock. She's got a key, Lucy whispers. *Let's get out of here.* The women dash through the kitchen to the back door, but not before hearing a shrill scream and the crash of china. As they bolt out the back, they get a whiff of gumbo.

Ricky stands up and walks around to the girl. I hope you're not trying to blackball me, he says.

She laughs. I think you mean black*mail.* If you're asking would I tell your wife that you took advantage of me then gave me a job, no. You give me a dancing gig here, pay me seventy-five dollars a week, and I'll quit my job at the salon and never see Mrs. Ricardo again. Unless she comes here, that is. The girl smiles with giant, white teeth.

¿Aye qué barbaridad, esta mujer loca, por qué no puedo dejar estas cosas en paz? ¡Y maldita sea dios, la muchacha sí puede bailar! ¿Por qué necesita ella a enseñar me el coño? Necesito una Jezebel esta noche, qué caramba.

He struts and flings his hands and she pulls out an emery board from her pocketbook and calmly files blood red fingernails.

Fred orders a piece of lemon meringue pie. The waitress's name is Inger. Summers when Fred was a teenager he used to visit his grandparents in Minnesota and he'd go down to the swimming hole and watch the Swedish farm girls with their thick blonde braids and robust bodies splashing in the water and then sunning themselves. He remembers a girl, Sassa, out in her father's barn, how he shot his wad on sight of those dark, pink nipples and that wheaten bush. He thought he could've been happy being a dairy farmer, wearing overalls and pitching hay, married to one of those robust Swedey-pies bearing him babies and fixing him meatballs. But vaudeville called him, and he never looked back once he met Ethel.

He had a dream last night that doctors had come up with a potion, one that got your pecker back. Would that be something. Fred shakes his head, eats his pie.

Huffing hard, Lucy and Ethel make it back to the Ricardo's apartment. Within moments, they hear the plaintive wails of Mrs. Trumbull out in the hall. We have to go out there, Lucy says. It'll be weird if we ignore her.

Lucy and Ethel venture out into the hall and call up the stairs. Anything wrong, dear? Lucy says.

Is Mrs. Mertz there? There's been a terrible accident.

Lucy and Ethel look at each other. Oh no, they say simultaneously. What happened?

It's Bertie, Mrs. Trumbull says. Mr. Ripley, I mean. I'm afraid we've lost him.

Ethel freezes, wide-eyed, open-mouthed and Lucy shakes her by the shoulders. Snap out of it, she says. Ethel gulps, comes to. The women go upstairs to the apartment. Gumbo and cornbread are splattered all over the place and Lucy is starving again. She wonders if any of that cornbread is salvageable and then winces when she sees the body. It's a heat sink and she shivers. It's a color drain and everything goes black and white. She looks at Ethel and she's a pillar of salt. Mrs. Trumbull has already phoned the police and soon two officers stride in. One examines the body and looks around the living room while the other listens to Mrs. Trumbull explain how she let herself in to bring gumbo and then found him like this. They ask her why she has a key to his place and she says that she and Mr. Ripley are very good friends; that she often fixes his suppers and he looks after her since she's a widow and needs a man's help from time to time. Blushing, she says they've even discussed marriage.

Ethel's jaw drops and Lucy pinches her.

A detective shows up and confers with the uniforms. He looks around, checks the coffee table, the angle of the body. He squats down and inspects the man's face, shines a light on his cheek. Looks like he was slapped, he says. See, he says to one of the cops, a handprint, frozen in death. The detective stands and slowly looks around the room. He asks if anyone knows who might've wanted to slap this guy.

Oh no, Ethel says. He was a good tenant.

Goodness no, says Mrs. Trumbull. I loved him very much. She starts to cry.

No sir, says Lucy.

A woman, the detective says. A man would use a fist. Women slap open-handed. So a woman with a grudge comes in, slaps him, he falls back and busts his head.

Everyone turns to look at Mrs. Trumbull, and she faints.

Ricky is desperate for a dancer. Connie is around to teach the girl the Jezebel routine and he's confident she could learn it for tonight's performance, sparing the audience Connie's pregnant belly and udders. The girl is perfect but he knows she's trouble too. He could kick himself for being so weak, but the lure of strange pussy is something he struggles with. He loves Lucy even if she drives him crazy. He chastises her for being suspicious, and then he gives her grounds. It's not easy being Ricky.

All right, he says. You start now. Try on the costume and have Isabel make any alterations. And then you'll work with Connie to learn the routine. But I'm warning you, what happened today will never be repeated. Do you understand?

The girl tilts her head. What you say, boss. She stands and sashays out.

Ricky will replace her as soon as he can. During his dinner break he'll swing by Bloomingdale's and pick up something nice for Lucy, that perfume she likes—or maybe some sexy lingerie.

Fred finishes his meal and Inger brings him the check. She smiles but her eyes look through him. But what's to look at anyway—paunchy, balding—cherubic, maybe, curmudgeon, more like it. He leaves her an extravagant tip, resisting the temptation to take half of it back, and then strolls out onto the avenue, feeling full and a little urpy. He can't handle pastrami like he used to. He sits down at a bench to catch his breath, wishing he'd brought his jacket.

He's too grumpy with Ethel; it's his way of dealing with his lost wood—making like Ethel doesn't stoke him anymore. She's probably got it figured out but now he's stuck in the grouchy, long-suffering husband mode. Ricky confides in him about this molly and that one. He'd never felt the urge to cheat on Ethel; she filled him up. Sure, he'd see some cute little tail and he'd wonder, but mostly it just fired him up for his honeybunch.

The coroner arrives, inspects the scene and bags up Mr. Ripley. When Mrs. Trumbull revives, the detective asks if she'd go downtown and answer a few questions. In a daze Mrs. Trumbull staggers out between the two uniforms, her hair disheveled, a rip in one stocking, her legs spattered with tomatoes and okra.

Gee honey, Ethel says, wringing her hands again. Do you think I should—?

Don't you dare, Lucy says. If you tell them they'll get you for leaving the scene. Hit and run. The whole ugly mess will end up in the papers. Don't worry, they'll figure out that Trumbull's innocent. It was an accident, anyway.

They're back in the Ricardo's apartment and Ethel rubs her rear where the doctor injected the penicillin. Dr. Gottlieb said he wouldn't put it on my chart, for privacy's sake, she says. That's good. He also said that Fred needed to come in for a shot, too. I'll call him next week and tell him Fred got a shot at the men's clinic. Fred's an old goat but it'd kill him if he knew what I did. Ethel's face knots up. I didn't want to die without ever getting laid again. I'm hoping after the change I won't care.

The change! We're *light years* away from the change, Lucy says. Come on honey, I'll fix us a sandwich. Liverwurst on pumpernickel and a couple of cold beers will fix everything.

Ethel pulls a hanky from her bra and blows her nose. Got mustard?

Fred feels better after a few moments digesting, so he gets up from the bench and strolls back toward his brownstone. The park is lush with spring and he takes a minute to smell the flowers. He's going to take a nice snooze when he gets home. Then there's a good fight on TV and then, Sid Caesar and *Your Show of Shows.* Fred rubs his palms and wobbles his head. Hotcha, he says. If he could leap and click his heels, he would.

That night the Jezebel number is a smash. The gifts for Lucy—a spray atomizer of Chanel No. 5 eau de toilette and a lace peignoir—are wrapped in silvery paper under Ricky's desk. He and the new girl take another bow and Ricky's hand slides too far down her backside. Then the finale with the Babalu number. Next day critics will write that Ricky and his new dancer lit up the stage like St. Elmo's fire. Boffo, they'll say.

In the morning, Lucy kills a jar of pickled pig knuckles and makes a loaf of French toast. Ricky's still asleep. She shivers and her groin gets lust-achy recalling last night. That man! Ethel comes to the back door, enters the kitchen and pours a cup of coffee.

I just saw Mrs. Trumbull, Ethel says. Get this: she says the detectives realized her hand was too small and delicate to have made the imprint. They said Bertram Ripley was a well-known blade in the homosexual circuit and any one of his poufs could've smacked him. They're ruling it an accident. She sits at the table and stabs a piece of French toast with a fork.

A*ha*, Lucy says. A *pouf!*

Ethel goes on. Of course she's mortified, poor thing. Know what? I'm glad he's dead, using men, using women, what filth. How dare he? Ethel pushes an entire piece of French toast in her mouth and then swigs syrup straight from the bottle. She chews and swallows and chews and swallows. She dabs delicately at her mouth with a paper napkin. Fred's acting weird, she says. He wanted to cuddle all night long.

Lucy looks dreamy. I love cuddling. I could fuse with Ricky; melt right into that Cuban dreamboat like hot cheese. She rests her chin in her hand and sighs. He brought me perfume and lingerie last night. You know what that means. Lucy lights a Phillip Morris and does an expert French inhale. He's feeling guilty over something. And I just kept my mouth shut like a good little wife and let him make love to me. Boy did he make love to me. I had to smother my face with a pillow to keep from waking up the whole building when he—

For crying out loud Lucy, do you really need to tell me this? Ethel stabs another piece of French toast. I just killed my—what's it called?—paramour. Now it's back to life as Sister Mary Ethel. She butters the toast thickly and then douses it with syrup. You know, for a man of that persuasion, Bertie sure knew what he was doing. She shudders.

Those dancers *throw* themselves at Ricky, says Lucy. And me packing on the blubber. And getting crow's feet. It's enough to make you want to—

She too, grabs another piece of French toast. You know, Lucy says, if we could master sticking our fingers down our throats and throwing up after eating, we could feast like queens and maintain our figures. We could start a new diet craze.

Hey, that's a great idea, Ethel says. Ricky loves you honey. You can see it in those bulging brown eyes of his. Men don't confuse love and sex like we do. Hell, I'd about convinced myself that I loved queer boy.

The women laugh with wide, full mouths.

And get this, Ethel continues. I couldn't resist. I asked Mrs. Trumbull if Mr. Ripley was good in bed.

You *didn't!*

I did, and she said that he never pushed her for sex, that he was happy to wait until they married. Then I asked her if she was feeling all right and getting to the doctor regularly and she said, oh yes, she'd just had a complete check-up and a little infection she'd had in her throat had cleared up nicely with a shot of penicillin. Do you think?

Lucy flings her head back and forth and stamps her feet. Ethel snorts and chokes. They finish the French toast and then ravage some left-over spaghetti.

BORGES IN INDIANA

Michael Martone

The Pan Am Stewardess Saying Good Bye in the Door of the Airplane at the Airport in Indianapolis

He paused on the platform at the top of the stairs and said, "Ah, Indiana. It smells like corn."

The Comp Lit Student Who Had a Car

From Indianapolis to Bloomington, about an hour trip, I counted between him and the prof, seven languages. But I was distracted by the new car.

A Farmer in a Field of Clover Near Martinsville Spreading Manure

I saw a big new car going by, south, fast.

The Pharmacist on Walnut Street

He says, indicating this other guy next to him, this is Borges, and he has a head cold.

A Grease Monkey at the Standard Station

The filler cap was hidden behind the license plate. Little flappy thing. I saw him in the rear seat nodding his head.

The Brakeman of a Northbound Illinois Central Freight Waiting to Set a Switch on the Other Side of the Viaduct as a Car Passes Beneath

Smelled like rain.

The Junior High School Art Teacher Supervising the Elaborate Painting of Fire Plugs to Represent Various Patriots in Honor of the Nation's Bicentennial

This car stopped, and he asked me, he had an accent, to describe what I was doing. Can you believe it?

The Track Team Manager Scooping Out Dollops of Analgesic Balm with a Wooden Tongue Depressor

A car went by honking its horn.

The Morning Baker at the Sugar 'N' Spice in the Memorial Union Serving Him an Iced Fruit Bar Cookie

He said, "It has no nuts, yes? I can't eat nuts. Nuts give me gas." Something like that.

A Student in Front of the Von Lee Theater on Kirkwood Watching Bees Collect Around the Trash Bin There Attracted by the Dried Syrup of Spilled Cola

I told him: Careful. Bees.

A Waitress in the "Frangipana" Room Explaining How the Perfume Was Popular at the Time Hoagie Carmichael Wrote the Words for the Alma Mater Changing the I to an A so It Would Rhyme with Indiana

No, I am wearing musk.

The Flagman on 3rd Directing Traffic Around the Asphalting Being Done There Near the Green House

They were rolling up their windows real fast. The kid who was driving didn't want to take the new car down the wet street. He had no choice, see.

The Audio-Visual Guy Running the Lights at the Lecture

He erased the blackboard then clapped the erasers together a couple of times which made a huge cloud of chalk dust which he then walked through which coated him.

A Student Who Had Broken a Leg Slipping on a Freshly Mopped Terrazzo Floor Listening to the Lecture From His Hospital Bed

He was just beginning to say how he was reminded of Buenos Aires when the orderly starts to slop the floor with Lysol. I told him to knock it off.

The Union Board Representative Leading Him to the Podium

He sniffed the microphone before he spoke, like it was a rose or something.

The Mayor's Wife Giving Him a Bouquet of Roses after His Speech

And then he held them up to his mouth like he was going to speak to them or eat them. I don't think he can see so well.

The Daughter of the Professor Who Sponsored His Visit (a Toddler at the Time) Recalling the Visit Years Later in Her Best-selling Memoir

With a crayon I had drawn on the wall and I was rubbing my little nose against it and this sweet old man with moth-bally clothes who can hardly see, my dad always says when he tells me this story, leans way over right next to me to get a good look at the wall with my scribbles.

A Librarian Who Brought the University's Collection of Books to Be Signed Standing in the Back of the Hall Cradling the Editions

He knew I was a librarian. How the hell did he know I was a librarian? I must have reeked of it.

A Freshman Who Was Required to Attend Falling Asleep and Dreaming He Was Mowing the Front Lawn of His Parents' House in South Bend

I can't remember.

In the Darkened Light Booth a Theta Making Love for the First Time Coming, Her Face Pressing Against a Humming Electrical Panel Where She Saw Out of the Corner of Her Eye the Twitching Needle in a Glowing Dial Indicating the Fluctuating Sound Levels Emanating from the Stage

It was great. Just great.

A Teenager Pissing into the Empire Quarry Thinking He Had Been Caught

I was naked and about to shit my pants.

The Stock Boy at the A&P Grinding a Big Bag of Eight O'clock Coffee

The old guy, he didn't say nothing but held his breath.

An Old Woman in the Back Seat of the Third Car of a Funeral Procession Seeing a Man on the Corner of the Square Eating Popcorn from a Bag

I thought it was my dead husband.

Her Father Sitting Next to Her

I thought it was me.

A Clerk in Howard's Bookstore Watching Through the Window of the Store and Through the Windows of the Passing Funeral Procession

I was licking my thumb, counting money in the till.

A Yearling Gilt Roasting on the Spit of a Portable Barbecue Set Up for the Occasion on Dunn Meadow

At Night a Group of Fraternity Boys About to Pour a Large Box of Detergent into Showalter Fountain

This big old car circles around and the geezer in the back rolls down the window in the back to have a look-see.

A Reporter for The Herald-Telephone Lighting a Cigarette

He spoke to me in Spanish. Asked me for a smoke.

A Doctor at the Heath Center Washing His Hands After Taking a VD Swab Out of a Young Man's Penis Telling the Person Knocking to Come In

It's a Borges in two. He says he has a head cold and fever.

Mr. Frango Mincing Garlic for his Pizzas

"Can I have change on the phone?" Honest to God, that's what he said. Honest to God.

A Graduate Student Who Was Reading Borges on a Bench Making a Mental Note to Give Her Dog a Bath When Her French Lover Who Left Her Two Years Before to Go to Algiers Sits Down Next to Her on the Bench

I said, "Philippe, what are you doing here?" And he said, "Looking for you."

A Trumpet Major Blowing the Spit Out of His Trumpet Just as Borges Presses His Nose Against the Small Window in the Practice Room Door

I said hi, but he couldn't hear me. Soundproof.

A Sophomore Poet in a Workshop Watching the Great Man Slap Himself in the Face with the Paper Each Time He Is Handed a Worksheet

It was a ditto, man. He wanted the high.

Twenty Years After the Visit, a Sound Lab Technician Listening to a Tape of the Lecture

This platform is the stone ages. Scratchy, you bet. How should we label it?

Borges, Calling Home from a Phone Booth in a Pizza Parlor in Indiana Inhales, as He Speaks, the Scent of Talc Left by a Previous Caller

"It is snowing here," he said in Spanish.

A Man at the Counter of the Gun Store Sighting Down a Barrel of a Surplus M-1 Garand at an Old Man Across the Street Looking Up at the Courthouse

It had been recently oiled.

A Fireman Flushing the Hydrants on 10th Noticing in Passing How Small People Are in the Distance

Jesus, these plugs. They're a disaster.

The Night Auditor at the Union Hotel Running Room and Tax on 415 at 3:07 in the Morning

There was a pick-up error of nine cents on that folio which threw the house out of balance. I found it around five before he checked out. It was direct billed so it didn't matter much really.

At RCA a Quality Control Inspector Fine Tuning a Set for Shipping

His head is blue. OK. His face is red. OK. And now it is blue. OK. Now it is green. OK. Now it is red again. And that's OK.

At the Waffle House Eating Corned Beef Hash a Graduate Student Translating Says He Said

The eggs. The sunny-side up eggs. They look like eyes. Like eggs. Look, like eyes. Something. Something. Something . . .

On an Indiana Bell Pole a Lineman Completing a Splice Listening

It was in Spanish, I think. Spanish. I don't really know since I don't really know Spanish.

An Undergraduate in the Language Lab Listening to an Elementary Tape

These guys come in and look us over. I couldn't hear what they were saying, but for a second it looked like their lips were moving to what I was hearing on the tape. You know, le chat est sur la table, stuff like that.

On the Edge of Town a Woman Selling Concrete Lawn Ornaments

There. There, a deer. A chicken and a chicken with chicks. A frog. A frog. A frog. Another deer. A deer, there, there, there, and there. Ducks. Two deers. This goes on.

A Dog Tracking Something on the Lawn of a Limestone Ranch House

The Engineer of the Southbound Monon Freight Waving at the First Car Waiting at the Grade Crossing on 15th

It was ditch weed, you bet. I told the Maintenance of Way. Plain as the nose on my face.

A Bum in the Open Doorway of the 23rd Car of the Southbound Monon Freight

Spoiled grain. Old cardboard. Never get off where there ain't no shade.

The Conductor on the Rear Platform Turning and Walking into the Caboose as the Gates Begin to Lift

Something's burning.

A Man at the Next Urinal in the Rest Room of the Airport

I couldn't say anything to him under the circumstances.

The First Officer Asking If He Would Like to See the Flight Deck

It was pretty close quarters up there.

A Woman in Seat 7A Turning Her Head Away in Disgust

Oh, I knew I was pregnant.

A Radar Operator Noting an Anomaly at 0744 and Informing His Supervisor

It smelled like trouble, but it wasn't nothing.

HUMPERT

Daniel Grandbois

Humpert Dumpert had a great fall. It was only natural because he was a puff of wind and loved the autumn. But Humpert had a problem. He wanted to push a giant egg off a wall, as his friend had done to Humpty Dumpty, but all the kings horses and all the kings men, and Humpty wasn't ever coming back again. There weren't others like him either.

By winter, Humpert Dumpert wished he could stop blowing altogether. Yet, the world kept turning and pulling on his feet.

Then, he remembered Alice, the little girl who'd met Humpty once and had since taken to perching herself on the porch wall of her grandmother's house, rocking back and forth with her knees to her chest. If Humpert could cause some mischief there, he might begin to feel more like a gust.

But when Humpert's blows were fierce enough and in the right direction, the girl was not on the wall. What was worse, she began to sit there less and less, as the years stretched her awkwardly up.

None too early, the wind puff's moment arrived. Alice, now a young woman and rocking like an egg for probably the last time, tipped forward just so, and Humpert Dumpert had his way.

It was not at all like Wonderland.

WHY THE MINOTAUR REMAINED A VIRGIN

J. Bradley

When the minotaur opened his locker,
he found a pile of used spankies
and a note: *You are man enough*
for all of us. Please say yes

The minotaur thought of the way
their arms would sigh like shackles,
how no golden thread could lead him
back from between their legs.

In shop class, he made a promise ring
out of the rib of his last offering.
If the minotaur lets you live,
he'll show you the inscription:

"Love is not an open axe wound."

Bartleby in Domesticity

Darcie Dennigan

I am looking for an honest clause.
The salesman counters: Would a word do?
If you've got an honest one.
Yes. He is chuckling. Yes:

There was a man who named his child Fetter for he knew he'd forever be tied down.
Six months later, the child was abandoned.

I add *Fetter* to our list and leave the wedding registry desk.

He gives me twelve red roses.
What do they mean?
My love, what do you think they mean?

When I think of roses, nothing stems to mind.

Honeymoon in Florida.

Breakfast in an orange grove with famous recluse lexicographer Laura.

Over OJ, we all say nothing.

Three empty glasses adorn the patio table.

Laura finally says, Skin & bones.

What? my new husband says.

I whip at him, Shush! We are starving the language.

The anatomy of truth, I say to her. Yes, yes, okay!

Laura says, Don't say okay. You don't know okay. You are mishearing the signs.

Okay.

Dear, what shall our car bumper motto be?

Peace?

Not quite right.

What do you suggest?

War is not the answer?

Isn't that the same as peace?

No. Clearly peace is not the answer either.

But—

But—

Knock knock.

Who's there?

Any.

Any who?

Anyhoo, let's go on.

Tell me again why we had to name the dog Bartleby?

Because he prefers not to do tricks.

He won't even bark at other dogs. Is barking a trick?

The dog says a crowd is untruth.

When the honest word eludes, try to substitute.

I substituted *porridge* for *marriage.*
On all household documents, tax forms, what have you.
The boiling down, the grayness, and yes, the fortification—more accurate.

For *child*, substituted *held.*
My held.

For she was, and she was, and she was.
Are you hearing *hell* in there? I am not. There is a degree of viseness that is quite agreeable.

My held.
Called it, during the fetus stage, *to hold.*

And so on.

I prefer and so on to etcetera.
The latter goes by too quickly to convey sub specie aeternitatis with accuracy.
And fails to suggest hope of an end. Unlike *and soon.*

Why don't you ever say I love you?
I have endearment demophobia.
Why don't you like it when I say it to you?
You have endearment agoraphobia.

I wish we could shut ourselves up in a closet together.

Great Aunt Eileen, in a codicil to her will, left me a gift uxorial.
It's for when he wants to and I'd prefer not to.

It was her favorite word: *In-effable.*

Tell me again why we had to name the dog Bartleby?
Those mild eyes of his make me want to kick him.

I meant to say kiss him.

You have done both.
I have done both.

What did one tea bag say to the other tea bag?
The kettle's a-boil! We must, we must du-ty.
There is a vast unwritten clause—that I race and pound and skip to—that I palpitate to—

My belief in that vast unwritten clause brought it into being.
I invented the clause that I needed to heed.

Well, what is it?
Well, it's a low talker. I can't quite hear it.

Knock knock.
Who's there?
(muffled muttering)
Who? Who?
Exactly.

I think often of little Fetter out there.
To be able to accurately answer *Fetter* to any number of questions.

We must, we must do tea.

Friends, I cannot entertain you eternally.
The knocking, the ringing and dinging, grow louder.
I want to go where the lemons taste like orange juice.
We must, we must du-ty.

Can I be honest?
You are that abandoned baby named for chains?
Maybe. Maybe not.
Maybe is awash with wishwashiness.
Fine. Either/Or.

No more.
What is the reason?
Do you not see the reason for yourself?

I want to hold my held.

Do not think that I do not believe in marriage.
I have read somewhere of a fabled porridge, of oats mixed with silver leaf.
And the eaters of this porridge live all their days shitting lovely silvery piles of luminosity.

I want to go where people say the sea is green.
Is their sea green there?
No. But their language has no word for blue.
Would you have loved me there?
Maybe, if they had a different verb.

Why did our goddamn dog never bark?
That wasn't his response to the world.
What was his response?
To lie down.

That was mine too. I put my lie down all over the house.
I love you. Yes. Oh yes. Yes, why not. And so on.

MADONNA AND THE SEVERED BITS

Peter Conners

It is my job to mind the severed bits and the jars. To be honest, it is not too involved. Between dusting William Burroughs' fingertip, and making sure that van Gogh's ear is floating in plenty of formaldehyde; between overlapping Iggy Pop's strips of flesh with Sid Vicious' and back again, I have plenty of time to ponder things. There are procedures she insists that I must perform. And between them is my life.

Gezundtheit.

Madonna picked me up three years ago at The Dungeon Downstairs; a club where I'd been working maintenance for two years, since I was eighteen. I'm older now though, old enough to weigh the pros and cons of each position. At The Dungeon I was made to dress in very high heels and a leather corset that pinched my testicles. And I wore that outfit, sometimes with matching hood and clamps, through the entire twelve hour shift. replacing frayed ropes and loose strands on the whips, making sure that all binding straps were secure enough to hold any customer. Oh, how they hated when those straps gave out - customers and staff both!- and they all blamed me. So I became skilled and efficient in my work.

That was how I caught Madonna's eye, so to speak, in the first place.

Madonna was flogging an overweight woman with a large head and leather zippered mask when a strap on Old Splitter gave out. Old Splitter had been a thorn in my side from the start, so I was nearby and prepared when it happened. The big-headed woman watched while Madonna flogged me as I worked; she could hardly believe when I finished the job before her partner could draw blood. The woman checked and double-checked but the straps held. Skilled and efficient. Finished flogging, Madonna asked for my name. I told her, but she called me something different, something vulgar, and slapped my face and tucked one hundred dollars into my corset and sent me away. I could tell that she liked me though. One week later the boss called me in and told me that I had a new job, to report that same evening to a new address. Three years later I'm still here, performing maintenance on Madonna's severed bits and jars. And the work keeps me quite busy too; Madonna adds to her collection at least once a month. So busy, in fact, I once I remarked to the Lady, *Soon the Chamber shelves will be out of space,* and lost a nipple for my trouble. So now I say nothing. I accept the pieces silently and catalog them and keep them clean and dry and well preserved.

In most ways, working for Madonna is better than working in the Dungeon. I never have a day off, but it is much better having only one person to answer to when something goes wrong. I avoid this at all costs though. Here is an example: when Jerry Garcia's fingertip was misplaced. After hours of searching the chamber I heard Madonna return upstairs and quickly severed my own fingertip to fill the space in the collection. This deception did not work, though. Madonna knew immediately what I'd done and was most displeased with me. As a result, the matching fingertip was severed and I was made to crawl around on both until Mr. Garcia's finger could be located. (Under the Austrian grandfather clock beside the chamber door, for those curious.) And Madam was right, as always: I did learn my lesson and I am a lucky man. My job is actually quite simple considering the compensation I will receive.

Once my music is released I will never work again.

There are five separate sections to the collection. The sections are labeled Artist Bits (this includes musicians, writers, painters, etc.), Actress Bits (Madonna's most fervent passion, the cuticle of a young ingenue named Lana Marlou the latest addition. I smelled their dinner through the ceiling vent, Beef Wellington, a lovely perfume, they laughed until morning), Business Bits (Trumps' semen, Ford's left testicle, Winfrey's pubic hair, Morgan's foreskin - always genital related, this section), and two sections of unlabeled bits, one known as The Beautiful Ones, and one labeled Ancients. I am most curious about these Ancients - there are pieces of flesh, digits, ears, and fluids, that would turn to dust if removed from their vials - but only Madonna knows their contents. And I know better than to ask. Suffice to say, Madonna is a most industrious woman. I never fail to learn from her, and, as she tells me daily, that is compensation enough. I am lucky for all that I receive.

Although she has yet to reveal the true power of the bits, I have an idea of how they work. I am ejected from the room beforehand, but I notice patterns. In a way, these bits are as much mine now as hers. I see how they are arranged in certain ways after Madam has used them: a bit of Barnum, a touch of Kitt, a strand of Monroe's hair before each performance; a mingling of robber baron essences before a meeting; a mixture of ancient seductress' fluids before a date; an overlapping of all five categories before she goes out at night to gather fresh Beautiful samples . . . There are combinations for every occasion. All I am missing now is the language, the ritual, but Madam has promised these to me eventually too. And I think that time is coming soon.

For the first time in three years, Madonna has just asked me to join her upstairs for dinner. She tossed an outfit of tight fitting black clothes into the chamber and told me it was time. To put it on and come up. It could be a trick, I have been made to dress in costumes for the Lady's friends before, but this time it is different. I can feel it. She used the Business combinations tonight, and handed me a vial to drink as well. It was yellow, but it was not her urine. This was different. And I can hear a crowd gathering upstairs and can feel the fluid pass through my veins as I dress in the outfit. And I notice disrupted vials in the Artists section, Sammy Davis, Ricky Ricardo, Errol Flynn, and some others but I am moving too fast, too eagerly, to make them all out. The sounds grow louder as I climb up from the chamber. One hundred guests, maybe more. And suddenly I am moving with new grace, my arms and legs strong and coordinated in a way they've never been before. And my pupils shrink as Madonna throws open the door, light floods the stairwell, and even as I hear my voice I do not recognize it as my own. I am dancing. Singing. And men and women in dazzling formalwear are applauding my every move as Madonna slaps my behind and announces, *Ladies and Gentlemen, Mr. Ricky Martin!*, and before I know it I am singing at the top of my lungs in Spanish, on top of the world, and I have my own boy in the chamber downstairs.

JACK AND JILL

Jim Ruland

Up The Hill

They stumble from the station drunk with exhaustion. They haven't slept in hours, but are full of self-congratulatory cheer. They have finally made it to Amsterdam.

They want to do everything at once. Eat. Drink. Smoke pot. Fuck. Jack would like a beer. Jill is craving pancakes.

Look at the buildings, Jack says, impressed with the oldness of the train station.

Look at the people, Jill replies.

Overwrought Americans drag their suitcases across the square, the tiny wheels getting caught in the cobblestones. French girls lick mounds of ice cream, two to a cone. German boys fight over fried potatoes swimming in funnels of mayonnaise. Rowdy Englishmen, already splotched with sunburns, call out the names of pubs. A crusty punk wearing a t-shirt of Vincent van Gogh with a mohawk invites Jack and Jill to take his picture.

Jack reaches into his pocket. Jill pulls him away. She is fascinated by a group of Nigerian women solemnly crossing the square. Back in Indiana they'd be a spectacle, but here in Amsterdam they are practically invisible. Jill has come a long way, this trip is proof of that, but these women have traveled farther. She watches Jack study the pretty Dutch girls cycling past. Trim up top and muscular on the bottom, almost regal looking. Jack adjusts his backpack, runs his fingers through wavy brown hair that is neither long nor short, what Jill calls his soap opera hair. Ew, she says, plugging her nose, you smell French.

Jack and Jill take a taxi to their hotel, embarrassingly close to the train station. They are too tired to care, too wired for sleep. They drop off their bags, and head for the lobby bar, which shares a pool room with a café that overlooks a canal neither of them can pronounce. Jack announces his desire to go on a boat ride, see the city, get the lay of the land. Jill laughs. She wants nothing to do with any of that *touristy crap*, as if she could be anything but. Jack orders a bottle of beer. He realizes he sounds like his father, if his father had the balls to leave Indiana. But is it really so terrible his idea of fun is anchored to the practical concerns? Jack resolves to loosen up. Be open to new things.

Like marijuana brownies.

They stand at a counter, the glass smudged with fingerprints, examining the soggy-looking cakes, cookies, bars and brownies jacketed in cellophane. There are a million choices to be made, innumerable temptations that neither one is strong enough to resist.

What should we get? Jill asks.

Something mellow, Jack says.

We're on *vacation*, Jill scoffs.

I think we should start slow and work our way up, Jack says. The dreadlocked woman with dirty fingernails punching numbers into a calculator behind the counter nods at Jack's common sense. Or maybe she's flirting with him. Everyone flirts with Jack.

Jill notices. Not for the first time it occurs to her Jack might be more beautiful than she is. That chin, those shoulders, the *hair.* This has never happened before, and she's not sure she likes it. Before they left Summerset, she'd dyed her hair white blonde and wore it in braids, but here in Amsterdam she feels foolish. The women here are gorgeous without trying to be.

We're at the *hotel*, Jill says. We don't have to be *careful.*

Jack has already come to dislike the way Jill stresses certain words, not to emphasize their meaning so much as to underscore her low opinion of the intelligence of the person she is talking to. Jack's only known Jill a week, and she's proven herself willing to take full advantage of the benefits of his doubts. Besides, he didn't say "careful." He said "mellow." There's a difference.

I want to live here! Jill exclaims, and then she laughs. Her laughter turns heads, ignites smiles. It's not for Jack, this good humor. It's for anyone who wants a piece of it. Jack joins her, but it already feels like an obligation.

Jill picks out the smallest, most expensive marijuana brownie in the cabinet. Jack pays, fumbling with the new currency. The girl gives the package to Jill.

Can we eat it here? Jill asks.

You can do whatever you want, the girl says as she gives Jack his change, deliberately stroking his fingers. Jack smiles. Jill smiles. They all smile.

Jack and Jill eat half the brownie and play a game of pool while they wait for the drug to kick in. Jack lets Jill win, a decision he regrets when a guy in leather pants challenges Jill to a match. His name is Hans. Of course it is.

Halfway through their game, Jill gets impatient and eats most of what's left of their brownie. Jack gulps down the rest because he feels it's important they go through whatever it is they're going through *together.* The beers are making him sleepy, and he doesn't like the way Hans compliments Jill after every shot she takes. Or maybe it's the way Jill accepts these compliments Jack doesn't like. Either way, fuck Hans. But his friends are nice. Gregor and Sam. They each buy Jack a beer, and Jack wonders if this means he's supposed to buy the next round, because he's not sure he's going to make it much longer. He sits down in a chair, a very comfortable arm chair. The game doesn't seem to be moving along; there are incomprehensible lags between shots. Jill keeps disappearing. Jack can barely keep his eyes open. Then Hans is there. Wake up sleepyhead, and something Jack can't make out. Everyone laughs. Jill is looking out the window, peering down at the water in the canal, lost in some reverie.

Let's go up to the room, Jack says.

Jill nods and Jack is so, so relieved.

The elevator car is tiny, the hallway narrow. Jack feels like a giant in a doll's house. Neither one of them speak. In the room, which is a bed and a bathroom and nothing else, Jack strips down to this underwear and climbs into bed.

Come here.

I'm going to take a shower, Jill says from the bathroom.

Jack grunts, closes his eyes, and the feeling he had in the elevator returns, of lurching and jerking in a tiny space. Please don't let the bed spin, Jack says in lieu of a prayer.

He wakes several hours later to a darkened room, unsure of where he is. The other side of the bed is empty, hasn't been slept in. Jill is gone. No, not gone. Gone is a bad word for something that was never there.

Up Jack Got

While Jill is in the shower, Jack leaves the hotel room to get a cup of coffee, and decides to stretch his legs, ramble about for a bit. He imagines Jill calling out to him from the bathroom, his name floating around the empty room. It gives him an anxious feeling, but what's done is done. They'd agreed to wake up early, but Jill slept all morning, and when she finally got up she sequestered herself in the bathroom. Jill was a methodical shower-taker and made daily use of the blow-dryer, a sound Jack loathed, especially in the morning. He marvels at the way she emerged from the bathroom a new person, but today he doesn't have the patience.

The smell of the canal, dank and dismal, rises up to meet him. He's pretty sure it's Saturday. At the corner, a pretty girl with a hustler's smile hands him a flyer for the Vincent van Gogh Museum.

Is it close?

Very, she answers, flashing a smile with lots of teeth in it.

Does it have a café?

Oh, yes. You should go.

I will, Jack says, and he does. But Jack isn't the let's-go-to-the-museum type. He buys a ticket and wanders around the galleries, watching the pretty girls look at the ugly art. There's something about the way they stand, absorbed and un-self-conscious, that arouses Jack.

He stands before a painting of sunflowers, convinced it's a scam. *This* is what all the fuss is about? Jack is pretty sure he gets it--it's a sunflower, what's not to get?--but he wonders what he's *not* seeing. All his life Jack has gone with the flow of expectations. In Indiana, he fit the mold of a hayseed jock. He excelled at lifting weights and fucking cheerleaders a bit too well. It's all that was expected of him, and he willingly gave himself to these pursuits. To aspire to anything more was the same as saying *I'm better than you.* But Jack wants more than the weight room can offer. The affection of girls who keep stuffed animals on their bedspreads no longer appeals to him. This is why he's so attracted to Jill. She's different from anyone he's ever met. More worldly, more reckless, more everything.

Looking at the painting on the wall, Jack feels like he understands it entirely. No weird symbolism to grasp. No half-formed figures to pretend to comprehend. This confuses him.

He expects more from a genius. Having grown up on a farm, Jack is no stranger to sunflowers, and these don't strike him as a particularly competent depiction. Look at all the paint van Gogh used. It looks like he smeared it on with a trowel. Jack wants it to be more complicated than it is.

In the museum bookstore he purchases a van Gogh biography. He takes the book to the Hard Rock Café. It rained while Jack was in the museum, but the sun has come out, and the sunlight glints brightly in the puddles on the sidewalk. Jack orders a Heineken and reads about Vincent taking up with prostitutes, Vincent drinking absinthe, Vincent roaming the streets of Paris with a pistol in his pocket. No question about it, Vincent was a crazy motherfucker. Jack will never go mad, and the thought depresses him a little. There are tales of lunacy on the fringes of his family. Gruesome examples of prairie madness. He has a cousin who'd cut his own throat during a thunderstorm. And someone's sister had hung herself from a ladder in a haymow. But it will never happen to Jack. Few things put him out. He has little or no ambitions to fall short of. He's never known guilt as a motivator. Jill is right: he's too careful.

He was raised by bootstrap Baptists who took a dim view of excessive invocations of fire and brimstone. His father believed it wasn't a good idea to become overly preoccupied with the next world, not when there's so much work to do in this one. As for his mother, Jack has no idea what she believed. He did his father's bidding, going along to get along. They all had, and now here Jack was in a strange city in a foreign land doing precisely the same thing with a woman he can only pretend to know.

Still Life

Jill is from the city; Jack comes from the country. They met in a place that is neither. Jill left to escape what she had become. Jack came to become something he isn't. They despise everything about the place. This is their one and only bond.

They met at a rave in Summerset, Indiana, years after raves went out of style. Jack didn't know. Jill didn't care. Her beauty didn't work on Jack, didn't give him a moment's pause. They were the best-looking people at the party. Jill could bide her time.

Jack and Jill went out for breakfast after the rave. Jill knew a place. As the sun came up and their first night turned into their first morning, Jill dug a brochure out of her purse and presented it to Jack. She'd been carrying it around forever. In old movies, people were always being asked for their papers. These were hers. She flipped through the wrinkled panels until she reached the map of Amsterdam in the back. Jill loves maps. When she first studied the brochure, she was surprised by the number of canals, all those rings of blue. She had no idea there were so many. Jill jabbed her finger at a place near the heart of the city. Here is where we'll stay.

Okay, answered Jack. Slowly, deliberately. When do we leave?

The dance beat that had been drumming inside Jill all these years jumped up a few notches.

When Jill Came In

Jack and Jill move into the apartment recently vacated by Hans's friend Sam. Sam had had second thoughts. About what Hans didn't say, and Jack was afraid to ask.

They pool their traveling money to cover the first month's rent, and the purchase of several hundred Ecstasy pills, which Jack and Jill peddle to tourists. Jack works the bars in the Red Light District, Jill the clubs. Jill sells twice as many pills as Jack, but he only works a couple times a week. Jill goes out almost every night and sleeps all day.

It's an unusual room. The walls are painted a dingy lemon yellow that matches the floorboards. The room has two sets of windows: one faces the street, the other gives out on to the hallway. Both sets have been painted shut with green trim. The bed is broken and lists to one side. At first Jack thought it was the mattress, sagging from all the traffic, but now suspects the frame is to blame. It isn't level. Jack finds it difficult to sleep in. He keeps rolling toward the edge, as if gravity is pulling him toward the floor. Jill has no trouble sleeping in it. She huddles near the wall and swaddles herself in sheets, like a cocoon on a twig.

Jack putters around the apartment, opening and closing cabinets he knows are empty, waiting for Jill to come home. To save money, Jack eats one meal a day, and he's hungry all the time. When Jack can't sleep, he reads, and when he can't read, he masturbates. When he's finished with the biography, he moves on to a collection of van Gogh's letters that Sam left behind. Jack doesn't know what he hopes to discover, but he's fascinated by the artist's schemes to get more money out of his brother, Theo. This reminds Jack of Jill. He can't put the book down, can't stop reading. As long as he keeps turning the page, he doesn't have to wonder where Jill is, when she's coming home.

The sun rises, migrates across the sky. Jack is hungry, but he doesn't want to leave. It's well past noon. Jill has never been this late.

Jack wrestles the bed away the wall and measures the length of the legs with a piece of string. It's not the bed. The bed is true. It's the floor that's screwy, slanting toward the canal-side wall like a drain.

The floorboards in the hallway creak. A shadow passes on the other side of the curtains. Jack pushes the bed against the wall as Jill comes through the door. Her eyes tell the story: darting and desperate. Something terrible has happened, she says.

No shit, he thinks, doesn't say.

I lost it.

Lost what?

Everything, Jill says.

Everything?

Money, passport, pills. It was all in my purse.

How could you, Jack says without thinking.

Jill collapses in his arms, hot tears spilling down his naked chest, and Jack wonders how something so beautiful can be so broken.

Jill Falls Down

Jill performs her first trick by accident. She is sitting in a train station depot, waiting for the cafe to open, when a man who'd caught her eye because he resembled her father, whispers *How much?* She feels wretched and looks worse, but doesn't hesitate.

Five hundred.

Dollars?

She meant guilders but nods anyway.

The man takes her to his hotel room across the street, and that is that. No big deal. A joyless kind of problem solving. Jill is accustomed to using her beauty like a shield, and this is no different. If she learned anything from her mother, it's that a smile from a beautiful woman can be more devastating than a scowl. Semi-self-interest, semi-self preservation. She's not sure which she's acted out of. At least the semi-self part is right. She even had the sense to ask for the money first.

Jill gets braver and bolder, more forward. She cultivates the look of a depressed party girl. She wears makeup that obliterates the circles around her eyes with darker rings. She wears boots in favor of heels. But she has to be careful. There are mornings when the image that confronts her in the mirror is dreadful. But Jill isn't an addict; she's one of those girls who never want the night to end. Amsterdam is crawling with them. As much as it kills her to admit it, she is by no means exceptional here.

Jill meets some of her best clients through girls just like her. They point the way, tell her where to go. The key, they tell her, is to work the district without becoming a red light girl. When that happens, they own you.

Jill sticks to the blokey bars popular with tourists. Sports bars and sailor bars and bars with photos of pugilists on the walls. Men gather here to drink and work up their nerve before approaching the women in the windows. Jill will pick out a group of footballers with funny accents, men from Belfast or Edinburgh or Liverpool. She'll watch them crash their pints together and slap each other on the back. When they start shouting team slogans at one another—*Don't let the bastards grind you down!*—she knows they're ready. Jill will proposition the most gregarious fellow of the lot, their de facto leader, and work out a rate. Then she'll go with them to their hotel and fuck them silly.

(One at a time; she isn't a freak.)

The first time Jill did this she made enough money to take the rest of the weekend off. She bought a shitload of hash and got a hotel room near the station. Jill spent the weekend in bed, alone, getting stoned and watching news dispatches from around a world more complicated than she ever could have imagined.

Jack On The Town

Jack goes to a nearby Internet café to check his e-mail, catch up with friends back in Indiana, figure out how to leave Jill, and get the hell out of Amsterdam.

At the café, he bumps into Olga and Elka, attractive cyclists from the Rhineland. They've been smoking hash and seem a little outside of themselves. Olga's cheeks are flushed; Elka keeps sweeping her hair back, her gray eyes crackling. They are pretty and forward, a combination Jack finds irresistible. They're all over him. Show us a good time, they say. Jack obliges.

They go out for drinks, take Ecstasy, go dancing. Jack and Elka make out on the dance floor. Then Olga and Jack. Then Elka and Olga and Jack. They mash their mouths together and sway to the beat of a song remixed so many times it feels both foreign and familiar.

In the cab, Elka hauls out his cock. Olga gasps. Jack closes his eyes. The map of the night unfurls like a silk flag, rippling and undulating in the secret wind.

They go to their apartment on the outskirts of the city. Jack's never been here. It's not a place tourists go. Off the map of Jack's world. There are no bicycles. When they are finished fucking, the women announce in bad English they have a confession to make.

We are not tourists, Olga says.

We are not even German, Elka adds.

No? Jack asks, pleasantly confused.

Olga shakes her head. It's a game we like to play when we get stoned.

German girls will fuck anything, Elka says by way of explanation.

Then who are you? Jack asks.

Olga takes a card from her purse and hands it to Jack. LIVE SEX SHOWS. You want to put that monster to work, give this number a call.

Ask for Ingeborg, Elka says.

Jack turns the card over, and there's the phone number. Then Olga asks him to leave.

In the taxi, Jack decides to call the number. He'll have the adventure he came here to have, and then he'll go back to Indiana.

Jack returns to the room he shares with Jill as the sun comes up. Jill wakes, tired and out of sorts. Where have you been?

Job interview, he tells her.

Red Lights

You will need a partner, Ingeborg says.

Jack hadn't thought of that. He runs his fingers through his hair, embarrassed to be so ill-prepared. Maybe she knows someone. Maybe--

We have a list of applicants you may consult, she continues, but the decision is yours. You must take full responsibility for your choice. It's a business arrangement, but of course it is more than just business.

Jack nods his head. He waits for her to say more, but that's it. Interview over.

He takes the list to a bar. It is Friday afternoon, and the district is starting to sizzle. Expectations charge the air over the canal-side sidewalks. A group of English tourists heckle passersby. Seated under a portrait of a clipper ship, Jack consults the photocopied pages. There are so many names. It staggers him that in a few days he could be fucking one of these women for money in a room full of strangers.

His eye is drawn to the least Nordic name on the list: Esperanza. He walks to the hotel he stayed at his first night in Amsterdam, and calls her on the house phone. She's not far, she tells him, just a few blocks away. I'm working. Come on over.

Jack heads east, gets there in no time at all. There she is in the window, inside a rectangle of red neon, hands pressed against the glass. She wears a white halter top, matching denim shorts. She is small and lithe, her skin darkened by tattoos he yearns to study. He catches her eye, winks. She waves him over to the door.

Esperanza meets him in a hallway so tight and narrow the patterned wallpaper seems to vibrate. Jack stoops to whisper, explains the situation. She's apprehensive. She tells him to keep his voice down. She is so small.

Let me see it, she says.

He unzips his trousers. She goes for it as soon as his fly is open, cooing in approval. Jack feels a twinge in the chest, a trapdoor opening. Esperanza looks up at him with eyes that are easier to admire than interpret. Her lashes are impossibly long, too disorganized not to be real. She catches him and smiles in girlish embarrassment. It's an act, of course. It has to be. She has his cock in her hand but blushes because he stares? Jack laughs and she gives him a second smile, as if she had been caught being bad and would relish the punishment. This unravels him, his desire filling him out.

I will fuck you now, she says. But you have to pay. I hope you understand. She casts her gaze at the bad wallpaper, the shitty carpet. She wants him to know she is trapped, but has not yet lost hope.

Yes, Jack says. He doesn't want to talk price. He doesn't care what it costs.

They crash into a tiny room with a high ceiling and a low bed. There is a red lamp on the nightstand. They kiss. The clothes come off. He plunges into her. They both cry out. She burbles something in Spanish or Portuguese, urging him on. She wants it. He gives it to her. Each movement is question and answer, call and response. A hitch of the hips, a shift in rhythm is met with a breathy exhalation, an urgent exclamation. Esperanza comes and the performance tears an orgasm out of him. Jack didn't think he was ready, didn't know he was close, but it flies right out of him, as if she willed him to come. Jack is still hard. Esperanza wants more. He gives her everything she asks for. They go at it for the better part of an hour. When they are done, he's pretty sure he's broken the headboard, and the sheets on the bed are soaked through with sweat. Jack fights the urge to curl up in a ball at the foot of the bed like a question mark.

Partners? Jack asks.

Ssshhh, Esperanza answers. It is still too soon for words. She reaches over, puts her hand on his breastbone where the hair on his chest is damp. I am not finished with you yet.

Self Portrait

Jill wakes up in the toilet. For a moment she lets herself believe she is back in the apartment. She imagines Jack in bed, a paperback steepled on his bare chest. She loves him this way. So handsome, so harmless. But Jack didn't come home yesterday. It's been… She doesn't know how long it's been since she's seen him. She has no idea where she is or how she got here. She is only wearing some of her clothes.

Jill opens the door and sees a man asleep in the bed. Her denim jacket is hanging on the back of a chair. She creeps into the room and slips it on. It is a tiny studio apartment. Bedroom. Bathroom. No kitchen. Only men can live like this. There is her bra on the floor next to his pants. She stuffs it into her jacket pocket. Her panties are wadded up in the folds of the blanket at the foot of the bed. She unkinks the black thong and quickly steps into them. It is like a game. Connect the dots. With each item she recalls a new piece of information from the night before.

Jill went to a café to score from Hans's friend Sasha. She likes Sasha. He is super-good looking but never hits on her. He wears tight clothing and shaves his head. Possibly, probably gay. She remembers meeting up with Sasha, and he took her to a party where she met… Someone. And here she is. That doesn't seem quite right. Jill recalls a bar, shots of something sweet. She spies the toes of her boots peeking out from under his jacket on the floor. If she can just find her fucking purse she'll be on her way. Jill is starting to freak out a little when she sees it hanging from the knob on the bathroom door. She checks to see if her pills are there and—surprise, surprise--finds a thick sheaf of guilders. So she did fuck him. Good for her.

Jill shuts the door with a click and hears her name being called from the other side. She doesn't know why this startles her, but it does, and she runs down the stairs. She hears her name again, louder this time, with a bit more urgency than she is accustomed. No instructions. No orders or entreaties. Just her name. Jill flees the tiny vestibule. She doesn't recognize where she is. There's a canal, but she doesn't know which one. She turns right, follows the water. She's five hundred meters away when she hears it again: *Jill! Come back!* Calling to her from a window, perhaps? She tries to remember Sasha's friend handing over the money, but she can't, which means there is a better than good chance she took it.

What are all these people doing in the street so early? It's a museum, a famous address. The Anne Frank House. She goes to the front of the line and buys a ticket. No one stops her. She convinces herself it's a kind of chivalry, the whole damsel-in-distress thing, but this is not the case. One look and they know everything. She's all distress and no damsel, another cautionary tale for the kids lining up alongside the canal. Well fuck *that.*

The museum is boring. Jill has no interest in the commercial concerns of the warehouse Anne Frank's father worked in before her family went into hiding. Jill could care less about the girl's diary, when she re-wrote it, who edited it. These things do not interest her, but in Anne's famous bedroom in the secret annex, Jill finds herself weeping. She did not expect this. She knows the story. She's heard it all before. Anne was sent to the camps, separated from her family, gave up hope and died. Less than two weeks after her death, the Allies liberated the camp. Tragic, right?

But that's not it. It's the ordinariness of the place that gets her, the little things that make it a home. The pictures on the wall, the sweater hanging on a hook. These things speak to her, awaken the past inside her. Anne hid from the world for two years; these are the rooms.

Jill wants to go back in time, back to old Amsterdam and

shake Anne by the shoulders. *Never lose hope*, she'd tell her. *Don't let the bastards grind you down!*

But if this is truly how I feel, Jill asks herself, why can't I stop crying?

Broken Crown

Jack works with Esperanza for a week, which is long enough to figure out he is completely infatuated. And then she disappears.

Esperanza doesn't show up for work, doesn't pick up the phone when Jack calls. Same story the next day. He looks for her in the club where they work together and the window where she works alone. Nothing. Jack goes back to Ingeborg, the woman responsible for the who's who of Amsterdam sex workers, but she's no help.

If I had any more information, she says, I wouldn't give it to you.

Jack is devastated. His feelings for Esperanza are complicated. Jill was an escape; Esperanza is… Jack doesn't know. Hope, maybe? The impossible made possible? If there's a better definition for love, Jack doesn't know it. Falling for a sex worker is the biggest cliché there is. This he knows, but it doesn't stop him. He takes to the district, going up and down the streets, peering in windows, prowling the bars. He is driven. He is obsessed. Perhaps there's a little van Gogh in him after all.

After searching for several hours, he stops and orders a beer, watches the people go by. In a window across a narrow alley from the bar, Jill watches Jack. There's something different about him, an intensity that wasn't there before. She adjusts her bra, tugs on her skirt, the one she bought for herself on Valentine's Day. Jill can't stand still. She lights a cigarette. Flips her hair. But Jack doesn't see her. It's like she's invisible.

At a table next to Jack, English tourists, besotted on Guinness and Strongbow cider, commence negotiations. They all want to blow their wads, both literally and figuratively, but no one possesses the courage to be first, to risk their mates' disapproval. For the moment they are content to make faces at Jill.

Look at this blond bird, a swaggering bastard calls out to his mates. You suppose the curtains match the carpet?

Aye, another says. I'd like to give her a jump.

Feckin' gorgeous, chimes another.

From three pints away she is, says the first. That gets them all laughing.

Jack turns and sees Jill in the window. Compelled by urges he doesn't understand, he rises to defend Jill's honor. His one and only punch takes two teeth out of the comedian's head. Jack turns to face the man's mates and is tripped up, kicked in the knee, brought down to the slippery floor where he is glassed, gashed, and stomped on before the bar staff muscles the mob aside and shoves Jack out the door. Though what Jack believes is beer sheeting down his face is actually blood, he isn't done yet. Jack has only just begun to put up a fight, to show these people what madness is made of. Come on out! he shouts. The Englishmen burst out of the bar and Jack knocks a few down before they bury him. They lift him up, two to a limb, and heave Jack into the cold canal. Gravity takes him down, down past the greasy murk, through the silt of centuries of filth, to black depths the light of no star has ever reached, and Jill comes tumbling after.

MY COUNTRY IN SEVENTEEN ROOMS

Samantha Hunt

Stephen Blumberg, the world's greatest book thief stood before the court while the judge sentenced him for stealing 23,600 extremely rare books and 10,000 manuscripts. See, the greatest. The judge raised his gavel, started to speak and, in that, moment, Stephen thought:

> I was taking a nap in Ottumwa when some words slipped from the books where they lived. Soon the air was thick, a bit musty. Some of these words came from the last history book that didn't mention Christopher Columbus. These words were old.
>
> The room was vibrating. The shelves, standing floor to ceiling, covering even the windows in all seventeen rooms of my house, looked funny. So many words made it tough to breathe. I got an "of" down the wrong pipe. First edition *Leaves of Grass*, in fact. I sputtered and coughed but the sound drew the words to attention. The room cleared. The words were stunned back into their books.

The judge licked his lips, drew breath. Stephen thought:

I could get a dendrologist, a lady who studies trees, to take a core sample across and through the stacks of my library. That'd be some sample. It'd say, "America, you're resourceful. You're cunning, dirty, brave and hungry."

I am hungry. I wish I had a Saltine.

Then he thought:

The past is like a warm tub of water. I sit and soak. Yellow light. Dead people watching over my good deeds, saying "Don't *forget McLoughlin and Old Oregon: A Chronicle.*"

"First edition *and* manuscript," another might add.

I didn't forget.

I remember how the 1480 Coburger Bible spoke to me in a high falsetto. "Save me, Stephen. Save me!" I spun, imagining that if I built up enough centrifugal force my superhero self would be able to rescue books everywhere. Instead, I just got dizzy. I sat down until the book shelves stopped spinning. "Hold tight, Momma," I said to the 1480 Coburger Bible. "I'm acomin' ta git ya."

Nineteen tons of books was the final tally.

The judge was speaking. Stephen tried listening. He was being scolded. Stephen went back to thinking:

All my heroes are dead.

And then he wondered:

Did they tie my horse up out front?

And then:

In every library a cushion of words lifted me , a little cloud carrying its champion. I'd give a royal wave to the stacks of American history, incunabula, special collections. King Blumberg.

And then:

That's right. People don't ride horses anymore.

Stephen thinks:

I am an insect. I could smell danger if danger were on the approach. After hours I stayed behind. I slipped into an elevator shaft moving quickly before a car carrying the last of the cleaning service crew crushed me. I carried dentist's tools. I pulled myself through a ceiling panel and waited until the lights went out. I found a University of Minnesota faculty ID and it was God saying, "Take this. Use this." I attached myself to a grappling hook, lowered myself down to a window I'd unlatched during the day. I gained too much speed too quickly. I almost missed the window. But I am a bird. I didn't miss the window. I slipped through, still attached to the roof. I dangled nearly thirty feet above a patterned marble floor, having run out of rope. I sniffed the air. "Smells like suffering." I spat down to the floor before jumping the remaining distance without incident or bodily harm. I am a cat.

> I am an insect, a bird, a cat.
>
> I bet most people can't even imagine what nineteen tons of books looks like.
>
> Carried horse pliers in a special coat. Metal surveillance tabs spiked into spines. Those really get me.
>
> Look, here's my hand worshipping the margin of an old book. I am writing something there. Look what I am writing. It says, "Genuflect, genuflect, genuflect."

And then:

> I know what those librarians are doing. They're downloading all the books.
>
> Fuckers. There's no leather-bound register of my times and accounts, as there is for, say, Nathan Hale or Jesse James or Brigham Fucking Young. They put me in the computer. Yeah. I'm gonna get someone for that.

The judge was spitting. His veins flushed purple. Stephen imagined he saw:

> A dictionary page that said "Stephen Blumberg" next to HERO and the definition in between —*95% of the libraries he stole from never knew their books were gone.*
>
> Where are all the missing books? If a person is missing we can write dead at least halfway, *de*, the electricity shut off and undetectable to radar. But a missing book still emits its message from a dark place or a mishelved place or a hostage situation. Like this: *Everywhere he feels his heart because it vessel run to all his limbs*
>
> -The Secret Book of the Physician from 1500 B.C.

My country in seventeen rooms in Ottumwa, Iowa, a town on a river. At one end of my house are the books about California, Oregon and Washington. Throughout the middle rooms Minnesota, Kansas, Texas. New England and the Atlantic States are on the other side of the house and the bathroom functions as an immigration center for processing new arrivals.

Will they have a library in prison?

Oh, the sketch I will draw — a tremendous statue of me, wearing my deep-pocketed coat. The statue could stand outside the Ottumwa library teaching children about the liberator of American history books.

Entering a plea of insanity is difficult when you are as clever as I am.

Stephen thought:

The Library of Congress at night.

And then:

When will someone from the government say to me, "Keep on stealing books Stephen! That's who you are! That's what you're good at! The greatest book thief of all time! If I were you I'd continue to steal books. I would steal books from the prison library. I'd steal books until the United States acknowledges that you are the finest at what you do and so deserve a promotion to ambassador or minister or greatest hero and at a State Dinner held in your honor all the ladies there would hold onto your hand a bit too long when they met you. And afterwards, on their drives back home the ladies would think about you and demand that their husbands stop at a convenience store. Here the ladies would give their husbands explicit instructions. 'Do not return to this car until you have stolen me a candy bar or a stuffed teddy bears or a six pack,' and she'd say it because she'd be thinking of you, brave Stephen."

The gavel reached its highest point. Then:

Nineteen tons

Then:

Oh. My trusty horse.

And the judge brought the gavel down like the slam of a heavy prison door or a country smashing into tiny, federal bits.

FIRE WALK WITH ME

Blake Butler

David Lynch is eating breakfast in bed. He is eating Oreos by twisting the top off of each cookie and scraping the white icing out of the center with his finger. He transfers the icing to the headboard of the bed where it sticks and globs together. It is mushed in corners, smeared on wood. He plans to eat the icing later, all at once, so he can fill his entire mouth.

David Lynch is tired. The blood in his legs is getting old. When he closes his eyes, he sees trees on fire. He does not want to have to think.

Some of the icing is coming loose and falling between the headboard and the mattress or getting gummed into the sheets. David Lynch is concentrating on the crackle of the cookie, the crunch against his tongue.

When he fits the whole husk of a full black cookie edge-up against the roof of his mouth, he can remember things he didn't know that he remembered. He remembers a girl with a firm handshake. He remembers saw teeth against glass.

Beside him in the bed I am sleeping with my mouth open. I am wearing a blonde bouffant wig, lipstick and rouge. I have been sleeping a long time. I flip and wriggle and tug the sheets off of David Lynch's legs. He has on dark blue socks with garters. He has something unintelligible scribbled on his right knee.

Above the bed is a chandelier.

The chandelier is affixed to the ceiling, and in the ceiling there is a crack. By following the crack with one's eye, one can see that it perfectly bisects the bedroom. The crack is ended only by the wall, as if suggesting that it continues elsewhere.

David Lynch crunches the Oreos with his mouth open. He smacks his lips and tongue against his palate. The sound does not stir my sleeping. There is gauze stuffed in my ears. The gauze is bloody, gunked with black.

I am talking in my sleep, though not quite loud enough to be understood.

Finished with one row of Oreos, David Lynch stands up over the bed and begins to do deep knee bends. Each time he stands fully, he bumps his head against the chandelier. Each time the chandelier stirs, the crack in the ceiling tickles open a little further. Plaster dust rains into the bed sheets. It intermingles with the cookie crumbs. David Lynch begins to sing. He sings: At last, my love has come along, my lonely days are over, and life is like a song. His voice is strong and enthusiastic. His brow is furrowed. He is excited. He exercises more vigorously, while continuing to disturb the lighting fixture. A small wound develops in his hair. Blood runs down his forehead; the same color as my blood. It drips down his face onto his nightclothes—blue silk boxers, a wife-beater, a dead corsage. It drips on the mattress. It drips on me.

Though still asleep, I begin to sing along. I sing in harmony, taking the higher key.

The ceiling begins to crackle.

David Lynch is sweating. His fists are clenched. He deep-knee bends so hard it shakes the bed. The frame begins to groan. It sounds briefly like a woman. The bedroom door comes open.

A white horse enters. It comes in only far enough to show its head. It stands in the doorframe looking. It reveals its gums and whinnies. It shakes its hair. The hair has bugs.

The horse moves slightly further into the room revealing a small man on the horse's back. He is riding without a saddle, facing backwards, face concealed. He has on a cowboy hat and bright spurs and a long scar on his neck. He spits on the carpet. He lights a cigar and puts the match out on his tongue. He begins to sing. He takes the lower harmony with our sing-song. His voice is beautiful, like a woman's. It makes the whole room seem to quiver.

The main crack in the ceiling has now split into several other minor cracks. It has spread over the whole room. The feet of chairs and sofa and coffee tables can be seen poking through the plaster. The chandelier is hanging lower, with its wires gone loose. The lighting flickers. It hisses, pops. The glass arms of the fixture rest against David Lynch's back, making him stoop.

David Lynch puts a piece of sugarfree peppermint gum in his singing mouth.

I am asleep. I am dreaming of summer. I am in a swimming pool up to my neck. I sip from a glass of iced tea and shave my mustache with a straight razor, both hands fulls. There are several children in the pool kicking. They kick so hard it's like the pool's aboil.

I have an Oreo in my mouth, soft and runny, sucked wet with saliva and great need.

The room is raining dust now. The bed is covered under. The pile slowly builds until I am also covered under.

The horse's eyes are bright blue.

David Lynch continues deep knee bending. He shakes and grins and groans. He chews the gum so rough his teeth go loose and begin to fall out of his mouth. With each loss he begins to shake a little harder, spasms, until he can't control his arms. He can't control his eyes or fingers. The ceiling has sunk down several feet. He stoops further and continues shaking. Blood is running from his lips and nose. It pours out of him like a faucet. The sweat beads in his hair.

The ceiling is so low now in the doorframe that the horse has to lie down. It rolls onto its side with the cowboy still position on its back. It crushes the cowboy's right leg. The bones break loudly, popping, spraying dust. The cowboy doesn't scream. He has already smoked the cigar down to a stump. He continues to smoke until he burns his fingers. His lips. His tongue. He and the horse gently wriggle on the floor.

The dust is pouring in so fast now that soon the horse and cowboy are also buried. David Lynch is up to his waist. He is still singing the same song. Under the dust, you can still hear both muffled harmonies. The chandelier is ripping holes in his back. The dust is piling higher. The ceiling is still sinking.

He blows a bubble with the sugar-free gum. Inside the bubble there is blood. Inside the bubble there are bits of Oreo cookie. There are teeth. There is the song.

David Lynch blows more air into the bubble. The pink bubble grows and grows and does not pop. He blows the bubble bigger. He blows until there is no room left to blow. The bulbs in the chandelier glow faintly through the pink film until they are crushed and sputter out.

In the darkness, there is a voice. It is the horse, speaking in horse tongue. The language is transmitted in subtitles, small white text on pure black: Oh, at last, the stars above are blue. My heart was wrapped up in clover, the night I looked at you. I found a dream that I can speak to. A dream that I can call my own. I found a thrill to press my cheek to, a thrill that I have never known.

WOOD WELL

Tom LaFarge

for Fiona Templeton
and Daria Faïn

Values.

The WOOD is the poem behind poems, locus of night & silence that WELL there. ATHENS is a weaving; seeks its fiber in the WOOD. FAIRIES are gestures of the WOOD. OBERON is the WOOD's most dissipated denizen, a figure projected upon a vapor of appetite circulating in many senses. PUCK is the condensation of this undirected willing.

The BLACK TITANIA is the dancer through absolute space. Her gift develops reciprocal answering. She is drawn to BOTTOM's creaturely words but thrown into shadow by the WHITE TITANIA, eidolon of BOTTOM's fabrication.

BOTTOM is the weaver of ATHENS, chief of the MECHANICALS. He would author unanswerably. TITANIA calls and answers him with night & silence.

ATHENS is always *left.* The WOOD is always *right.*

Prologos.

ATHENS, *left*, is dark, a skyline of turrets and battlements against the night sky, where the full moon hovers. It contains a flickering image, Hippolyta Queen of Amazons, advancing upon her torturer, wounds and bruises appearing on her, and then receding, those wounds fading. The WOOD sprouts, *right*, in plumes and sprays of silver vapor. On these are projected images of leaves, of beasts, of weather, of war, of food cooking, of stones breaking, of feet treading a path, of the same feet running, of footprints in sand, of water in currents and eddies; of OBERON. Midstage between ATHENS and the WOOD opens a WELL of light.

A monotonous music of viol and tambour. BLACK TITANIA climbs out of the WELL and dances around it, while PUCK wheels out first a "bush" made from light-scaffolding, which he rigs upstage WOOD-side, and then a tall writing desk with a reading lamp, ATHENS-side. As he clicks on the lamp, the WELL is extinguished; BLACK TITANIA dances now invisible and illimitable. PUCK unfolds a script on the desk and begins to read.

Puck:
"See-eth sow...NO!"

No, that is ⌜difficult to pronounce⌝:
"… see-*est thou* thith tweet … NO! *sweet!* sight?"

WHITE TITANIA, a body to project upon, stands within the "bush" facing front.

"I do begin to pity."

A projected hand masks her face.

"For meeting her awful late behind, NO! For meeting her OF late behind the wood, I did upgrade her … NO! I did up*braid* her."

Red lips and a black eye appear on the back of the hand masking WHITE TITANIA's face.
PUCK squints, uncertain.

"with … coronet of flesh and flagrant, NO! *fresh* and *fragrant* … flowers" — AAAH!

The hand is snatched away. The lips and black eye remain. Bouquets grow over her pubis and armpits.

"and that was wont to smell — " no, NO! To *swell* — "to swell like round and orient tears" — AAAH!

Drops of water shine in her hair.

"When I had had my pleasure, NO! When I had AT my pleasure tainted … *taunted* her … "

Hand-shaped shadows black out her breasts; a grinning monkey-face is stamped on hers; the map of Argentina unrolls down one leg; clock-works move on her belly; water falls down her other leg.

"… I then did ask of her her … "

She is eclipsed; corona. PUCK studies the text; what is this word? Jangling? Ching-a-ling?

"… CHANGELING, which straight she gave."

WHITE TITANIA turns; an alluring boy stretches his body on her back.

PUCK turns and sees the boy; he shakes his head and starts to erase.

"And now I will undo … this … hateful … imp, er, fiction …"

The boy's image is wiped out in successive strokes.

"… make that 'IMPERFECTION' … take this transformed scalp …"

BOTTOM's face with ass's ears is projected on one buttock; OBERON grins on the other.

"… and think of this night's ass-kiddings, no, ACCIDENTS, butt-ass! … "

BOTTOM's projected face turns red.

"… or rather 'but as' … "

BOTTOM's projected face turns yellow. PUCK turns and looks.

"… fear's vacation." Looks back, reads more carefully: "FIERCE VEXATION!"

PUCK, cross, clicks off the lamp, wheels off the WRITING DESK. The WELL is lit, BLACK TITANIA returns into it, it goes dark again. In the "bush" WHITE TITANIA is entirely blacked out except for BOTTOM's mottled livid face on the one buttock.

Scene 1.

PUCK, adjusting the light-“bush”:
Who is here.

BOTTOM consolidates. BLACK TITANIA peers from the dark WELL, but WHITE TITANIA speaks from the lighted BUSH.

WHITE TITANIA:
Out of this voodoo knot desire tug oh thou shalt, treeman.
Here weather, thou wooder!
Know I am aspirative, no calm in rate.
The summer’s still death; tend upon my state and die.
Dual love, th’air foregoeth me.
I’ll give thee fare. Reason die! Will purge!
Th’eye, mortal grossness, sew that!
Thou shalt like an hairy spear. It.
Go, please, possum, fetch!

BOTTOM breaks apart and runs off in all directions.

Scene 2.

BOTTOM is a wild ass tangled in the LIGHT BUSH, kicking. PUCK wheels out the WRITING DESK again.

BOTTOM:
Little love and company nowadays keep reason together.
Wait.

PUCK scribbles.

BOTTOM:
Nowadays little reason and love keep together company.
Wait.

PUCK scribbles.

BOTTOM:
Keep together, love company, and reason little nowadays.
Wait.

PUCK scribbles.

BOTTOM:
Love, reason, and company keep little nowadays together.
Wait.

PUCK scribbles.

BOTTOM:
Keep little company, love nowadays together, and reason.
Wait.

PUCK scribbles and BLACK TITANIA dances:
Thou art! Ass-wise ass, thou art beautiful.

Scene 3.

BOTTOM, with very long, crooked ass's ears, stands at his WRITING DESK across the WELL mouth from BLACK TITANIA who reclines listening to the mating noises that issue from it. BOTTOM also listens, ears cocked that way, and scribbles furiously as if he were copying what he hears.

BOTTOM mutters while he writes; the following phrases should be read in an improvised order:

when wheat is green
that in a spleen
yet he gives me love
with the golden head
the raging rocks
to be to you translated
things base and vile
it is a dear expense
stranger companies
wings and no eyes
come to confusion
never did run smooth
an I may hide my face
shall break the locks
and shivering shocks
to their eyes
the more he follows me

sickness is catching
call forth your actors
for I am slow of study
here are your parts
my eye your eye
a tyrant's vein
of great revenue
emptying our bosoms
play it in a mask
wishes and tears
by another's eyes
painted blind
shall shine from far
most gallant
and a merry
I'll speak in
name what part I am for

your tongue's sweet air
to enrich my pain
which burnt the Carthage queen
the jaws of darkness
thoughts and dreams and sighs
decking with liquid pearl
upon faint primrose beds
swift as a shadow
her silver visage
unfolds both heaven and earth
thoughts and dreams and sighs
that which knitteth souls
a lover or a tyrant
fright the ladies
but let the audience look
a monstrous little voice
obscenely and courageously

[For instance:]

here are your parts...wings and no eyes...a monstrous little voice...things base and vile: the raging rocks which burnt the Carthage queen most gallant...a lover or a tyrant shall break the locks...a tyrant's vein never did run smooth, emptying our bosoms, decking with liquid pearl that which knitteth souls upon faint primrose beds...and shivering shocks come to confusion...name what part I am for...and I may hide my face to enrich my pain, my tongue should catch your tongue's sweet sickness...jaws of darkness that in a spleen unfolds both heaven and earth...it is a dear expense and a merry to be to you translated, my eye your eye...call forth your actors when wheat is green...stranger companies fright the ladies...play it in a mask, swift as a shadow, but let the audience look...I'll speak in her silver visage with the golden head...sickness is catching thoughts and dreams and sighs, obscenely and courageously...

Scene 4.

BOTTOM still writing sings a duet with BLACK TITANIA who is down the bright WELL so that her singing echoes.

BOTTOM: The woosel cock
TITANIA: would set his wit
BOTTOM: to see a noise he heard.
TITANIA: Who would give a bird?
BOTTOM: Why do they run away?
TITANIA: Sing a gain.

BOTTOM: The wren
TITANIA: on the fur-stuff you
BOTTOM: (wit not so true)
TITANIA: wakes me from my
BOTTOM: lie, though he cry
TITANIA: "And I do love thee"

BOTTOM: To make an "as" of me!
TITANIA: And thy fair virtues force …
BOTTOM: aren't Gitanes equal? …
TITANIA: me from my flow re-bed
BOTTOM: To fright me, if they could.
TITANIA: Out of this wood!

BOTTOM: Mine ear is much.
TITANIA: The more the pity, that.
BOTTOM: So is mine eye.
TITANIA: I love thee, thou.
BOTTOM: Have little reason!
TITANIA: I have enough to serve.

Scene 5 (homage to the rich art foreman).
I'm falling down this very well!

FAIRIES applaud

So, have you … lost the use of your legs?
No, I lost x years using them. But … I forget.
How many do you have left now?
Well, now I don't know.
Years left or left legs?
I really can't tell well.
What counts?
They all can count.
[falling forever]

PUCK:
Customs are like floors. Like … elevator floors.
They carry you from one story to the next.
But this … is like the elevator floor that beat you to the ground.

BOTTOM:
To the ground story.

PUCK:
There is no ground story.

MUSTARDSEED stuffs a meat-grinder, cranks.

LOVE IS CATCHING COLD

TITANIA:
You keep it cold in here.

BOTTOM:
Everyone keeps it cold. That's consensus.

TITANIA:
I like well-sounding words. Speak some more.

cobwebs hung with viscous drips

And the flood?

When does the flood start?

No, it isn't like that.
Madness?
Yes. It isn't like that.
Is that it?
That's right.
I like that better.

TITANIA: can you sound quiet?
Enter MOTH, a bear. The quiet bear sounds well
MOTH: Quiet sounds down two feet.
TITANIA: Well sounded, MOTH.
NIGHT CLOTHES ALL REFLECTION.
BOTTOM: I can't see bottom.
TITANIA is robed in mylar
TITANIA: Bear down lightly.
The bush is filled with light. Dreams

Dream light clothes love! That's more like it.

AT THE INTERSECTION

BOTTOM: Is there a bottom to this dream?

He finds it

Exodos.

The MECHANICALS' voices are heard in polyphony, while vapors spiral the dark WELL from which BLACK TITANIA climbs to dance as BOTTOM still stands writing at the WRITING DESK.

Tom LaFarge

Well in a wood loves leap in all eyes
Dreams sound very fancy, dreams spell lies
Shadow slight bodies thought lies with a skin
Mind chance sounds that still well in
Fancy skins reason of a play an ass weaves
Love chants trouble and right love leaves
    Dream loves well
    Write love leaves
    Right thoughts play
    Love dreams well
    Dream loves well
    Love   dreams   well

TROPIC OF CANDOR

Shya Scanlon

2:37 AM	Henry: Tania, are you still up? Tania: [is away]
2:38 AM	Henry: Fuck. Well, I'll talk anyway. Just got home, and I'm singing for your forgiveness. Tonight was magical! But I know it wasn't all you expected it to be. Tania: [is away]
2:40 AM	Henry: I know I said I'd ream out every wrinkle of your cunt, and I wanted to, for realz. Tania: [is away]
2:41 AM	Henry: I wanted to send you a fat letter full of big words. It's just that I've been finding it difficult, lately, to "form a sentence." :P Tania: [is away]
2:43 AM	Henry: Sigh. I've got to get out of this place. My mom is driving me fucking crazy. My room is full of lice. My house is an intoxicated palace of rot… Tania: [is away]
2:45 AM	Henry: When I graduate, things are going to change. I'm gonna get away from all this decay and all these sewer rats and I'm going to go somewhere to find a little peace so I can write the big book, the Last Book.

Tania: [is away]

2:49 AM Henry: I don't know. Maybe this is all just the dyke's fault. I went to the dyke's apartment yesterday before I came over. I always think it's going to be different, that I'm going to show her what's up, but she just makes me feel stupid. What the fuck does "a rose is a rose is a rose is a rose" mean? I want to pack her hairy cunt with TNT and see what she thinks about roses then!

Tania: [is away]

2:51 AM Henry: jk re: the tnt. ;););)

Tania: [is away]

2:52 AM Henry: But seriously, where does she come up with this shiz? And why do people sit around and take it? Nodding like bobble heads. Like rubber balls. I'll walk into the room and swat those balls down the staircase and out into the street, one by one, and they'll carom off the sides of flatulent immigrants pushing steroidal strollers to the park, knocking them to the ground like fallen soldiers.

Tania: [is away]

2:55 AM Henry: Also Boris has been making me feel bad about being poor. Boris with his girlfriend so fat you could find lost cities in her snatch! Whole societies up there, gasping for air, straining for light, withered by the musty mucous and praying for death. Still the kid has the stones to stop in at Ray's for a slice every five minutes. He shoves them into his face, one after another, then sheepishly looks over at me without offering so much as a bite. And he never once gains a pound! It's like the pie goes straight from his mouth into his girlfriend's thighs. How I wish to surrender myself to those brilliant white thighs! To suffocate myself between them, hungry and alone...

Tania: [is away]

Henry: It's all good, though. I'll show him. I'll write a book that will swallow him and his fat girl. It will swallow Manhattan in one gulp, and burp out Brooklyn.

Tania: [is away]

2:58 AM Henry: If I tell you something, will you promise me—will you swear to god—you won't tell anyone? Actually, forget it.

Tania: [is away]

3:06 AM Henry: I'm back. I raided my mom's liquor cabinet. At least that wretched bird has a taste for good booze. She asked about you the other day, did I tell you? She asked whether you've "matured." I wanted to show her the pictures we took! LOL!!!1! That would tell her something about maturity. I want to take her on a walking tour through the cathedral of your shaven cunt.

Tania: [is away]

3:08 AM Henry: We'd stop at the temple of your clit and say a prayer...

Tania: [is away]

3:09 AM Henry: We'd bless ourselves with your stinking holy water...

Tania: [is away]

Henry: We'll dive into... shit. I'm sorry. This is just gross.

Tania: [is away]

3:11 AM Henry: I swear to you, Tania, that when we finally fuck it's going to completely destroy both of us. It's going to shake the world and rattle all the dying, gold bones on Wall Street.

Tania: [is away]

3:21 AM Henry: The whiskey is catching up with me. Why won't Boris buy me a slice? Just once I'd like him

to offer. I'd refuse, of course, on principle. But it's the gesture I want, I need. Doesn't he see that?! LLLL
Tania: [is away]
3:27 AM Henry: A rose is a rose is a rose is a cunt.
Tania: [is away]
3:23 AM Henry: When we do it, it's going to be beautiful. I won't fail you! I won't fail you. I won't fail.
Tania: [is away]
3:27 AM Henry: What if I fail you?
Tania: [is away]
3:28 AM Henry: Shit. Okay, here goes. The truth is I'm a virgin. There: I said it. I'm a virgin! I'm a half-man, a crippled pickle, a cipher. Please don't tell Boris. Please don't tell the dyke. Please don't laugh at me. I don't think my heart could stand it. I'd die if I weren't already dead.
3:30 AM Tania: Henry, I just woke up to pee. OMG are you chatting with yourself? LMAO. What the hell are you doing?
Henry: [is away]

THE DEVIL AND THE DAIRY PRINCESS

Pedro Ponce

Toward the end of the nineteenth century, in the upstate village of Eligius, a dairy farmer, whose name has been lost to posterity, broke off from his labors to rest. This particular day in early summer was unusually cold. Mist roiled over the pasture as Ayrshires tore at the moist turf. Perhaps it was the farmer's exhaustion that imbued the herd with a strange intransigence. Jaws pulsed blindly in the thickening mist; flanks shifted and twitched in unsettling congruence as if at any moment, the obscurity would part to reveal the bloated paunch of a prehistoric grotesque. The farmer was apprehending, un-reined from the rubric of industry, the grim alchemy of ruminant digestion, eternal consumption and eternal expulsion, a bestial indifference that had existed since the first dawn, and would doubtless supplant the most monumental of human designs. He recalled the admonition about work and idle hands, but too late to escape the approach of enormous hooves. The hooves supported a pair of disproportionately tall legs, a dark topcoat, and a bowler hat drawn low over the eyes.

A leathery hand pawed the side of the choicest milker. Handsome specimen, mused a deep voice, which seemed to reach the farmer from high along a nearby silo.

The farmer was at first too afraid to protest as the hand descended to cup a pair of udders. Who are you? he finally managed.

A harbinger, responded the voice, dispatching him to fetch the Reverend Jonah Cooper immediately for an audience. If the messenger felt any indignation at the speaker's presumption, it was impossible to discern from the urgency of his steps towards town.

Reverend Cooper was just settling in for his afternoon nap when he was roused by pounding at the rectory door. He did little to hide his irritation with the waiting messenger, who seemed oblivious to the Reverend's displeasure. Cooper followed the farmer reluctantly to his pasture, nevertheless greeting all they encountered with the sagacious alacrity familiar to his flock.

They arrived to a circle of bovines, legs tented in obeisance to a hulking silhouette in their midst. The figure scratched idly at a raised muzzle. The Reverend appraised the assembled supplicants, the solid shade of the stranger's clothes, the amused bellow that resonated through the earth as a calf lapped hungrily at an outstretched palm arrayed with oddly attenuated fingers.

Pardon me, the visitor said. I have my followers, just as you have yours.

No one follows me, the Reverend responded. We follow the one true Lord.

I'm pleased to hear that, answered the visitor, who now stood and approached the low wooden barrier between them. Below the hat's brim, the Reverend could discern a bulbous forehead and a neatly trimmed beard.

What is it you want? asked the Reverend.

Your impertinence surprises me, replied the visitor. I find it hard to believe that you, of all people, need instruction on civility from one such as I. Allow me, all the same, to introduce myself—

I know who you are, Cooper replied.

Well of course you do. How silly of me. I find your weekly insights from the pulpit quite enlightening. They are, in fact, the reason I'm here.

Go on, said the Reverend.

Thus revealed, the Devil explained that he was ready to admit defeat. He had been flushed out by the citizens of this, the godliest part of the country. He could no longer depend on subterfuge if his quarry were so alert to the usual tricks. So he had decided to conduct his business out in the open, like any tradesman. He still required sustenance, certainly, but he now had no choice but to yield to the contingencies of predation, culling only the weakest and least necessary. He would endure eternity on the leavings that were his due, while those who prevailed would be left in peace to pursue the New Jerusalem.

Reverend Cooper craned his neck to look the creature right in its eyes. He could not find them and instead settled his stalwart gaze on the dark space veiled by the bowler's brim. What then, asked the Reverend, do you propose?

To be your humble servant, answered the Devil. The people of Eligius would be granted prosperity for all their earthly days, until the Lord of all returned to claim his Kingdom. All that was required in exchange was one soul per year, of the town's choosing, in whatever manner the good people deemed fit. And there was an exception even for these minimal terms: for should the offered sacrifice be pure in heart and spirit, he would be rendered powerless to enforce his part of the contract and required to hunt for souls elsewhere, leaving the town's abundance intact as a token of righteous defeat.

No town had as yet been courageous enough to accept. The Devil shook his head in disappointment, running scaled fingers over a splintery fence beam. He had been greeted with skepticism throughout his travels, but more often with fear disguised as humility. For many, the thriving of future generations was no solace for the loss of a single soul to the demon's minions. And who could claim the purity required to successfully breach the bargain once made? So had gone countless offers over numerous miles. Was there no community that actually lived by the faith declaimed in song every Sunday? Surely somewhere there must be believers willing to allow him the little that was his due, or to challenge him altogether for even this pittance?

Reverend Cooper could not help but be flattered. He was well aware of the Biblical interdiction against testing the Lord. But this wasn't really testing the Lord, was it? Really, it was he himself being tested, along with all who claimed allegiance to his teachings. What if, in fact, this test had been arranged by the Lord Himself to measure the worthiness of his flock? A new century was imminent and with it, perhaps a new urgency to fulfill the visions of Scripture.

What say you, Reverend? asked the Devil, extending his left hand.

The Reverend, saying nothing, reached for the proffered claw. His fingers caught on one of the demon's long, flinty nails. Blood poured from the wound, seeping into the earth below.

Cooper returned to town just in time for dinner, where he regaled his family with the tale of his otherworldly bargain. Abigail Cooper, for her part, relished every detail of her husband's triumph, flinching only briefly at the announcement that the inaugural sacrifice would be their eldest daughter, Theresa. The Reverend, seeing anxiety trace itself across his wife's brow and the faces of their six children, was too sated with purpose to admonish them. He took Theresa's hand and assured her that no harm would come to her. He knew that her sacrifice would be untenable under the Devil's bargain. If Theresa wept as she accepted her father's will, it was surely feminine fragility and not the pliancy of faith that betrayed her.

The appointed hour arrived. The people were instructed to wait at the border of the surrounding woods for the Reverend's signal, which would let them know that all were safe. The combatants entered the moonlit forest goaded by hymns and spontaneous acclamations. Jonah Cooper lit the way with his torch, followed by his daughter and Nelson Flynn, whose proposal of marriage Theresa had just accepted. Refusing to let his fiancée weather this trial without him, he entered the woods bearing the carved oak cross that had crowned the steeple of Eligius' church for nearly two centuries. The gathered watched Reverend Cooper's flame fade slowly into the shadows. When it was gone altogether, they linked hands and prayed, first for their Reverend, who had brought them fearlessly to the threshold of redemption. They prayed in thanksgiving for the souls of Nelson and Theresa and their generous sacrifice, which was not really a sacrifice at all if one was truly blessed by faith, which they all assuredly were. They prayed for the pending marriage of Nelson and Theresa, that it would be blessed with prosperity and love and abundant progeny. They prayed for the progeny of Nelson and Theresa, that they would always remember this day, when the seeds of their bright and abundant future were sown. There was a brief pause as several of the assembly looked into the darkened woods, where the promised signal had yet to appear. They were quickly wrenched back from distraction by calls to pray for the coming prosperity that would result from the present trial, that it might be used prudently and always in keeping with the spiritual guidance that had led them to prevail. A deep rustle within the forest dampened the chorus of amens; a pair of broad white wings rose from the branches overhead and veiled the dwindling moon. Perhaps it would be prudent to pray for the nation as a whole? asked a matron through the shiver that tensed her shoulders. Yes, agreed the wavering circle, hands numbed by frost. One wouldn't want to forget the nation.

Before the nation could be blessed, however, a bright light flared in the distance. The exhausted assembly squinted to ensure that this was no illusion. Indeed, the light persisted and spread, edging a trail through the dense trunks. The people cheered and followed the light, laughing as they stumbled over unseen roots or felt the slap of low branches. They emerged into a clearing about a mile into the forest. A large elliptical stone rose vacantly at its center. To the left of the stone, a figure crouched in the light of blinding flames, shifting feebly on its knees and outstretched hands. A neighbor recognized the Reverend and rushed to help him up. Cooper made no effort to stand, despite his rescuer's appeals; instead, the Reverend turned his face to the silenced gathering and screamed through the bloody maw that remained of his mouth. The flames doused themselves in the graying dawn, revealing what was left of the town cross, sheathed in a dripping mass of coals.

So began the longstanding détente between the Devil and the people of Eligius, who, at the very least, were never betrayed by the surviving party. The town's fortunes rose steadily into the next century, even as those of the nation waned. Through Dust Bowl and Great Depression, not a single of Eligius' fields lay fallow; its herds boasted record milk production. The vague sulfur taste, attributed to local innovations in the science of feed, could be substantially mellowed during pasteurization, and some experts found the raw savor essential to the area's finer cheeses. Over the years, the sacrifice in the woods took on the fanciful implausibility of myth or senility as witnesses—never forthcoming to begin with—aged and went on to an afterlife that, they could only hope, offered the solace of annihilating sleep. The Eligius they left behind had always been a fertile oasis in the wilderness, always producing for those with the vigor and resilience to tame the land. The people had always taken pride in their industry, always tempered with the humility to recognize their debt to divine providence. And every June, always the week before the nation celebrated its Independence, the town celebrated the bounty of the preceding year by electing one of its own to promote dairy products to surrounding communities. The post of dairy princess was among the most coveted in the region, unless you were one of the four community scions apprised of its actual purpose. Since the mysterious disappearance of Theresa Cooper and her fiancé in the summer of 1894—a likely elopement, youth having always been so impetuous—discretion was required to sustain the original bargain. The Dairy Commission convened formally for the first time in the autumn of 1901; its four lifetime appointees were primarily responsible for enforcing the rules of election and assuring neglect by the public and press. The closest call in the Commission's history came in the winter of 1972, when a cub reporter for the *Barrettown Bugle* began investigating a sizeable payment made by the then mayor of Eligius to the contest coordinator, who subsequently eliminated the mayor's 17-year-old daughter from competition due to questionable interpretation of an obscure bylaw. The daughter's outrage—this was her last year of eligibility after a string of disappointing placements as second and third runner-up—was quickly assuaged with the promise of a new car. The *Bugle* reporter was not so easily deterred, even after receiving a parcel with a Washington, D.C., postmark during the first week of March. Had the reporter actually opened the parcel, the contents would have at least merited a one-inch squib in the "Washington Roundup" column toward the back of section A: inside was a blank sheet of White House stationary sleeved around an unmarked reel of audiotape. Before the reporter could reach for his letter opener, however, circumstance intervened when word reached the bureau that a dog had fallen through the ice at Brasher Inlet; in the ensuing rush to the scene and two weeks of spot and follow-up coverage—the dog survived—the sealed package was lost and never recovered.

The rest of the Commission's responsibilities involved planning the annual coronation ceremony. Reverend Cooper lived to see the dedication of Theresa Cooper Pavilion in 1954; the Pavilion, financed by the first group of Commissioners, boasted dark neoclassical columns, a travertine floor, and elaborate pastoral friezes animated in relief by the dimmest moonlight. Cooper made a comical dignitary as he dozed through remarks by the Mayor and a medley of patriotic favorites performed a cappella by the local Tonic Tillers. The Reverend had not slept a full night since his daughter started visiting him shortly after her assumption into the underworld. It wasn't so bad, she would assure him, crossing the sleeves of her loose crimson gown, her face scarred by the shadows of maple branches. Her master was quite solicitous actually, and very understanding about her early deficiencies as a spouse. She had since been amply instructed, she added, looking at the lush lawns outside. By the way his daughter shifted slightly in her stance, the way her garment gathered and hung over her bare feet, he knew she was naked underneath. He keened over the stump of his tongue, an attempt to ask after her mother, who had died in her sleep in the early spring of 1902. Her expression as she neared was either dutiful discernment or mock incomprehension. He never got the chance to find out as he awoke alone to his mute reflection against the darkened window.

At the subsequent reception—which set the standard for all subsequent dairy court festivities—the Reverend was congratulated by a representative of the Dairy Commission. Despite the humidity of the April afternoon, the representative wore a dark three-piece suit. His brow was dry as it brushed idly against the bunting strung along the pavilion's Corinthian capitals. He looked down at the progenitor of Eligius' great fortune and extended a hand in greeting. Cooper gripped the armrests of his seat, saying nothing. Aging had done little to improve his manners, the representative mused. He gave the Reverend's shoulders a brusque, encouraging shake and complimented his wisdom in choosing the devil he knew. That night, Reverend Cooper at last chose the one he didn't; his housekeeper and sometime nurse discovered him the following morning, hanging from a second-story handrail.

The turn of the subsequent century introduced a new fervor among Eligians, who perhaps had always lived with the guilt of easeful existence, even if its actual source was never widely known. The prospect of a new millennium was seen by many as an opportunity for repentance, or the consoling excess that precedes apocalypse. Something of both was heard in the sermons of Terry Dillon, an excommunicated priest who proudly enumerated the dozen countries where he had performed exorcisms, a practice restricted by the obfuscating bureaucracy of a Vatican that Dillon saw as irredeemably corrupt. His Church of the Exorcism was only radical if one accepted the dilution to which all the major faiths had succumbed in recent years; he and his followers were merely witnesses to a truth too many had forgotten: evil was only as inherent as the common cold or grippe. The expulsion from Eden was ultimately a side effect of the poison ingested and passed on by Eve. But it was pointless to continue blaming the weakness of woman, however deserved. The defeat of the Devil now depended on purging him by increments through the sacrament of exorcism. Every Sunday, the faithful of Eligius would gather in an abandoned granary to share reports of suspicious behavior witnessed in the preceding week. The incidence of strange disturbances, particularly at the wooded fringes of town, convinced parishioners that the demon was indeed in their midst. Dillon led them to the desolate edges of Eligius every first night of full moon to chant and pray in warning to whatever creatures dared to breach the beams of their storm lanterns. The darkness yielded owls, skunks, the occasional raccoon, but no sign of the promised quarry. The former priest raised both arms, his lantern hooked loosely on his outstretched thumb. Never mind, he admonished; vigilance would, in time, be its own reward. His admirers nodded, squinting into the sway of light.

Agnes Hadley fell in step behind her mother as the procession made its way back to town. Georgina Hadley was exchanging marble cake recipes with one of her fellow tellers at the AgroBank branch on lower Main when, at a cluster of recently opened condominiums, she saw her daughter dragging her steps. For the parishioners of the Church of the Exorcism, tonight was one skirmish closer to Revelation; for the rest of Eligius, it was a Friday. Music and neon light ascended from the distant doors of both of the town's legal drinking establishments. Once over the glossy thresholds, the light and noise were muffled by the starless expanse above. At Agnes' age, Georgina would have followed the boots and high heels, the music and cigarette smoke, the drunken laughter and fumbling at damp dollar bills. But this was how she had met Agnes' father, and she was determined that her daughter cultivate early a fervor for resignation, distilled of the passions that, inevitably, taunt us longer in recollection than in real life. She commanded Agnes to rejoin the group immediately.

There was little danger of Agnes losing her way. She had none of Georgina's sensuality, which even now took effort to disguise under drab suits and opaque stockings. Agnes was so unlike her mother that town gossips often spent slower weeks revisiting rumors of her adoption. Agnes was more her father's child, a muddy brunette with flat features and a parsimonious figure no dress could enliven. Glasses might have given her face much needed character, but excellent vision was the one perfection Agnes did possess, and Georgina refused to even look at the fashionable cosmetic lenses recommended by friends at school.

The Hadleys found their front door open and a pair of black loafers crossed casually in the doorway. Xerxes, their 180-pound English mastiff, barked feebly at the seated stranger from the dimly lit vestibule. The barking grew louder when he spotted his masters walking hesitantly up the narrow driveway; Xerxes continued to sound his alarm as he bolted over the front lawn and crouched anxiously behind them. While Agnes tried to calm the dog, Georgina withdrew the pepper spray from her purse and took the three steps up to her open door.

The door was unlocked, the stranger said. I hope you don't mind.

Georgina certainly did mind, but when she tried to express her annoyance, she found herself incapable of speech. Her grip slackened on the spray, which dropped to the floor and rolled to a stop against her guest's reflective shoes. The stranger stood and introduced himself as a representative of the Dairy Commission.

By now, Agnes had managed to coax the mastiff to the threshold of the house and was struggling to bring him in again by the collar. There was a snap and a scatter of pads across the vestibule floor. Agnes emerged into the living room staring at the torn collar hanging limp in her hand.

The dairy representative stepped toward the door and helpfully closed it behind her. Almost had him, he said, with a wink. You must have some grip.

I guess, said Agnes. She recognized the tricolor pentacle on his lapel pin and froze, suddenly conscious of her disheveled appearance and the damp rusty smell Xerxes had left on her face and hands.

I was just about to tell your mother how much we look forward to seeing you for registration at the Pavilion next week.

You were? Agnes looked at her mother.

Agnes was sick last year. That's why—

Of course, said the representative. You were right to keep her at home. Our bylaws are very clear on the need for all contestants to be in peak health. But your daughter looks quite eligible now. He was distracted briefly by the thatch of dark hairs visible across the girl's upper lip.

With all due respect, Mr....

He nodded agreeably. I'm with the Commission. He resumed his seat on the faded floral lounger.

Yes...As I was saying, my daughter and I aren't really interested in your competition.

But a girl—young woman—has only three precious years

of eligibility to represent Eligius. It would be a shame to see her miss yet another opportunity.

Georgina looked at her daughter. I know what an opportunity this is. I was third runner-up to Beatrice Watson in '95.

Well, congratulations! The Commission still remembers that as one of the most difficult years to judge. So many worthy candidates.

I remember. A shame what happened. Did Bea ever manage to get better?

The representative shook his head. Overdose I'm afraid.

I thought she was getting help.

Oh, she was, the representative insisted. The Commission never turns its back on one of its own. We spared no expense. We thought she would benefit from one of the more remote treatment programs. Unfortunately...well, I can't say more without violating our obligations to the Watson family.

Of course, said Georgina. She contemplated an empty seat opposite the representative, but she could not get her knees to bend. She tried dissembling her awkward stance by brushing at dust specks on the mantle. They say it's cursed, she said, her back to the room.

What is?

The crown. The contest. All of it. Even when I was a girl. The old people especially. You win and either leave and never come back. Or you end up dead.

The representative emerged at full height from the lounger. Georgina watched him blot the periphery of her vision with a practiced restraint.

Make no mistake, the representative said evenly. Winning is a serious responsibility that should never be assumed lightly. Some are elected and recognize ambitions in themselves they would never before dare admit. Others come to appreciate the seriousness of their position and begin to question their worthiness. And sometimes, though not often, some take their questioning too far. That's understandable, isn't it?

Georgina nodded. The representative regarded her a few moments before turning to Agnes.

The world is changing, he observed. The Commission believes the post should reflect these changes. We stress—have always stressed—that this is not a beauty contest. Or, rather, the beauty we assess can manifest in any number of ways. Tell me, Agnes, what do you dream of doing?

Agnes' grin revealed a spackling of strawberry pulp from that night's dessert. I never really remember my dreams.

The representative chuckled amiably. A sense of humor, he said. Another plus in the eyes of the judges. But seriously, dear, what do you dream of accomplishing? In the future? You strike me as one of those shy girls who end up discovering a cure for something. Still waters and all that.

Agnes grew nervous at his eagerness. I don't know, she answered, staring at her shoes. She tamped at a dog-eared corner of the living room rug. The corner rose stubbornly with every footfall.

Of course, said the representative as he stooped to smooth the carpet by hand. You choose to live in the moment. I wish we all had such free spirits. Your daughter has the soul of a poet, he added, just before his hand was crushed under Agnes' ill-timed heel.

Georgina was roused from her strange stupor by the familiar need to correct her daughter's clumsiness. She helped the representative up and guided him back to his seat, apologizing profusely. Agnes was too embarrassed to join her mother; she froze in place, ensuring that the offending foot would cause no more damage. The representative eased into the lounger and made a tentative fist.

Are you sure you're alright? Agnes Elizabeth, go get this man some ice.

No. Please. That won't be necessary.

It's the least she can do. I insist. Agnes—

The representative opened his hand and raised it in dismissal. Not until the night of her daughter's coronation would she remember how strangely his fingers met the air, his nails trimmed acutely, the pads wavering slightly at the tips, like the beads of flame from a burner set on low.

He asked Agnes to hand him his briefcase. With his good hand, he slowly undid the latches and withdrew a densely printed form, thick with carbons. There was no need to apologize, he assured them. Accidents happen. But the secret of success is knowing the difference between accident and opportunity. Avoiding the former merely prolonged the interval between unavoidable obstacles. Avoiding the latter condemned one to a life of mediocrity and regret. Surely this was not the fate Georgina Hadley wished for her daughter? Agnes tried to conceal her growing excitement as her mother took the offered papers.

The transformation of Agnes Hadley was as subtle as it was unexpected. Cosmetics did not conceal and soften her imperfections so much as imbue them with a gaudy polish. If she maintained absolutely rigid posture, the fit of her sweetheart neckline gown appeared, from the right angle, almost flattering. She had never fallen testing her mother's heels on her own feet, although she never did master the glide the judges looked for in evaluating poise; at her most practiced, Agnes' steps had the stolid adequacy of the bovines with whom she would be sharing the stage over the next year. Her biggest challenge, after the "Whey Out Dairy Facts" qualifying challenge, would be the second-round extemporaneous speech on a randomly assigned industry topic. The three-minute time limit was strictly enforced, and many promising candidates succumbed to nervous prolixity or baffled silence as the warning light console went from green to amber at two minutes and 30 seconds. Regretting her consent the moment the Dairy Commission representative snapped his briefcase shut again, Georgina watched helplessly as her daughter vacillated between paralyzing doubt and feverish hope.

The evening of the competition, a dozen candidates approached their respective podiums at Cooper Pavilion. From her place onstage, the audience was a field of tilting banners and digital flickers. The four judges were visible as featureless silhouettes in the foreground. Agnes felt the stare of the tallest silhouette and could even make out the faintest of nods in her direction. The mayor of Eligius took the stage with a crustacean's undersea grace.

The rest of the event seemed charged with the same airy expedience. Whether quizzed on "Lactose Lore," "Bovine Biology," "Milk In History," or "Icons and Innovators," Agnes answered with an unaccustomed confidence, placing second overall and easily winning a berth in the next round. She was a competent student, but her disquisition on the 21st-century dairy alluded to pending advances familiar only to specialists. Her interview question during the third and final round ("Why do you want to be dairy princess?") was considered one of the most difficult to answer with zeal and originality at this late stage of the competition. But once again, Agnes proved herself a knowledgeable and engaging promoter of dairy to a community, both local and global, that needed to go back to nutritional and moral basics. By now, she had the crowd substantially on her side. Georgina Hadley watched from a seat five rows back as her daughter finished her interview to clusters of whistles and standing applause. She humbly nodded, acknowledging the looks of other parents who recognized her as Agnes' mother. She allowed herself a glance or two at the expressions of approval and envy that typically marked such occasions. But the looks she was given were strangely muted, edged with something else that she told herself was inscrutable.

By the time of the coronation, the crowd's cheers took on a fearful expectancy. The mayor shouted into his wireless microphone his thanks to all the contestants, to the judges for their judiciousness, to the Dairy Commission for all its hard work, and to the community for its attendance and commitment to local industry before dismissing them all with promises of next year's spectacle. The stage behind him was vacant. Georgina watched her daughter's tiara retreat amid a coterie of shadows. The exiting crowd pushed her further back as she struggled to catch up.

She finally managed to sidle out between a pair of columns. In her rush towards a rank of departing cars, she caught someone's shoulder. She stopped to apologize and saw it was Terry Dillon. Dillon tried to arrange himself into the severity appropriate to his clerical station, but he could not ignore Georgina as she excused herself and bolted for the parking lot. Publicly, Dillon disapproved of the vanity that the annual dairy festival encouraged in the community's young women; privately, he, along with many Eligians, was curious to see just what would result from Agnes Hadley's unlikely bid for princess, and he was hopeful for a passing word with Georgina, whose attractions had begun to perturb him during weekly meetings at the granary. He held her fast by the shoulders and asked her what was wrong. She was distracted briefly by Dillon's boldness. Dillon, loosening his grasp, repeated his question. Georgina Hadley replied with a confused and fragmentary recitation of clues, hints, signs, and insinuations that concluded with a single tangible fact: Her daughter was being taken. The pastor needed no further convincing.

In Dillon's truck, they followed a silver sedan to the border of the woods. The sedan slowed before a nondescript expanse of trunks. Dillon stopped his truck about half a mile behind. Georgina panicked and fumbled for the passenger door lock. Dillon grasped her hand in the darkness. He knew where they were going. Over the years, he had mapped every possible gathering space for nocturnal conspiracy. In this sector of the woods, there was only one place where they could gather, a clearing which could be accessed discreetly by one or two hikers from a nearby trailhead.

They each took a flashlight, but after several minutes of gently rising terrain, these were no longer necessary. A coppery fluorescence illuminated their steps between gnarled roots. An open field emerged in the distance, ending in a thick trunk that seemed to bead and drip into the crimson grass rustling below. The trunk detached itself from the surrounding trees and reached the prostrated form of Agnes Hadley in two cloven strides.

The figure stood over his prize and hooked her tiara with a single extended claw. He threw the bauble into the grass with disgust. How he hated when his due was delivered in the feeble finery of mortal hands. He preferred them natural, unadorned. He yoked Agnes' face between two fingers and lifted her to her feet. Her cheeks were streaked with blood where his rough skin abraded hers.

The Devil hesitated at the abject girl in his grasp. Are you feeding these things? he asked, turning to the four suited silhouettes waiting at the edge of the clearing. I've never understood the fashion for emaciation. Very well then.

This being the one soul he could claim for the entire year, he had to consume it with appropriate ceremony. He began with a mock recitation of baptismal doxology. Tell me, he began, do you believe in the one true Lord which guided your forefathers in the extension of His Great Work? For every affirmative answer, spoken in the agonies of last hope, he would tear at layers of embroidery, beading, and skin, until the soul was relieved to his command.

To Agnes Hadley, death was an iconic abstraction, as palpable and solemn as a window dressing Father Christmas presiding at a nativity scene. She was old enough and lonely enough to have romanticized her own death, the despair of others as they mourned, which she would somehow be able to enjoy from a comfortable perch in the great beyond. But there was nothing of comfort in her imminent demise. She tried to swallow back the dryness in her mouth, managing only to tighten the searing noose formed at her throat by the

Devil's fingers. His catechismal taunts recalled to her, with brutal clarity, the whisper of earth beneath the feet of Terry Dillon's disciples as they patrolled the bordering woods, their songs and Scripture dampened instantly as echoes of a greater silence.

Agnes Hadley regarded the Devil's damp beard. No, she answered. She did not.

The Devil loosened his fingers slightly. Do you, he continued, vow to live by the Creed you took at baptism for all your earthly days as witnessed by parents, proxies, and the community of faith at large?

Agnes, suddenly afforded breath, answered more loudly this time, so that her voice carried to the fringes of the clearing. No, she repeated.

The Devil, foiled in his vanity for surrender, jabbed the soft dip of her neckline and made a diagonal slash across the front of her dress. Agnes collapsed before the towering shade, which seemed to bloat slightly at the edges.

Look at me, the Devil commanded. When Agnes did not move, he poised two fingers over her neck, but held back to resume.

Do you vow to be always vigilant against the inroads of evil, in yourself and others, whether in word, deed, or intent?

Agnes stood, her arms crossed over her chest. She hesitated in what at a distance resembled the guarding of wounds. But when she lowered her arms, causing the top of her dress to fall away, her skin was unbroken, its moonlit pallor softening the hair on her nipples to a downy silver.

Agnes met the Devil's stare and answered a third time, No.

At this point, extant accounts vary widely. For some, the ceremony in the woods coincided with a strange tumult all along Main Street. Cornices on public buildings crumbled, groceries toppled to tilting floors, likely provoked by numerous herds that escaped in panic to parts unknown, leaving many of

Eligius' most productive pastures empty, as if the missing had been absorbed into the very earth itself.

Others claim that late in the long night, angels descended to a clearing deep in the woods, their vestments and swords the blue of ivory, to send the demon back for good. In some versions, the girl is rewarded for her faith—asserted bravely in the face of the Devil's torture—by bodily assumption into heaven. In others, the girl refuses to answer to the Devil altogether, vowing to answer to the Lord alone; she is martyred grotesquely before her soul is freed to its rightful home and Eligius is liberated from a century's spell.

In still other versions, Eligians rise early to an ordinary morning. The sky is only beginning to lighten to deep blue. The first cups are being poured from percolators. A barn door is coaxed open with a reluctant grate. Routine is interrupted by a group passing by on foot. Their faces are familiar, but they regard the town's outskirts like travelers arriving from a long journey. Perhaps they have been here before, perhaps they were born and raised here, but they have been away so long that their anticipation in return is tempered by fear of all they will fail to recognize and all who will fail to recognize them. Nevertheless, approaching the only destination at hand, they continue over the narrowing contours of dirt road, aiming their steps in the direction of what remains.

DOWN AT THE DINGHY

Molly Gaudry

It was my job to console Lionel when, a month after Christmas, one of his presents died. The present, a Grow-A-Frog, had arrived in the mail courtesy of our absentee mother. Lionel spent Christmas and the days following captivated by the egg and its aquarium, asking, *How long until it hatches? What will it look like? Does it really grow into a frog? How big will it be? What kind of frog is it? When's Mom coming back? Does she really have to work on Christmas?* My father and I exchanged shrugs, not wanting to spoil the holiday with the truth, that it would just be the three of us from then on, so we distracted Lionel with questions of our own: *Where should you keep it? In the window or by your bed? Do you think it will be a girl or boy? Don't you want to try your new bike? What are you going to name your frog?* It was this last question that proved worthy enough for serious consideration. Finally, after A Charlie Brown Christmas, Lionel announced, "His name is Tannenbaum."

"O Tannenbaum," I cried, standing beside Lionel on the bank of the river. "You were loved."

"O Tannenbaum," he repeated. "I'm sorry I failed you." Although only seven, Lionel was a smart kid, and failure was both a concept and phrase he understood well enough in reference to our mother that it broke my heart to hear him say it again: "If only I hadn't failed you, Tannenbaum."

Lionel poured the contents of his aquarium into the river—water first, then Tannenbaum--who had by then hatched and grown hind legs, the left a bit larger than the right--and finally every last multicolored pebble. As they plopped, I couldn't help but think that it wasn't Lionel who had failed Tannenbaum but my mother who had failed us all. It was the first of many such realizations to come during those next days, weeks, and months while we adjusted, but as Lionel and I stared together at a dinghy in disuse bobbing in the distance, toes freezing in our rubber boots, offering our prayers to a tadpole named Tannenbaum, I felt also, for the first time, like the woman of the house, and I thought it quite possible we would be better off without her.

Big Blue

Steve Himmer

You could hear his heart breaking like thunder. And I don't mean "like thunder" the way a poet might mean it, no, I mean it actually sounded like thunder because he was just that damn big. And his heart was that much damn bigger. There's nothing poetic about a man that size falling apart, not for the folks down below who may as well live in the shadow of a dam held together by cracks.

The vet spent all morning climbing up to his ear, and by the time he arrived with the bad news that the big ox was dying, the big ox was already dead. Those last breaths shuddered so hard from his body that windows shattered and houses shook free of foundations and a tree fell right over on somebody's roof, but no one told him about that. Nobody asked him to pay for the damage because we could see he was already spent. He fell to his knees and we all saw it coming and held onto whatever we could -- armloads of fine China, babies in their bassinets, vials of copperhead tears we'd paid too much for and kept in hope they had some longshot use -- and we braced ourselves for the impact. His fall split a canyon straight through this land; it's become famous in parts far from here where folks don't recall how it happened and think it's a beautiful thing, which is dumber than paying good money for copperhead tears.

He spent a long time on his knees, the best part of a year, and moss crept from his soles to his shoulders like a green blanket the earth had pulled over. He stretched his back once and its creaks and cracks echoed the length of the valley. Folks along the river thought winter's ice broke up early and came rushing outside to celebrate spring, only to be buffeted by swirling sharp winds and blown back into their houses, buried by deep drifts of snow in their own living rooms.

In our logging camps and at the bar, under the safety of eaves after dodging his tears in the street, we asked each other what we could do. No one volunteered to climb up to his ear. No one offered to deliver kind words to the sky because we had no words to offer. What do we know about losses that big way down here on the ground, in this village raised up in the valley he cleared with a swipe of his axe just because we asked him to do it, along the river he carved with a boot heel when our crops began to dry out? We owed him something, but what? He can't stub a toe without shaking the world, and none of us know about that.

He's so tall women love him like ants love the sun. His whispers work up into gales and tornadoes before ever reaching their ears. When he sighs it blows the roofs off our houses, and when he coos the sweet sounds of love the town's tenderest eardrums all rupture and rip. Only that ox was big enough to stand beside him, to rub his gnarled horns on the lumberjack's leg and let those great trunks of finger scratch behind his blue ears -- what woman could he touch with those fingers, who could he caress without breaking their bones?

When he finally stood up in the spring, he turned away from our town without saying a word and dragged his feet for the forest, leaving us acres of fresh ground cleared for farming. Now he stays out among the tall trees, the tallest of them only up to his waist, and figuring he wants to be left alone we go on as if we can't see him towering over everything else in our world, as if we can't hear the rumbling roll of his murmurs when he has a bad, lonely dream late at night. As if we don't pretend that it's only the river, roaring down over the falls, and go back to sleep side by side in our beds.

Law & Order: Viewers Like Us

Tim Jones-Yelvington

About

Law & Order: Viewers Like Us arose from series creator Aaron Davis's theory that younger viewers, having been raised by mass media, were more engaged by their own television-watching habits than by television itself. At the time, police procedural/courtroom drama *Law & Order* and its spinoffs were witnessing a decline in ratings, particularly in the coveted eighteen- to forty-nine-year-old demographic.

Davis considered the popularity of reality television and speculated that "millenials" were a self-referential generation. They'd grown up watching *Law & Order*, and would feel naturally drawn to characters like themselves who also grew up watching *Law & Order*, and whose lives remained shaped by their viewing habits.

A recent graduate of the screenwriting program at the University of Southern California, Davis pitched his concept to *Law & Order* Executive Producer Dick Wolf, and after Wolf green-lit Davis's series, NBC picked up the pilot, pleased by the show's minimal production costs; shot on a single set with a two-person cast of lesser-known actors, the series was significantly cheaper to produce than the average nighttime drama.

Law & Order: Viewers Like Us profiled a young college dropout named Simon Smith, who along with his best friend, Jools, was an avid fan of *Law & Order* and its spinoffs, especially *Law & Order: Special Victims Unit.* Simon's character arc builds gradually over the course of the series toward the revelation of a secret from his past.

The series debuted with strong ratings, then saw a steep drop-off following its second episode. Ultimately, only seven half-hour episodes were produced before the show was canceled. Nonetheless, *Viewers Like Us* developed a strong cult following, most especially among academics and on the Internet, where fans continue to dissect its plots.

Tagline
In the criminal justice system, there are the police who investigate crimes, and the viewers who watch television shows about their investigations. These are the stories of viewers like us.

Episode Guide

1. "Who's Watching?" (Pilot)

Synopsis
The pilot introduces viewers to Simon Smith, a rabid viewer of the *Law & Order* series, particularly *Law & Order: Special Victims Unit* (*Law & Order: SVU*). In his opening voiceover, Simon calls *Law & Order* his "comfort food," and says he watches it to relax.

As the pilot begins, Simon is watching an episode of *Law & Order: SVU* in which detectives discover the sexually violated corpse of a young female retail worker inside a residential trash compactor. Via voiceover, Simon muses that a compactor would cut down on the trash piled outside the window of his garden apartment.

On television, *Special Victims Unit* cuts to a commercial for a phone sex service that advertises, "Girls standing by waiting to talk to you." Simon picks up his telephone and dials. The woman at the other end asks Simon what he's doing, her bright red mouth all that's visible to viewers. Simon tells her he's watching *Law & Order: Special Victims Unit.* The woman asks Simon whether *Special Victims Unit* is the show about sex crimes, and wonders what fascinates him about sexual violence. Simon quickly hangs up.

Immediately, the telephone rings, and Simon answers anxiously. A woman at the other end, older than the phone sex operator, asks Simon whether he's all right, and viewers discover she's his mother. Simon tells his mother everything is fine. His mother asks how his job search is going, and Simon answers evasively.

Quotes
"I'm supposed to be a grownup now. Every morning, I look at myself in the mirror and repeat what my high school P.E. teacher Mr. Clemenson always used to say: 'You're with the big dogs now, little puppy.'" —Simon, opening voiceover

"You want to sex-crime me, baby? Tell me how you want to crime. You want to ravage me in a dumpster? You want to part my labia with a melon rind? Stuff my mouth with dirty tissues? Stuff me, baby." —Phone sex operator, addressing Simon

"What are you eating!? Dr. Oz says raw almonds are the new superfood. Dietary fiber, Simon! They sell canisters at Costco. Canisters, Simon! I'll send you a care package." —Simon's mother, addressing Simon

Trivia

~Before the series' budget was slashed after its third episode, *Law and Order: Viewers Like Us* produced original scenes from *Law & Order: Special Victims Unit* "episodes" Simon viewed. Although the actual cast of *SVU* was employed in their production, these are not considered *SVU* episodes in the strictest sense, as they occur outside *SVU*'s continuity, and none were filmed nor aired to completion.

~In the SVU segment from *Viewers Like Us*'s pilot, the trash compactor where detectives discover the young woman's body is labeled "Compactrax," a manufacturer owned by the brother of *Viewers Like Us* creator and showrunner Aaron Davis.

~When the pilot first aired, viewers questioned whether a commercial for phone sex operators would appear during a primetime network drama. In response, Aaron Davis clarified that Simon was watching late night *SVU* reruns in syndication on a local station, "emblematic," he said, "of the character's urban alienation." Davis has not responded to the ensuing Internet speculation about whether Simon's mother would realistically call him so late at night.

2. "The Viewing Party"

Synopsis

In this episode, viewers meet Jools, Simon Smith's best friend and fellow *Law & Order* aficionado. Jools arrives at Simon's doorstep bearing ice cream for a *Law & Order* viewing party.

She tells Simon he has no idea the week she's had. Simon tells her he can imagine, as he's had quite the week himself.

The friends commiserate, ripping open the ice cream container and consuming its contents. They watch an episode of *Law & Order: Special Victims Unit* in which Olivia Benson and Elliot Stabler infiltrate a satanic cult where young women are raped, mutilated, and offered as sacrifices to Lucifer. The cultists contend the women volunteer to be sacrificed, and so the sex and murder are consensual. At the station, Benson and Stabler argue the case's ethics with detectives Munch and Tutuola.

While watching the scene, Jools expresses her sexual attraction to Christopher Meloni's Stabler. Simon asks Jools how her boyfriend Daniel would react to Jools' declaration. Jools confesses her love life is in crisis, as she and Daniel have not had intercourse in seven weeks. Simon tells her she's lucky she has someone. Jools consoles Simon, reminding him the love of his life is "out there" and it's only a matter of time until they meet.

Quotes

"The interrogation room, the evidence locker, hell, I'd do him nasty all over the precinct."—Jools, regarding Elliot Stabler

"All I've ever wanted is somebody to eat ice cream with." (Jools glares.) "I mean, with tongue." —Simon

Trivia

~The character of Jools appeared in an earlier version of the pilot, but her scenes were excised following the firing of *High School Musical*'s Vanessa Hudgens, the actress initially hired to portray her. Hudgens' departure ignited a public feud with series creator and showrunner Aaron Davis, in which Davis accused Hudgens of "diva tantrums," and Hudgens called Davis a "talentless hack whose series is destined for cancellation." Shortly after the edited pilot aired, Hudgens was replaced by Canadian actress Cassie Steele, best known to audiences as *DeGrassi the Next Generation*'s Manuella Santos.

Ironically, Steele was originally cast as Gabriella Montez in *High School Musical*, the role Hudgens herself made famous, but bowed out to shoot her fifth season of *Degrassi*. Steele's role on *Law & Order: Viewers Like Us* made her the latest in a series of former *DeGrassi* actresses cast in starring roles on American series. Prior to Steele's appearance on *Viewers Like Us*, Nina Dobrev (*DeGrassi*'s Mia) and Shenae Grimes (*DeGrassi*'s Darcy) starred on the CW Network's *The Vampire Diaries* and *90210*, respectively.

~Jools brings Simon a carton of Ben and Jerry's "Mission to Marzipan," a flavor that actor Chad Wilson, Simon's portrayer, once promoted as his favorite. Viewers cried product placement, but Aaron Davis denied Ben and Jerry's paid for the publicity.

3. "The Sculpture Gardener"

Synopsis

Simon watches an episode of *Law & Order: Special Victims Unit* about a serial rapist and murderer who victimizes men he solicits for sex online. The perpetrator sculpts his victims' genitals into elaborate centerpieces he leaves behind on victims' dining room tables, while disposing of what's left of their remains .

Just after the episode begins, Simon receives a phone call from his mother. He sighs, visibly annoyed she's interrupted him watching television. His mother asks whether he's had any job interviews this week. He tells her he interviewed for two retail positions, and both interviews felt solid. Through voiceover, Simon admits he hasn't left the apartment in over a week. Simon's mother reminds him that she and his father cannot support him forever. She understands if he's reluctant to communicate with strangers, given everything he's endured. Simon tells her he can take care of himself and hangs up the phone.

While watching the rest of *Law & Order: SVU*, Simon surfs the Internet. He loads Manhunt.net, a Web site where gay men cruise for sex. A chime sounds, and Simon receives a text message from a beefcake named NYCStud69. Quickly, Simon closes his laptop and thrusts it aside.

Quotes
"You had better not be lying, Simon. You of all people should know the wages of deceit!" —Simon's mother, addressing Simon

"I wish they'd show the dick sculptures." —Simon, watching television

Trivia

~After the revelation of Simon's homosexuality, a spokesperson from the Gay and Lesbian Alliance Against Defamation (GLAAD) said that by "outing" himself early in the series, Simon was a significant improvement over the *Law & Order* franchise's previous gay contract character, the original series' A.D.A. Serena Southerlyn (played by Elisabeth Rohm), who after four seasons announced she was a lesbian immediately before departing the canvas. "However," GLAAD's spokesperson continued, "it remains to be seen whether Simon's depiction will be wholly positive, given the implication that a dark secret is lurking in his past."

~After Simon's "outing," viewers questioned why, in the pilot, a gay character would've called a female phone sex operator. "Can't a gay dude be curious about the ladies?" Aaron Davis replied."What, will somebody revoke his gay card? Frankly, I think that's a little close-minded. It's like … reverse discrimination or something."

4. "Critical Theories"

Synopsis

In this episode, Jools engages Simon in a critical conversation about *Law and Order: Special Victims Unit* in which she attempts to deconstruct their mutual fascination with the series. Jools says that by producing the same anxieties it allays, the series is complicit in the so-called "culture of fear." According to Jools, this "culture of fear," which exploits middle America's terror of urban crime, has enabled the United States to incarcerate more citizens than other "First World" nations do, while establishing the construction and operation of prisons as profit-generating enterprises. Jools argues that while *Law & Order* helps stoke the culture of fear, the franchise's ongoing popularity also results from this same culture, generating a self-perpetuating cycle.

While Jools talks, Simon checks his e-mail and social networking Web sites, consumes snacks, and handles his cell phone, presumably sending and receiving text messages.

Quotes

"Sure, the characters of color kick ass, but did you ever stop to think they're kicking ass for the same criminal-industrial complex that disproportionately incarcerates them?" —Jools

"This popcorn is totally burnt. It tastes like ass. Here, taste it." —Simon, addressing Jools

Trivia

~Although the script was credited to staff writer Elaine Wilkinson, Aaron Davis later admitted this episode was in fact written by intern Dharma DeSantis, an undergraduate cultural studies major at New York University. Davis said he wanted to air, as an experiment, an episode of *Law & Order: Viewers Like Us* written "by and for viewers like us." Though panned by critics and viewers alike, the episode has since become the subject of numerous scholarly treatments, and is a frequent topic of conversation at the annual *Law & Order* Studies conference at the University of Hawaii.

~Viewers criticized Jools' behavior as out of character, given this episode was the only time she'd appeared at all critical of *Law & Order.* Actress Cassie Steele rejected these criticisms, saying, "People think pretty girls can't be smart, but Jools has a brain. She's complicated. She thinks things."

~Although Simon's television remains muted through the episode, *Law and Order: SVU* continues in the background. Astute viewers recognized the silent episode as Season Seven's "Storm," in which a group of sisters are kidnapped from New Orleans and brought to New York City following Hurricane Katrina. This was the first time Davis's crew did not produce original *SVU* clips to air during *Viewers Like Us*, a practice that would continue through the series' final three episodes.

5. "Necessary Categories"

Synopsis
In this episode, Simon Smith reorganizes his iTunes library. He assigns his music to one of four categories: "exuberant," "ponderous," "tranquil," or "obscure." He retypes the track titles and artist names using all-lowercase letters. Through voiceover, he informs viewers that the lowercase letters calm him.

While reorganizing his library, he watches an episode of *Law & Order: SVU* where a young boy witnesses his stepmother's rape and murder. Midway through the episode, Jools telephones, and Simon mutes the television to speak with her. Jools asks him what's up, as she hasn't heard from him all week. Simon says he's been busy. Jools says he's lying, she can hear it in his voice. She tells him he's been acting strange lately. He denies her accusation. She reminds him he can tell her anything. He hangs up the phone.

Quotes
"Are you getting laid and not telling me!? Tell me the truth! Don't think I won't anal rape you with a broken Izze bottle!" —Jools, addressing Simon

Trivia
~When the camera focuses on Simon's laptop monitor, he can be seen recategorizing tracks by an artist named Emily Bezar, a little-known singer-songwriter from the Bay Area. Bezar was a family friend of staff writer Tina Schiller. Bezar's music is somewhat similar to artists Kate Bush and Tori Amos, but more influenced by jazz and avant garde composition. She has since become a favorite among *Viewers Like Us*'s remaining Internet fan-base.

~Visible in a stack of books on Simon's desk is *Severance* by Pulitzer Prize–winning author Robert Olen Butler. *Severance* is a collection of short fiction based upon famous historical decapitations, and features a story about the automobile accident that killed Jayne Mansfield, mother of *Law & Order: SVU* star Mariska Hargitay.

6. *"Secrets and Liars"*

Synopsis
The episode begins with Simon in the bathtub, hunched beneath a running faucet, washing black dye from his hair. A buzzer sounds. Simon calls down to ask who's there and Jools announces herself. Simon buzzes her up and puts on his bathrobe to answer the door.

Immediately upon entering the apartment, Jools asks Simon why he altered his hair color. He tells her, For the hell of it. She tells him, Bullshit, and says she knows he's been hiding something. She has come to confront him, she tells him, and to discover what's been going on with him.

After a sequence of entreaties and denials, Simon finally tells Jools he dyed his hair because he feels safer when nobody recognizes him. He tells her whenever he leaves the apartment, he has the sensation that somebody is following him.

He tells Jools that he moved to New York City because something terrible happened at home. When Simon was fourteen years old, he began a sexual relationship with his older cousin, who at the time was twenty-one. Shortly after Simon's seventeenth birthday, his parents discovered the relationship and prosecuted Simon's cousin as a sexual offender.

Simon left for college the following year, but never felt secure. Unable to focus on his studies, he failed his second term. Moving to New York City, he tells Jools, was his therapist's idea, an experiment in independent living.

What Simon has never told anybody is his relationship with his cousin was consensual. On the stand, Simon called his cousin coercive so as not to upset his parents, but in reality he was in love with his cousin and misses him terribly. He has been haunted by guilt since the trial, feeling responsible for his cousin's incarceration. Because of this guilt, he feels self-conscious in public spaces, as though everyone knows his misdeeds and is judging him.

Jools tells Simon perhaps his parents were correct, and he was too young to knowingly consent. He shouldn't blame himself. Simon says maybe Jools is right. Simon falls asleep with his head in Jools' lap, watching an episode of *Law and Order: Special Victims Unit* where a piano teacher is arrested for molesting his students.

Quotes

"There were times I'd look at him and hope ... I'd hope his face was all I'd see forever." —Simon, regarding his cousin

Trivia
~A spokesperson from the Gay and Lesbian Alliance Against Defamation denounced the revelation of Simon's secret as perpetuating the conflation of homosexuality with pedophilia, incest, and related forms of sexual deviance.

~A group calling themselves the United Federation of Cousin Lovers (UFCL) sent Aaron Davis a letter thanking him for his "honest depiction of an experience far more common than anybody realizes." Shortly thereafter, a representative of the organization named Clive MacGuffin appeared on the *Today Show* to give testament to "the bonds of amorous fealty" that bound him to his father's brother's son. When *Today Show* co-host Meredith Vieira asked whether his relationship constituted incest, he proclaimed, "That's a bull*bleep* cultural construct!"

~Simon uses "Earth Tones" hair dye, an ecologically sustainable brand promoted by former *Law & Order: Special Victims Unit* actress Michaela McManus, whose ill-fated turn as A.D.A. Kim Greylek ended after only fourteen episodes.

7. *"Seen Assailant"*

Synopsis
As this episode begins, Simon is watching a *Law & Order: Special Victims Unit* episode in which detectives discover the decomposing body of a sexually molested five-year-old girl. His telephone rings just before a commercial break. Simon answers. A recording asks him whether he'll accept a collect call from "Gavin Carlton." Simon blanches, then approves the call.

An unseen male asks whether Simon is there and if he can

hear him. Simon grunts affirmatively. The man tells Simon he loves and forgives him, and viewers realize the caller is Simon's incarcerated cousin. Simon is quiet. His cousin asks whether he is still on the line. Staring at the television, Simon slides his finger onto the switch hook button to disconnect the call.

Moving in an almost zombie-like state, Simon opens his laptop, logs onto Manhunt, and views a message from NYCStud69. Simon types, "Come over?" After a jump cut, a stocky white male dressed in black clothing arrives at Simon's apartment. Simon invites him in and they begin making out. The visitor violently spins Simon and kicks his lower back. Simon collapses, and the visitor yanks off Simon's blue jeans. Simon cries out, but his assailant muffles his screams.

After another jump cut, viewers see Jools outside Simon's door, pounding and calling his name. Finally, she pulls a key from under his doormat and pushes inside. She finds Simon unconscious and bloodied. She panics, grabs the telephone, and dials 911. As the episode ends, Simon is wheeled into an ambulance. A paramedic informs Jools he's in critical condition, and may not survive the night.

Quotes
"Simon? Simon, are you there? I want you to know I forgive you. I want you to know I think about you. I think about you every day." —Gavin, Simon's cousin

"Simon? Simon!? Don't die on me, you asshole!" —Jools

Trivia

~When this episode was written and produced, Aaron Davis believed the series was entering a two-month rerun cycle, but after several months, NBC announced *Viewers Like Us* would not receive a full-season pickup. Many viewers continue to resent the network for leaving them with a cliffhanger, while others speculate about Simon's fate. In earlier interviews, Davis said that rather than following a single protagonist throughout the series' run, he intended to present a different "viewer" each season in order to represent a more diverse cross-section of *Law & Order*'s viewership. Thus, Simon's survival was far from a fait accompli.

~Many viewers have continued Simon's story in fan fictions posted on the Internet. One group of young women call themselves the "Simools" and speculate an alternate reality in which Simon is alive, heterosexual, and married to Jools.

~"Slash fiction," erotica stories in which male characters are paired with one another, are also popular. Most revolve around Simon's relationship with his cousin, Gavin Carlton. An entire subgenre of *Viewers Like Us* slash fiction takes place in prison; in the majority of these stories, Simon has deliberately committed a crime in order to land himself behind bars, and shares a cell with Gavin. These tales are often wrought with romantic *sturm und drang*, as Simon and Gavin confront their emotional demons and shared history. Inexplicably, most slash writers describe Gavin as resembling the actor Christopher Walken. In fact, Gavin Carlton's association with Christopher Walken has become so deeply entrenched in particular subcultures, "walken" has become a verb used to describe incestual bonds similar to Gavin and Simon's. The Web site Urban Dictionary defines "to walken" as "to mack on one's own cousin, e.g., 'My cousin's a total hottie, I want to walken him up.'"

DISTRACTUS REFRACTUS ONTOLOGICUS:
THE DISSEMINATION OF MICHAEL MARTONE

Josh Maday

1 Michael Martone is Michael Martone.

1.1 Michael Martone begins, middles, and ends Michael Martone.

1.12 Michael Martone is this, that, and the other Michael Martone.

1.13 Michael Martone is not, however, every Michael Martone.

1.131 A Google search will support this, though not conclusively, because this Michael Martone may in fact be that and/or the other Michael Martone—Michael Martone the locksmith, the winemaker, the writer, the judge, the hockey player, the teacher; the fourth grader staring at the mirror reflecting the image of Michael Martone back into Michael Martone, where Michael Martone is appropriated, refracted, disseminated. Or vice versa.

2 Michael Martone is a fiction.

NOTE: Any similarity to real persons, living or dead, is coincidental due to the fact that Michael happens to be a very popular name, and Martone is unlikely to have been the invention of any particular Martone alive in the past century.

Michael Martone, despite and due to the wishes, imaginations, and varying qualities of effort of Michael Martone, is consumed, digested, and defecated; absorbed and reconstituted by the system, his acidic formal content neutralized by commodification in the capitalist market economy.

2.01 Marilyn Monroe, Marilyn Manson, Eminem, etc, etc, [. . .] Michael Martone.

2.011 George Orwell, George Sand, George Eliot, Lewis Carroll, Stendhal, Saki, J.T. Leroy, Dr. Seuss, etc, etc, [. . .] Michael Martone.

2.0111 ((([. . .], (Descartes), (Leibniz), (Rousseau), (Hume), (Kant), (Hegel), (Kierkegaard), (Nietzsche), (Husserl), (Heidegger), ((Blanchot), (Deleuze), ((Foucault), (Jacques Derrida)), (Barthes))), [. . .], Borges), Barthelme, Barth, [. . .], Michael Martone, [. . .], etc, etc, [. . .] . . .)*

*NOTE: This is only a single thread, one meandering stairway in the Escherian algorithm of world history. A comprehensive schematic can be found running backwards through any prism, or by playing a vinyl record in reverse. Or watching a rope maker at work. Or tracing a birth (live, still, or partial) back to its origin.

ALSO NOTE: The universe is located in the ellipsis, the comma, and the space.

FURTHER NOTE: God lives in the footnotes (but not intratextual notes such as this, so God is not here).

2.012 Michael Martone is a certain, specific, particular Michael Martone who is particularly particular about being referred to as Michael Martone.

2.0121 Michael Martone is fond of the name "Michael Martone" said in just this way, though with varying emphasis depending on where in the succession of Michael Martones a certain Michael Martone is situated.

2.0211 Michael Martone is a mantra, a rosary, a repetition, an incantation that grows slippery, slimy, and begins to dissolve and fall apart somewhere between mind and mouth like a piece of over-chewed chewing gum (this is to say nothing of flavor (well, nothing further, Your Honor; however, *taste* may in fact factor into this)).

2.0212 The task is and is not to differentiate the who of Michael Martone from the what of Michael Martone.

Good luck.

3 Michael Martone is the function of Michael Martone.

Consider the proposition: 'Michael Martone (Michael Martone (*Michael Martone x*))' where Michael Martone = Michael Martone.

Only the name 'Michael Martone' is common among the functions (numbingly common; in fact, anaesthetizing), and the name by itself signifies nothing (except, of course, in relation to publishing and among experimental literary circles, where meaning is legion, a snake tangle, and hearing the name spoken at social functions manifests mental images and words, setting off synaptic fires along the hearer's neural chains the way a giant spider causes its entire web to tremble when scurrying after stuck prey, quickening said hearers' heart rates and sending beads of sweat down the valley of the back toward Mordor—and the dark ring spreads from the underarms, signifying in return these hearers who are 'in the know,' and Michael Martone may in fact have experienced this as a hearer himself, as one 'in the know,' listening to the name being spoken (sometimes by himself), and wanting very badly to finally meet this fucking guy named Michael Martone.)

The above proposition can also be said, "Michael Martone feels alienated from himself."

3.1 Michael Martone is the simultaneous proliferation and subsequent reunion of Michael Martone—the conglomeration, amalgamation, and corporation of Michael Martone.

3.2 Michael Martone enjoys swimming through, shooting at, and hiding in the subterfuge of Michael Martone.

3.21 Michael Martone is a video game akin to *Centipede, Space Invaders*, etc.

3.3 Michael Martone is the red ribbed plastic shell casing with brass head, primer, powder charge, and wad, as well as each individual pre- and post-fired buckshot bearing: potential, kinetic, and residual Michael Martone.

3.x (also 3.01) Michael Martone is a signifier, a semiotic configuration, positing, depositing, calling, recalling, presenting, representing that which is meant by, imagined to be, and conceptually categorized as Michael Martone.

3.4 (also .01, or BMM (Before Michael Martone (but not that Michael Martone)))*

Michael Martone was born, named, held upside down by his ankles and spanked in front of up to a dozen adult human beings.

*NOTE: This asterisk indicates that the note previously occupying this space has gone on to The Great Footnote in the Sky.

3.401 Michael Martone is the linear progression of a circular argument, i.e. conflict with self.

X.X Michael Martone is everyone.

3.401a Michael Martone is simulacra.

3.4011 One day at school, Michael Martone was herded with the rest of his class to the cafeteria. All the lunch tables and benches had been folded up and locked into their compartments in the walls. The students were directed in an activity meant to teach them the value of teamwork (while also introducing them to the symbiosis inherent in social contract). The teacher called this particular exercise the Circle Sit-Down, where the children formed a circle and sat on each other's knees, positioning them at once as the chair and the one sitting on the chair. This paradox troubled Michael Martone the chair, but comforted the seated Michael Martone, who began formulating plans for the mass production of the former Michael Martone.

3.4012 Michael Martone dressed as Michael Martone, taking meticulous care to get the details just right, and stood before the mirror. Based on three basic principles he'd learned at school—power in naming, numbers, and repetition—he turned around three times at midnight and spoke the name "Michael Martone" at the commencement of each revolution. After completing the final revolution he stood facing his reflection and waited. Rumor was, the one he invoked would come forth from the mirror and murder him.

3.41 "Michael Martone was born in Fort Wayne, Indiana . . ." --Michael Martone, *Michael Martone*, pp. 11, 15, 19, 23, 27, 37, 41, 45, 49, 53, 57, 59, 61, 65, 69, 73, 83, 87, 91, 95, 99, 103, 107, 111, 115, 123, 127, 133, 139, 143, 149, 151, 155, 161, 167, 171, 175, 179, 183, 187

3.411 Many Michael Martones have lived in Indiana, where possibly every Michael Martone in history has lived.

3.42 Indiana was first on Michael Martone's list.

3.43 Michael Martone destroyed Indiana and replaced it with what you do and do not see there today.

4 Michael Martone is the center of Michael Martone's universe, as well as the numerous satellites orbiting Michael Martone, including the spinning, fragmentary arms reaching perpetually around for just one hug before everything falls apart again, before the dust gravitates toward and settles around some other center.

5 One particular Michael Martone wrote things about himself and other Michael Martones and gathered them into a book entitled *Michael Martone.*

5.01 It is the case that Michael Martone experienced certain phenomena. Said phenomena made impressions on Michael Martone, who interpreted, categorized, and stored the impressions chemically. Then, many years later, Michael Martone recalled stored chemical data, filling in blanks where needed and/or desired to suit his purposes of recollection and representation. This idea became physical motion became symbols on paper became characters on a computer screen became narrative became manipulated text tightened around a center: all of which became manuscript, the idea moving beneath the surface of the text having been bounced back and forth between Michael Martone and text similarly to dribbling a basketball while walking, including the loud noise of simultaneous smacking and beating.

5.011

5.012 Michael Martone is penciled in freehand above the solid black line, below which in all caps is the word "NAME," also in black, infinitely deep against the starched white paper, each character an abyss punched into the pulp.

A mistake is made.

Michael Martone is that remaining graphite pressed into the pores of the paper, that still-visible, ever-visible residue haunting the page regardless of what will be written over it, always hovering in the background drawing eyes to itself, past the façade of new writing and reflecting the reader's attention back in time and back off the page to the writer, to the initial inclination, intention, revealing the slippage of process, haste and trepidation—the eraser chewed, bitten, and nibbled, worn down by the dialectic of thought.

5.013 [: . :]

5.02 Michael Martone lied and may quite possibly be lying at this moment about Michael Martone.

6 Michael Martone is Michael Martone's experiment.

6.xx Michael Martone gave birth to himself (à la Artaud): he was born again, and again, and again, a piece at a time, first an arm, next a pinky toe, then an eye, now a full-grown head of hair, and so on; however, the parts were not assembled in the order in which they came, but rather in the manner of a puzzle.

6.01 Michael Martone is Frankenstein's monster, whose name is Michael Martone.

6.02 Michael Martone, this particular Michael Martone, is an entity similar (and sometimes identical) to Michael Martone.

6.03 Michael Martone's conception of Michael Martone took place when Michael Martone became aware of Michael Martone as Michael Martone, but not necessarily the Michael Martone known as the Michael Martone who wrote or is depicted in *Michael Martone.*

6.031 Michael Martone had had a bad day at school during his fourth-grade year when his too-small spectacles had made a spectacle of him, the subject and object of derisory discussion by classmates (against whom he vowed revenge by becoming more brilliant and talked-about than they ever could, and then, finally, they would be sorry they had ever said nasty things about his glasses, his person, and his mother) in a modality of Fort Wayne, Indiana. Michael Martone came home and went straight to his bedroom.

6.0311 Michael Martone was fertile soil, and the world was the tree of life reaching deeply with its roots, pushing its greedy fibrous capillaries between every grain of Michael Martone's being, trying to sap out everything.

6.03xx Michael Martone had reached the saturation point.

6.04 Michael Martone wanted to keep himself, not lose his self a la carte at the hands and eyes and mouths and minds of the world.

6.24 Therefore, Michael Martone [took] *hold of himself, clutching his own self to his breast,* and [removed] *that self to a safe place.*

But when *the safe places became ever fewer,* Michael Martone abandoned them for the refuge found in *a complex system of optical illusions,* the *manipulation* *of cunningly illuminated facets*, donning the façade of *feign*[ed] *translucence.**

*Italicized words from the work entitled *Invitation to a Beheading*, arranged by Vladimir Nabokov.

6.54 Michael Martone sat slouched on the side of his bed, hands in his lap while he listened to *The Dark Side of the Moon*. Studying the album cover, how the prism split a single ray of light into such varied, glittering, attractive, distractive colors, Michael Martone decided to clone himself—create hundreds, thousands of clones, splinter away his accidental qualities and develop them as he pleased, sending them into the world while the essential Michael Martone remained safely intact at the center of things.

6.789 And while the album cover remained still, static, a frozen moment, Michael Martone manipulated the image, reversing the light back through the triangle, and the prism gathered each thread of light back together, weaving it into a perfect whole, something he knew did not really exist, but was the most beautiful illusion he had ever seen.

6.999 After defiantly foregoing dinner in order that his head would shrink to better accommodate the hugging arms of his spectacles, a melancholy Michael Martone found a mirror and looked at the reflection—and reflecting on that reflection, he said over and over in a whispered, undulating scale of (Mar)tones: Michael Martone . . . Michael Martone . . . Michael Martone . . . I'm Michael Martone . . . I am Michael Martone . . . Michael Martone . . .You're Michael Martone . . . You're Michael Martone . . . Michael Martone . . . Hello, Michael Martone . . .

My Secret Life as a Slasher

Henry Jenkins

As an academic, I've often written about the curious genre of slash fan fiction. Slash fans actively reread and rewrite popular media texts with a homoerotic twist. They typically take relationships which are explicitly framed as homosocial – what we might call "male bonding" or more recently, "bromance" stories – and reimagine the characters as engaging in carnal relations. In most cases, the sex becomes a way of expressing the intimacy between these characters that fans feel has been repressed by the original story. Often, the act of opening up to each other sexually also involves opening up emotionally and in many cases, these stories depict sex as transformative, curing past hurts, overcoming distrusts, opening the characters to new perspectives and experiences. In short, these stories are not simply about sex between bodies but sex between characters, characters that are already known well to the readers and writers of such stories as a result of their appearance in other texts. So, we are talking about Kirk and Spock, Luke Skywalker and Hans Solo, Snape and Harry Potter, and so forth.

Not so very long ago, I was interviewed by Emma Grant for the Slashcast podcast and spoke openly about the fact that I have one published story out there in a relatively obscure little zine called Not What You Think.

Now that the cat is out of the bag, I would like to present some excerpts from the story itself along with some reflections and critical commentary on the nature of slash.

The story is called "Golden Idol." It was first published, if you can call it that, in 1998 and promptly disappeared into obscurity.

Here's how the story starts:

"Another Idol has displaced me," the fair young girl in the mourning dress exclaimed, her eyes misted with tears. 'If it can cheer and comfort you in time to come, as I would have tried to do, I have no just cause to grief.'

He gasped, stung by her sudden revelation. She knew! Nancy had found out the secret that he hadn't uttered aloud even in private, and if she knew, who else might know? Did he? He trembled at the thought and then tried to mask his discomfort with a half-felt denial.

"What idol has displaced you?"

He wanted to probe, hungered for an answer, and yet feared to find out how much she knew. He was certain in any case that she would not be able to put what she knew into words. His secret, as he had always known, was unspeakable and so her language was circumspect. She hinted at things without saying them directly.

But how could she know? He had always acted the part of the perfect gentleman with her, since that day long ago when they first spoke of marriage and began to imagine a future together. He had taken her to dances and let her show off her new beau to her blushing friends. He had brought her flowers and had dinner at her house. As time passed, they had moved from speculations of marriage to treating it as something that would happen someday, then soon, then in a matter of months, whenever he got his affairs in order, whenever he was sure he would be able to support them. He was eager to believe that things could work out between them, that they were in love, even if he often had trouble finding those feelings inside himself, even if his emotions towards her lacked the intensity with which romantic love was described in books or songs.

He danced the dance -- did it matter so much that he didn't really quite hear the music? He held her hand, on occasions when it was deemed appropriate, and stroked it softly, admiring her slender digits, running his fingers ever so gently along her wrist. He kissed her playfully on the ear when that was appropriate, uncertain if this was too much of an advance for someone in their position or not enough of one. He always played the part, always aware of an audience that included her but also many others. He tried to convince her (not to mention himself) that all of this came naturally, spontaneously, grew from honest emotions (which he was increasingly doubtful that anyone in his position really felt.)

Yet somehow he knew he was lying, and more to the point, somehow she knew he was lying. That much was certain. The sham was unveiled, and with its demise had ended his hopes of settling comfortably, easily, respectably, into married life. Perhaps she had known even before he had known himself. But that only increased his guilt since this meant that perhaps she knew him better than anyone else and had come to understand his emotions, his thoughts -- even his desires? -- from the inside out.

The seconds seemed to linger in the air, and she was not responding to his question. She looked at him with hurt, perhaps a little anger, though less than he would have expected under the circumstances. Did he imagine a little pity in her eyes, or was it dread? He waited and she waited and then he asked again, "What idol has displaced you?"...

"A golden one," she said, again speaking ambiguously, telling only what was necessary to extract both of them from their painful circumstances, moving forward with a dignity that was mixed with more than a little denial.

A golden one. How tangled that one remark seemed to him at that moment, for there were two economies at stake in this discussion. There was the economy of business, of profits and loss, of red ink and black ink, of ledgers and columns; and there was the economy of desire, of things saved and spent, of things consumed and yet remained to be consumed. There was the gold, silver and copper that he could hold in his hands and count, and there was the gold, silver, and copper that he desired and yet could never touch -- the gold of Jacob's wild shock of hair pulled up in a tail, the silver of his eyes so keen and shrewd, and the copper of his glistening skin flushed with sweat. And there was the gold that passed between them, the coins that had touched the skin he dared not touch and that passed into his own hands still warm from Jacob's body.

He tried to pretend that they were speaking only of crowns and shillings and so protested that the world was unjust in issuing almost as much reproach to those who worked hard for their money, who labored and earned and saved and counted and stored away their money, as they did to the poor and worthless, lazy and lame. Perhaps she was, after all, simply protesting the many hours he spent at his work, the hours he neglected her to earn money. Yet he knew he could not extract himself that simply.

The time he spent earning money was not only time he had not spent with her; it was time he had spent with Jacob. He always found excuses to prolong it. They worked side by side in silence, often for hours on end, so close to each other that he could feel his partner's breath on the back of his neck. He would lose count, counting instead the ebb and flow of his partner's breathing, straining to hear the sound of his heart beating, to be aware of his body, until Jacob would speak, jarring him back to consciousness, pulling him back to the world of bargains and investments. Jacob never rebuked him for his dreaminess, for his inattention to the hard facts of the matter at hand but laughed softly, a gleam in his eyes.

If the hour was late and the day's work had been sufficiently profitable, they would close the big leather books and walk out into the streets together, stopping at their private club for a few drinks. Those who knew them rarely saw one without the other, and after a while, many of them had trouble remembering which was which. They had been partners in business for a little over a year at that point. Still he had trouble remembering when it had started since those arrangements had become so comfortable that it was harder and harder to imagine when they had not been together. He had already forgotten what it was like to be alone -- to be without a partner, to be without a fiance, to be working for old Fezziweg as a clerk, to be away from the warm glow of Jacob Marley.

Part of the pleasure of publishing the story for the first time in the context of a multimedia zine was to let people slowly discover for themselves who this story was about. I got the idea for writing a Scrooge/Marley slash story while listening to a tape of Patrick Stewart's one man show version of the Christmas Carol. Suddenly, for the first time, the scene when Scrooge breaks up with his finance Nancy had popped out at me. It was one of the few times in the entire novel that we hear from someone who can see inside Scrooge and really understands what he is thinking. Normally what characters say about Scrooge is projected onto him from a more distanced perspective. I was intrigued by this phrase, "a Golden Idol," and the way that she presents this "idol" as if it were a flesh and blood rival for his affections. She most likely is referring to his workaholic tendencies and to his greed, those traits we most associate with Scrooge, yet what if she wasn't? What if there really were a secret rival who stood between Scrooge and his intended bride?

Every line in this scene comes directly from the novel. What I was doing here was recontextualizing Dicken's original language to offer up an alternative interpretation of what the characters might have been thinking -- this integration of original dialogue and internal monologue is a common literary device in fan fiction. I was rewriting it for the purpose of critical commentary and in the process, I was trying to include as many elements from the original novel as possible while offering explanations for the character issues which have long concerned literary critics writing about the book. Even the idea that the partnership between Scrooge and Marley might have a homosocial/homoerotic undertone would not seem radical in the era of queer literary criticism. (For more on this point, see the slash chapter in Textual Poachers). But from an academic perspective, the fact that I used a fictional form rather than an analytic essay to construct this argument might have seen nonconventional.

The Victorians had been very interested in using economic vocabularies to talk about the expenditure of bodily fluids that took place through sexual encounters and so I played with this to describe the relations between the two men.

Let me continue further with the scene we started:

He had met Marley years before when they had been schoolboys, he an upperclassman who tried hard to teach the young Jacob his proper place but instead had been charmed by the lad, captivated by his quick wit and warm smile, fascinated by the workings of his mind, and stirred by his developing body. They had enjoyed a closeness then that no adult could know, become intimates in every sense of the word, sharing everything, withholding nothing, until the whole school was atalk about their crush, until the threat of scandal had loomed large on the horizon and begun to play upon even Scrooge's mind. Then his father, perhaps hearing gossip, perhaps getting a report from the schoolmaster, withdrew him from that school, took him home and 'made him a man.' His father was harsh and unloving, knowing little of matters of the heart. His mother had died when he was young, so there was little to bring joy into that house. His young sister, sweet little Fan, had done her best to reconcile the two of them, not really ever understanding the differences that kept them apart. Inevitably, voices were raised, harsh words were uttered and neither man could find reconciliation. When he had been younger, after his mother died, the old man had beaten him, punching him in the ribs, slapping him in the face, until he ran away and hid. Yet when he had returned home to find a father who no longer drank and who had discovered religion and so had learned to contain his violent rage, Scrooge found that some things hurt even more than fists. His father prayed for him every night and made certain that he knew that he knew that he had fallen far short of the old man's sense of what was proper, normal, respectable. His father's harsh whispers, not able to confront the problem directly, not able to forget it either, bruised him with their intensity. His eyes, stone hard, merciless, unforgiving, cut into his flesh.

At last Scrooge left, seeking his fortune elsewhere, looking for some place where he could escape his forbidden feelings for Jacob and avoid his father's wrath and judgment. He had gone to work at Fezziweg's, starting as a young apprentice and gradually gaining more responsibilities. Scrooge found in the red-faced, round and jolly man a second father, one as kind-hearted and generous as his own father was bitter and brutal. Fezziweg trusted him and through his trust, Scrooge had learned to trust himself again and had opened himself up to friendship, this time with a young man named Dick Wilkens....

Dicken's novel includes surprisingly few elements, tell us relatively little about Scrooge. We are expected to see him from the outside -- as a cranky old man -- and not from the inside -- as someone who is described as deeply lonely, even as a boy. I wanted to use this story to examine that loneliness and to use that loneliness to explain what happened between Scrooge and Marley.

Part of what interested me was the doubling that occurs in the book as we see Scrooge as an old man watching himself within scenes that occurred when he was a much younger man and the sense of powerlessness he must have felt reliving those moments without being able to change them. And this led me deeper and deeper into thoughts about being haunted by memories, about wanting to say things that had gone unsaid or do things that hadn't been done.

As I thought about what kind of slash story I could construct about Scrooge and Marley, I realized it needed not to be a love story per se but about the story of a romance that almost happened and that Scrooge, so much concerned by the judgment of the world, had backed away from. It became a story about how one internalizes homophobia and how it blocks one from the experience of one's desires.

Here's more:

Scrooge, now an old man, his face hardened into a caricature of itself, had trouble remembering times in his life when he had not been alone, cut off from the others around him. As a young boy, crying in the school house rather than return home to his father, he watched through the window as a parade of mummers passed, bursting with Yuletide spirits. As a young man, having at last found his one true friend, he was forcefully removed from the boarding school by his father and isolated once again, this time in a suffocating realm of Bible verses and condemnations. As a young clerk working for Fezziweg, trying to play the part of the respectable adult, he learned that the illusion of friendship and community could be maintained only if one didn't inspect it too closely or demand from it more than it was prepared to give. As a young suitor, he fumbled to convince the world that he was very much in love; as a young businessman sitting at night in the club by himself, he pretended not to care that no one invited him to join him for a drink.

My story contains very little sex in the end -- this is unusual for slash but not unheard of. What interested me was the emotional life of the characters and that is certainly the driving force behind most slash. I have them make love one time in a burst of enthusiasm on Christmas eve and then have Scrooge, alone in the dark, feel shame and crawl away, never to speak of the experience again. The closeness they feel is shattered by their efforts to consummate their relationship sexually (the reverse of what happens in most slash). And this prepares us for the last phases of their life together.

In his later years, after that fateful night when everything had come apart for them, Scrooge and Marley became simply a business concern. The two old men worked side by side yet scarcely spoke as they pored over their books. Marley came to communicate with him only through his clerk, Bob Cratchet. In the years since Marley's death, there was no more hope for them, no possibility of changing what had been said or finishing what had gone unsaid. Marley had died, and he had gone on living, though he had, by that point, become so paralyzed that he could scarcely be called alive. He went through life snarling at those who demanded from him what was no longer his to give, angry at those who enjoyed the happiness and good fellowship that he was denied, and harsh towards those who wanted what he had without being prepared to pay the brutal price.

I was fascinated that Marley returns from the dead to communicate with Scrooge and then shows him nothing of their life together, even though on other levels Dickens hints that this must have been the most defining relationship of Scrooge's life. One reason why people initially struggle to imagine a Scrooge/Marley story is that we never see Marley in his prime, as a young man, and have only the image of the rotting corpse with the slack jaw and the chains. So, in the story, I have Scrooge trying to read through the lines, looking for the scenes that Marley doesn't show him, and in the end, this is the level on which they communicate with each other.

He was confused. What was the meaning of any of these scenes that the Ghost had brought him to witness? Why these scenes, not others? What pattern was being slowly but surely developed form these fragments of time, bits of old memories, many of which he had long ago forgotten? It seemed to him that these choices missed the point somehow, did not fit within the narrative had had constructed to make sense of his own life, seemed to point consistently to a life he had not lived and the lies that he had tried to tell the world. But where was the truth? Perhaps some outside observer might look upon these as turning points in his life, but surely Marley, of all people, knew better.

Marley had returned from the dead -- for that was certain, Marley was dead, dead as a doornail, dead as a coffin nail, dead. Yet he had come back to him, at no small cost he was certain. To what purpose, what end?

Marley had sought to warn him about the cost of denying the world its due, about the price he had paid for hardening his heart and shutting out his feelings. He was prepared to learn that lesson as best he could and act upon it insofar as was appropriate.

But these were the wrong moments. Removed from context, they made little or no sense. He could witness the actions, hear the words, but he could not feel the emotions. The people around him meant even less to him than they had the first time. Could the truth of anyone's life be summed up in a few scattered moments without looking at what had come before and after? Were the words that had been said so many years before adequate to the occasion when he was powerless, as a mere witness, to rewrite them, to modify them, to speak them again but try to convey their meaning more fully? What mattered ultimately, he feared, was not what he had said and done but what hadn't happened, the silences rather than the utterances. What mattered were the gaps which fell between the scenes that the world chose to remember. That had always been the problem....

The Ghost had not offered him the chance, which he would gladly have taken, to relive that moment when he saw Jacob again at his club, that firm embrace, that happy reunion, or the time when they agreed to become partners, or those heady first days as a company when the two together gained the success that had been denied them both separately and they felt as if the world were out there waiting for them to pluck it like a bauble. The Ghost didn't let him hear Marley's laughter again or see his smile or watch the sparkle in his eyes. Instead he was forced to watch himself pretend a love he did not feel and try to accept the release Nancy was offering him with appropriate grace and appropriate regret.

None of that mattered. At that moment all that mattered was Marley and the time they had spent together and the scenes the Ghost was omitting from this journey down memory's crooked pathways. It was as if Marley had never existed, had not been part of his life -- the best part, the most important part, the only true and meaningful part. It was as if Marley was shoving him away with all of his might towards the life that might have been his if he had simply forsaken his unnatural love and conformed to what was normal and expected of him.

Everything in the next passage is there in Dicken's novel. There's a lot that seems psychologically odd about Scrooge's relationship to Marley if we read the novel closely yet these are the passages that get skipped over in the dramatization of the story. This is a good example of how slash writing requires the marshalling of evidence, the presentation of data, which supports the slash interpretation -- again, like other forms of critical commentary. The actions I describe are in the book; the motives I ascribe to them come from my analysis of the book through the slash interpretation.

Scrooge could not bring himself to paint out Marley's name on their sign, so he still went by Scrooge and Marley some seven years later, and people still came there looking for Marley and settling for Scrooge. He could not bring himself to fire Cratchet, even though his very presence was painful to him, since it reminded him of the times when he and his partner were unwilling or unable to speak to each other. He snarled at Cratchet and he punished Cratchet because he needed to strike out at someone and Cratchet was at his mercy. He wanted Cratchet to go away and take the memories of Marley with him, but he could not fire him, no matter how much he grumbled about giving him a day off at Christmas or using too much coal to light the wood stove. He couldn't fire Cratchet because, for all of the sad memories he provoked, Marley had hired him, had trusted him, had valued his friendship, and he could not undo what Marley had done. Scrooge moved into Marley's house to be close to him, to feel the presence of his spirit in the things the man had accumulated, and Scrooge slept, when he was able to do so, in Marley's bed, the bed curtains still hanging there as they had that night. He grew to hate Christmas as he did no other day of the year because it had brought him nothing but misery and stood as a reminder of how out of favor he was with the world's expectations.

In the end, I am impressed by the healing which Marley offers Scrooge in returning from the dead and offering him back memories of his life while it is still possible to change. Several writers have theorized that slash is a genre about nurturance, about men trying to heal each other of the pains caused by their repressed sexual and emotional lives, often in the forms of nursing each other back to physical or mental health. Seen through this lens, Marley's return to Scrooge is a great romantic gesture -- certainly embodying the idealized notion of romantic male friendship that many writers have found in slash.

Marley had come back from the dead to speak with him again, after all those years of silence, those years when the office had been like a tomb and those years when Marley had been buried in his tomb, as if it mattered, in the end, whether the silence between them was shared with a body that was living or dead. What must Marley have gone through to win that right denied so many other doomed souls, to return for even a moment to the world of the living, to intervene in the affairs of men and set them right again, to try to heal Scrooge before it was too late. But then Marley had always been a gifted negotiator and a good man for a bargain.

Marley had, miracle of miracles, come back for him, to him, still cared about him, still loved him above all men, still cared about what he did and what he felt and what fate befell him, still remembered the days and hours of his life and still lamented the times that they had not spent together or that, spent together, had come to nothing but painful silence.

So there you have it - a slashed up *Christmas Carol*, just in time for the holidays. I would offer the whole story but I no longer have it in an electronic form, only in hard copy. But I wanted to at least retype these bits to give you some sense of what the story was like and what it taught me about the nature of slash.

MONA TERESAS

THE *MONA LISA* RETOLD BY

Teresa Buzzard

Art photos by Jessica Ramage

"Mona Teresa,
Korova Milk Bar, 1977"

"Mona Teresa,
Rainbowland, 1984"

"Mona Teresa, Kyoto,

Teresa Buzzard

"Mona Teresa,
Kabul, 1996"

"Mona Teresa,
Toyboxes everywhere
since 1952"

"Mona Teresa,
Cotton Club, 1925"

"Mona Teresa,
Long, Long Ago in a
Galaxy Far, Far Away..."

"Mona Teresa,
Woodstock, 1969"

"Mona Teresa,
Hollywood, 1953"

"Mona Teresa,
Under a Pineapple in
the Sea since 1999"

From the Suicide Letters of Jonathon Bender, 1967–1999

Michael Kimball

[1973]

Dear Easter Bunny,

My mom and dad got mad at me because I couldn't stop looking for Easter Eggs around the house and in the backyard, but I thought that you were supposed to come to every kid's house. I was hoping to find those plastic eggs with the candy inside them hidden behind the curtains or in the bushes or in the long grass in the backyard. I thought that there might be jellybeans or marshmallow bunnies or those little chocolate eggs wrapped in different colored tin foil. You knew that I lived there, right?

Dear Tooth Fairy,

I was afraid to pull the loose tooth out of my mouth even though I knew that you would bring me a quarter for it if I left it under my pillow. I wanted the quarter, but I was afraid of the blood and I was afraid that I was going to start losing all of my teeth and that they wouldn't grow back and that I would have to get fake ones like my Grandpa Bender did.

Dear Santa Claus,

Thank you for bringing me the bike with the banana seat for Christmas and for putting training wheels on it so that I didn't fall off of it when I rode it. I knew that there was too much snow on the ground for me to ride it outside then, but I was so excited that you knew where I lived and that you thought that I had been a good enough boy to get a bike that I pretended to ride it in the living room. Did you see me? I was turning the handlebars back and forth as if I were going around corners.

[1974]

Dear Grandma and Grandpa Winters,

Thank you for giving me the Etch-a-Sketch for my seventh birthday. I liked drawing with it better than drawing on the walls, but I always felt bad when I shook it and everything on its magic screen disappeared. It reminded me of how my dad would grab me by both of my shoulders and shake me until everything went blank inside of me too.

Dear Robert,

Do you remember when we saw *Planet of the Apes* on television? I remember that I had difficulty separating the apes in the movie from the guerillas that I would sometimes hear about on the evening news. I knew that we were fighting a war then, but I didn't know that you could spell guerillas that way or that when you did it referred to people. I knew that gorillas were apes, but I didn't know that guerillas and gorillas were different things. I didn't understand why everybody wasn't as afraid as I was.

Dear Robert,

Do you remember that snowstorm in December, 1974? Do you remember the snowman we built like the kids did in that TV cartoon? Do you remember how the sun melted the snowman the next day and made his charcoal buttons fall off of his coat and his carrot nose fall off of his face and his stick arms fall out of his shoulders? I wanted him to come to life like the one on the TV did.

[1975]

Dear Scott Poor,

I'm not sorry that I hit you over the head with my Scooby-Doo lunch box and cracked your head open with it. You were a lot bigger than I was then and I was afraid of you and I wanted you and your brother to stop picking on me on the way home from school. Did the doctor show you what it looked like inside your head? I bet it looked mean.

Dear Mom and Dad,

I wore that crown from Burger King for most of the summer of 1975 because I really thought that I was the Burger King. It couldn't have been anybody else. Nobody else was wearing a crown.

[1976]

Dear Dad,
Do you remember that time our house almost burned down? It was me who did it. I took the newspaper that you hadn't read yet and I stole the matches from the pocket of one of your jackets and I started a fire with them in the bushes that were next to the house. I thought that it was going to be more than a regular burning fire, though, and I still don't understand why God didn't appear in the flames of the burning bushes to talk to me or why the bushes actually just burned up since that isn't how it happened in the Bible. I had some questions that I wanted to ask.

THE PLOT TO KIDNAP STONEHENGE

Corey Mesler

1

Randolph—Good morning, Sir.

Merlin—Morning? Hmph, is it?

Randolph—Indeed, Sir.

Merlin—Breakfast then.

Randolph—Yes, Sir. Soft-boiled quail eggs, dry toast, a banger.

Merlin—Quite.

Randolph—I'll let you eat in peace.

Merlin—Wait, Randolph. Mm, this quail's egg… um, tell me, what's on the agenda today?

Randolph—Full day, as usual. Perhaps moreso than yesterday or tomorrow, as the case may be.

Merlin—This living backwards.

Randolph—Yes, Sir.

Merlin—What's up first?

Randolph—Let's see (rattling pages)…9 a.m., the King's mandolin lesson.

Merlin—Poor Wart. He's horrible, of course. Well, that shouldn't take long. He gets frustrated quickly, smashes the instrument and we have to send for another. Okay. Then?

Randolph—You have an eleven o'clock with Mordred, Sir.

Merlin—Oh, hell. That little eelshit.

Randolph—Yes, Sir.

Merlin—Do you have any idea what that's about?

Randolph—No, Sir. No idea. He seemed quite hot to see you.

Merlin—Of course, he did. Why doesn't he take this up with Wart, er, Arthur? I'm not the fucking king.

Randolph—No, Sir.

Merlin—He's afraid of Arthur, of course.

Randolph—So it seems.

Merlin—Well, see if we can wiggle out of that one, eh?

Randolph—Um, yes, Sir.

Merlin—Problem?

Randolph—Mr. Mordred, Sir. He can be so unpleasant.

Merlin—Oh, fie and damnation. All right.

Randolph—Yes, Sir.

Merlin--What else? Give me something to look forward to today, Randolph. Mm, this banger is especially succulent.

Randolph—There's Guinevere at 1, Sir.

Merlin—Ah.

Randolph—Yes, Sir.

Merlin—She is one spicy little queen, isn't she, Randolph?

Randolph—I've heard tell, Sir.

Merlin—A regular nymphomaniac.

Randolph—I cannot speak so plain, of course.

Merlin—Just between us, eh? Randolph? Have you ever seen a better ass?

Randolph—(blushing) No, Sir. No, I haven't.

Merlin—She fucks like a wild animal, Randolph.

Randolph—Indeed, Sir?

Merlin—Gets on you and moves that great behind around. Ah.

Randolph—Yes, Sir.

Merlin—Well, that's something to look forward to anyway. Lancelot must be away?

Randolph—No, Sir. He's about.

Merlin—And she still wants Old Merlin, eh? That little minx.

Randolph—Yes, Sir.

2

Merlin—Come in, Mordred. How are things in Cornwall?

Mordred—(bowing) Quite satisfactory, Merlin. Rain, lots of rain.

Merlin—What is one to do, eh? Everyone talks about the weather—

Mordred—Of course, you could do something about it.

Merlin—You sweet-talk.

Mordred—Not at all.

Merlin—So, what's on your nefarious little mind this morning? Why so passionate to see Old Merlin?

Mordred—Off the record?

Merlin—If you wish.

Mordred—I have a plan. A monumental plan. Something that will make Camelot great.

Merlin—Camelot is already great.

Mordred—Well, the word on the street (here, Mordred lays a finger beside his nose) is that the whole Round Table idea is old hat. There's talk of the Queen's concupiscence. Many say Arthur isn't the King he used to be.

Merlin—Blasphemy.

Mordred—Yet, there it is. Covetousness, perhaps, but the word on the street…

Merlin—Right, right. What is this plan?

Mordred—Well. (Mordred moves slightly closer while Merlin unconsciously moves slightly away.) Perhaps you've heard of the Irish Giants?

Merlin—So.

Mordred—They're Giants. And they live in Ireland.

Merlin—Get on with it.

Mordred—Well, word has it that they have built something. Something miraculous, full of marvel and portent.

Merlin—The clock thing.

Mordred—(after a pause) Perhaps. A clock? Perhaps.

Merlin—An astrological clock.

Mordred—You continue to impress.

Merlin—I hear things.

Mordred—This is no ordinary clock. It is mammoth, built of bluestone and hand-carved sarsen-rock. And it stands a full ten men high, with lintels weighing 5 tons.

Merlin—Indeed. Well, there are wonders in the world. What has this to do with us, Mordred? (Merlin is impatient, thinking of the afternoon tryst with the Queen.)

Mordred—We can make it ours.

Merlin—(Surprisingly taken aback) Ours? Well, that wouldn't sit well with the fucking Giants, would it?

Mordred—They wouldn't know what him them. You spirit it away. Whoosh! You can do it, Merlin, only you can do it.

Merlin (hand to chin, rubbing furiously)—As much as it pains me to say this, I'm interested in what you propose, Mordred.

Mordred—Thank you, Sir. It will be greater, more mystifying than your Cerne Abbas Giant.

Merlin—A good jape, that.

Mordred—That it is.

Merlin—Fucking Giants, eh? What?

Mordred—Exactly.

Merlin--Where would we put the damn thing?

Mordred—Well, there's this nice space on Salisbury Plain. Lots of ground, slight promontory, nice long path for an entranceway. Some shrubbery.

Merlin—Salisbury, yes. Yes, that might work.

Mordred—Thank you, Sir.

Merlin—What's in it for you, Mordred?

Mordred—The pride of Camelot.

Merlin—Don't bullshit a bullshitter.

Mordred—Well, I *would* want a finder's fee.

Merlin—Ah.

3

Merlin—My Queen.

Guinevere—Are we alone?

Merlin—Quite, my Queen.

Guinevere—Ok, drop the "My Queen" crap and undo that robe.

Merlin—You little minx. (He opens his voluminous gown.) Where is Lancelot?

Guinevere—Jealousy doesn't become you, my Naked Necromancer.

Merlin—It's only that, well, never mind.

Guinevere—Never mind, indeed. That's quite a stout birch-branch, you've got there, Magician.

Merlin—You've never complained before. Unclothe thyself, my dear.

Guinevere—Make yourself young first.

Merlin—Oh, stuff and incense. Here then.

Guinevere—Yipes. I love those pecs, my Lothario. (She slips out of her silks.)

Merlin—And you turn around and let me see it. The Royal Rear.

Guinevere—You rascally conjurer. (She turns and bends slightly at the waist.) Here 'tis.

Merlin—Holy cats, My Queen. That is a formidable fundament.

Guinevere—And that is a thick staff. Is it legerdemain or tribute to my pallid backside?

Merlin—. Ah, Guin. It's all for you, my pretty. As round as Norval's shield, as white as Albion moonlight, as alabastrine as the cliffs of Dover.

Guinevere—Flatterer. Bring that bludgeon here.

Afterwards

Guinevere—Ah, Merlin, no one quite fucks like an archimage.

Merlin—You're not bad yourself, Toots.

Guinevere—That part where you turned briefly into a bull.

Merlin—Unintentional.

Guinevere—Inspired.

Merlin—Thank you.

Guinevere—Now, my horny magus. What is this I hear about a granite moon-mirror?

Merlin—Bah! Are there no secrets in Camelot?

4

Randolph—Good morning, Sir.

Merlin—Morning? Mmmph. What day is it?

Randolph—Thursday.

Merlin—Thursday. (He shakes his hoary head.) What happened to Friday?

Randolph—You slept through it, Sir.

Merlin—Indeed. It's very confusing.

Randolph—It is. You were powerful tired, my Lord.

Merlin—Indeed, I was.

Randolph—Well, anyway, Sir. Light schedule today.

Merlin—Fine, fine.

Randolph—The King at 10. He wants to congratulate you on the piece of art you erected on Salisbury Plain.

Merlin—It's *not* a fucking piece of art.

Randolph—Yes, Sir.

Merlin—It's a timepiece. An astrological wonderment—oh, never mind. If you have to explain magic it loses its, its…

Randolph—Luster, Sir?

Merlin—Precisely.

Randolph—At any rate, it is the talk of the town, Sir.

Merlin—Well and good.

Randolph—Mordred is taking credit left and right for it, of course.

Merlin—I'm going to turn that turncoat into a stoat.

Randolph—Quite right, Sir.

Merlin—After all is said and done, we have it now, don't we? It's ours. It's Britain's.

Randolph—Rightfully so, Sir.

Merlin—Can't help feeling a little guilty over the Irish though.

Randolph—Send them some rainbows, Sir.

Merlin—Randolph, you have a keen grasp of International Politics.

Randolph—Yes, Sir. Thank you, Sir.

Merlin—And it's popular, eh?

Randolph—Quite. I hear the tourist trade is up 37% in just one week. There's talk of an inn, a roadway, and a couple of food stands.

Merlin—Good, good. An unequivocal hit, then.

Randolph—Ye-es.

Merlin—You seem hesitant.

Randolph—There was a suggestion about the entranceway, lining it with topiary in the shapes of the Twelve.

Merlin—Inappropriate.

Randolph—Yes, and, well the name, Sir?

Merlin—Yes.

Randolph—Some people want to call it something else. Woodhenge was such a bust, there's talk that we need a catchier moniker for this one.

Merlin—Hm. I'll think on it, Randolph.

Randolph—Quite right, Sir.

Merlin—Anything else?

Randolph—I hesitate to mention it, Sir.

Merlin—Randolph.

Randolph—Well, the blood sacrifices, Sir. Some people are taking exception to them.

Merlin—Nitpickers.

Randolph—Yes, Sir. There's also talk about Avebury wanting one, too.

Merlin—Imitation is the sincerest form, eh, Randolph?

Randolph—Quite, Sir.

Merlin—(striking his forehead) The Giant's Dance!

Randolph—Sir?

Merlin—For the name.

Randolph—Ah. Quite euphonious.

Merlin—Oh, and Randolph, is the Queen about?

Randolph—Yes, Sir.

Merlin—Can we squeeze her in before the King?

Randolph—(allowing himself a small smile) I believe so, Sir.

Merlin—Tell her I am ready to show her the Bull again.

Randolph—The Bull, sir?

Merlin—She'll understand. The Bull, Randolph.

Randolph—Yes, sir.

ALIAS: THE COMPLETE SERIES

OR, SOME HEARTS ARE FAINTER THAN OTHERS

Roxane Gay

She waits until she feels so twisted inside she loses herself. She dresses carefully to take a walk in a dangerous neighborhood. She paints her face and slips into a low cut dress. She keeps her legs bare and wears a pair of very high heels that make every step a delicate matter. She tucks a few bills in her bra, carries no purse. She walks through her well-appointed home, past the pictures of her happy family and happy life holding up the walls, holding the house together. She binds her heart with the love she feels but sometimes, like now, struggles to hold on to. She gets in her car and grips the leather wrapped steering wheel, enjoys the luxury of German engineering.

She drives to the wrong side of town and parks on the edge of trouble, hides her keys in the gas tank. She walks past broken buildings and broken men who don't even have enough heart to pay her any mind. She walks past women who sell what she's going to give away. They see who she is even when she can't and she loves them for that. She wants to hold them in her arms and kiss the track marks on their arms and drown in the scent of their cheap perfume. She finds a bar—loud and humid and rank. She forces her way through the crowd. She orders a drink, lights a cigarette, talks to an ugly man with yellow fingers. She says things that make her heart beat fast. The ugly man puts a hand on her thigh, pushes her dress up, squeezes, she lets him. His fingers are cold. She feels nothing. She drinks more, smokes more, her throat hurts, her head hurts. She excuses herself to the bathroom and stares at her reflection in the mirror. She presses her hand to her waist, feels the thinly braided scar from where her youngest child was cut out of her. She finds another man who is better looking. He buys her drinks and leans in real close and keeps his hand against the sweaty small of her back.

As she leaves the bar, her ears ring loudly. Her daughter has a ballet recital the following evening. She has to finish the costume before she goes to work in the morning. She still feels nothing but her skin warms. Her body feels heavy. She leaves a trail of breadcrumbs with the unsteadiness of her steps. She waits until a strong pair of hands grabs her, pulls her into a dimly lit, sour alley. She feels relieved. The ringing grows louder. She lets herself be pushed against a dirty dumpster. She doesn't turn around. Her dress is raised, her legs kicked apart. She feels hot breath on her neck, unfamiliar hands on her breasts, holding her hips. She bites her lower lip, remains silent except to say, "Punish me." Her request is granted. She is punished. When he is inside her, forcing her body to open to him, she exhales slowly. She endures. When he is done, he calls her crazy and she smiles, recognizes herself. She listens as he buckles his belt and walks away. She straightens her clothes. She finds her car and gingerly slides behind the wheel.

She returns to her happy home and slips out of her high heels. She walks on the tips of her toes and looks in on her three sleeping children, her husband, asleep in their beds. She soaks in a hot bath, studies the fresh bruises—on her thigh, the imprint of a belt strap. She aches everywhere. She feels a certain loneliness in her happy house full of people. She does not know if they are happy. She does not ask. She ponders adding a bit of lace to the hem of her daughter's ballet costume. She will wear a flattering but modest dress to dinner with her husband and friends over the coming weekend. She will wear a diamond necklace her husband gave her for their tenth anniversary. She will slide her hand onto her husband's lap while she smiles and nods and chats pleasantly. She will lightly stroke his cock through his wool slacks and, because he is conservative in his tastes, he will eventually push her hand away. She will pretend that does not hurt. She sinks beneath the surface of the cooling water, closes her eyes as the tightness in her chest loosens, just a little bit, just enough. She understands some hearts are fainter than others. She holds her breath and hears the beating of her own heart. It is bright and good and strong.

THE CONFUSIONS OF YOUNG JOSEPH

Joseph Riippi

Teacher

His English teacher is blind and reads from school texts in Braille. Her hands move as she lectures, coaxing couplets and rhyme from thick pages. Better? Different? Does she read enough to build calluses? Jöseph has, and he has calluses—his fingers feel less in places. But on her, what would they? She cannot see how disgusting his face is, she cannot see, so she will be waiting when he comes home. He'll be the one who sees—her fumbling at his fly, her smiling and undoing blouse buttons. She closes the bedroom door and turns on the lights—how does she know? She reaches with antennae arms; her calluses feel wet face, open eyes. She reads to him from his acne.

Varsity

Tell it again, the stronger boys order, and the smaller one submits: I am a pussy, he says. Repeats it once more. Good, they respond, and kick him again. There is blood in his nose and mouth, a clot caught in the back space where snorts form. He coughs, looks to Jöseph for help, but Jöseph, his brother (but step) only watches with the rest. Jöseph made varsity as a freshman, too; he came home bleeding and pale. So this is what happens, the smaller thinks now. He hears someone yell, Say I am a fat bastard! There is laughter and more kicking. They cheer. He looks for Jöseph again and Jöseph is wishing he could stop it; Jöseph is wishing he could but he can't.

Božena's Boy

The coffin drops, slow, surrounded by Astroturf skirt. The men whose job it is to gather and stack the folding chairs stack and gather while smoking. Like thugs after a school assembly, Jöseph thinks. His instinct is to help; to be the one in a mourning suit who helps. But Božena is here. She is with him. She looks at him and speaks: Thanks for being here, she says. He nods, not feeling anything, not really. Why should he? He has cried. When it was his brother (but step), he cried. He and Božena have this in common now. He can imagine it for her. But does he look right? To Božena? He puts an arm around her and she lets him. He watches her mother and father holding each other in two chairs the thugs haven't stacked. He watches his father and mother watching him and Božena from the cars. Božena pulls closer, leans. He can feel her chest against him and he thinks to kiss her. She is that close, that pressed. Does she want him to? They watch the coffin settle. It's a part of life, she says. He nods. That's what the priest said, he responds. He could cry if she wants him to. Does she want him to?

Imaginary numbers

Multiply an imaginary number by itself and you'll get something real, the professor says, and Jöseph copies that down. Three days later, he opens a notebook and remembers, revises: Multiply your imaginary and make it real, he writes. He takes his courses and reads the syllabus books; he sees the version of himself his parents want him to be and tries to imagine. They see a doctor and a wife; they see themselves, and he sees: what? Sometimes a girl in the library takes off her tanktop and throws it at him; sometimes a bra and red skirt. Sometimes the skirt is blue; sometimes tight jeans. He leans his head to the desk and revises.

Törless

He reads Musil's *The Confusions of Young Törless* in a back storage room at the top floor of the library. Back beyond where he thinks anyone else goes, beyond where a girl's clothes might fall, in a space he believes no one else knows. It is quiet there. Dark. Sometimes he uses candles. But yesterday, someone else: someone larger sitting in another broken desk, not a larger boy but a man, full-grown and girthed. He has discovered how to turn the lights on. Jöseph stares, confused. A boy that is a man. The man stands and points, and Jöseph flees without thinking, as if this weren't where he were coming at all, as if there were some other, darker, even more secluded and secret room further on. He can imagine it, that room, and imagining, that—always! always!—is enough to keep going.

NOT THE STUFF OF FAIRY TALES

Timothy Gager

Lauren sat in the mud inside the pen of the three pigs. The pigs were fresh and small. It would take months to fatten them up. She and the pigs were not yet the best they could be. Her pants, a sponge, inefficient for the water, grew warm against her. She remembered how it felt when she let him in; Billy's thighs slapped against her as he broke her.

She wadded up a ball of mud in her hand as Billy approached holding two cups of coffee. Lauren aimed at the first pig but changed her mind, threw a strike, knocked one of the coffee cups out of Billy's hands, onto his white shirt. It made him wince for a few seconds.

"I didn't mean for that all to happen," Lauren said, lobbing a lazy mud ball toward the second pig. He offered her the other cup. "It's yours," she said and rubbed her stomach.

"I really don't want it. Do we? Do we want it?" He pulled the warm brown oval away from his thorax .

"I think we can do it, Billy. I mean you're solid, like a stone. Ain't nothing going to blow you over."

"Yeah, but we talked about it. About there being an us. I'm

older and you're still a kid. And you'd have to leave here." The sky darkened as dust swirled in the distance, blocking their view of the farmhouse.

"I'm twenty-one. Where do you think I came from… Momma's forty-two," she said, freeing the humid hair off her forehead so it could be caught by the breeze.

"I'd have to get a job somewhere else."

"Hey, remember the mother of those pigs?"

"Huh?"

"Their mother. She was fat and we roasted her. Her children will grow, be just as well."

"Damn." He kicked the fence post slowly and methodically five times. "I don't think we can do much better."

"You should have never told me how good you were."

When he looked down at her he wanted everything. The wind kicked up some sticks and straw. There was thunder. The pigs jumped.

A & P, Come Again

Heather Fowler

Languid like the summer heat, Annalise, Mitzi, and Lacy strolled past the sand of the beach and into the parking lot. They'd already decided Anna was to drive, because it was Anna's mother's car, so she took the proffered keys from Lacy's fat fingers and unlocked the Lexus, hopping from foot to foot on the simmering cement.

Outwardly she smiled, but inwardly cringed, remembering her mother's careless remark that morning: "You'll never drive my car, Anna, because you'd crash. When you turn sixteen, I'll buy something more suitable. A tank, maybe? Clumsy, girl."

She had looked at Laurence then, her mother's young boyfriend, who stared away and sighed, so she felt humiliated, calling to Mitzi and whispering, "Catch me if I stumble; I feel weak."

But that was hours ago. Now, she, Mitzi, and Lacy would steal her mother's car, and Anna laughed a cold, dry laugh, as Lacy, Lisbeth Dryden's frequent key-holder, said, "Don't you get me in trouble, Annalise Dryden. I'll tell her this was your idea if she asks."

"Oh, shut up," Annalise said, the moist pads of her toes crisping with each step. Already, the bottoms of her feet were black with the asphalt, and in the heat of the afternoon, even the leather interior looked fit to bake a potato. "Shit! Shee-it," Annalise said, taking a in lungful of Sahara air. "My feet are toasting!"

"We should have brought our flip-flops," Mitzi said, but getting in the car, Anna stretched her feet on the driver's carpet, cool after the asphalt, and told Mitzi to do the same. "It's cooler in here."

Her mind zipped ahead. If only they could get to that little store without trouble—and what was that place, the A & P? Some suburby shack with insular people popping in and out, heads down, faces plump, in fashions too ridiculous for words? The phrase "the wrong side of the tracks" popped into her head, but just as quickly, she submerged it, cranking open her window and draping her arm out.

Half a second later, she yanked it back, squealing, "Ouch! Oh damn! That thing just burned my arm!" Lacy and Mitzi gaped as she held up her arm to show them, a hot pink diagonal from the door's metal frame seared across her skin, and "It's true," Mitzi said, sighing, "it's steamy here and not getting any cooler."

Mitzi looked calm and collected, like she always did, with her turquoise, cat-eye sunglasses dipping half-way over her sultry eyes, wearing her creamy two-piece, and displaying that half-pretty poise. She let her expansive look take in the Thursday afternoon lot, and, "Hot, hot, hot," she said then, looking at Anna. "So, let's hurry."

"Ditto," Lacy said, holding her springy hair off her shoulders with a polish-specked hand. Trying for cool, she looked more like a rabid Shephard.

Annalise rolled her eyes, said, "Shut up, Lacy. If I wanted your opinion, I'd ask," but Lacy just gave Anna that dumb-cow look she had so mastered, the one that came right before pitiful tears, so Anna felt a tinge of guilt, but Lacy promptly ruined the nascent guilt by shaking her head and saying, "You're the one who thought of leaving our stuff on the beach, Annalise. It was your idea."

"Be quiet, you fat brick," Mitzi replied, saving Anna the trouble. The two then exchanged a simultaneous-best-friend thought: they should have left Lacy on the beach. The trouble was, the alternatives to taking her were not compelling, and their "enemies close" philosophy had served them well over the last five summers with the girl, and besides, Lacy would never have dispelled Lisbeth Dryden's fears, only enflamed them to a shore-wide search if left alone, which they hoped to avoid.

Still, just thinking about Lacy's blabbing made Anna feel constipated, as if she didn't have enough trouble already, and a wallop of pain/fear/gas hit her stomach when she reflected on how the second secret Lacy was about to learn could prove equally damaging.

Lacy would need her lips stitched shut if she found out, kind of like what they did for corpses, to stay quiet. Normally, it had been Annalise, who kept Lacy tolerable, but under the weather as she was, Mitzi had picked up her slack this morning, so Annalise mouthed thank you to her best friend, who winked in reply and touched her arm.

"You two are touchy feely today," Lacy said, leaning up from the backseat. Her breath stank like tuna, and she said, "You know, this is illegal what we're doing. But I think we should just relax. Hey girls, what would Lisbeth think if she saw us here now? Three girls having a good time!?" Lacy opened her mouth wider to launch another stream of idiotic banter, but—oh Lisbeth, oh her mother, Anna thought, screening out the babble, her mother was the queen of Antarctica, mountain-peak-snow-hag extraordinaire, and how Lisbeth would lay on thick the icy talk of personal responsibility if she knew any of this...

She would apply the subtle shaming she was famous for, having perfected it for ten long years on Anna's father, and no wonder he took off and no wonder Anna had this problem now, because Lisbeth Dryden, A.K.A. Evil, Unrelenting Mother, would be fuming to the tips of her cool turquoise nails if she knew anything about what Anna'd done the last two months, and would be fuming like a chimney if she had any inkling her own posh keys had just slid into the Lexus starter, keychains chiming, so that Ms.Annalise Dryden, her fourteen year old, sex-fiend deviant of the Boston Drydens, could drive out of the tiny lot without even her permit. "So I think we should get ice cream after this," Lacy said. "Maybe get a bite to eat. What do you girls think?"

Despite her fear, this thought gave Annalise a jolt of amusement, so she stared at the dials and knobs on the dash then started the car. When the engine purred to life, for a blissful second, it drowned out the tremulous noise of Lacy's continuous voice, so Anna decided she liked the view from the driver's seat. The power. Mitzi, because she was the closer friend, sat close to Anna on the passenger side, but Lacy had taken the backseat.

Annalise stared at Mitzi then, adoring her all the more because she was not Lacy, and Lacy was forever getting things wrong, basic things like talking on and on when someone was stressed and casting blame after a deed was done, and trying to push her nose into other people's confidences.

Mitzi had tact, but Lacy was the girl who shouted, "Hey! You got a tampon?" in a crowded restroom (as if the other person was perfectly happy to have their menstruation announced). Yes, Lacy was a fact-stealing, motherly-suck-up, who should either leave them alone or die a miserable death, but they were never that lucky, which Anna and Mitz had often discussed.

In a way, Annalise pitied her intolerable cousin, but at the same time, Lacy's green, two-piece looked horrible, made for a girl thirty pounds smaller, so Anna felt embarrassed, again, to be seen with her and glad for her own looks, coupled with Mitzi's semi-cool pizzazz, which protected them from unfavorable associations.

Still, as she drove, she stared at Lacy's dumb face - Lacy, who, even then twisted her nappified hair around her index finger, sucking it like a baby - and how gross, Anna thought then, so said without thinking, "Knock it off, Lacy, would you? That's disgusting," then riveted her attention to the light in front of her.

"What am I doing now?" Lacy asked, her tone exactly like the build-up of emergency sirens.

"Just be quiet," Anna snapped, "I'm driving." She had a brief fantasy of the car wrapped around a tree, but "What am I doing now?" Lacy bleated, insistently louder this time.

"Breathing," said Mitzi. "So cut it out, loser."

Mitzi and Anna fell into giggles and clutched their sides with hilarity, but Lacy turned red, furious in the backseat, shouting, "That's not funny! That's mean. You two are mean."

"I'm sorry, Lace," Anna said without meaning it, but then she forgot about Lacy and asked, "Can you believe it? I'm driving my mom's car! We are out in my mom's car!" She pounded the dash, blaring the radio locked on the oldies station as Mitzi shouted, "You're right, Anna! This is too cool," but Lacy just stared out the window, planning a late and ineffectual comeback that would invariably not affect them.

And so what? Annalise thought. So frigging what? She applied pressure to the gas and cruised through several green lights. Overall, this trip had started well, and how easily everything had fallen into place—one second she tanned on the beach in coconut oil, and the next drove down the road in her mother's car while her mother and Asshole Laurence played in the waves (or, on second thought, who knew what they did in the waves—but it didn't bear speculating), and Laurence, as Annalise well knew, should drown in his own handsome vomit, ending his life with the sludge he came up with.

Still, even that would be too good because at this moment, there were few people she hated more. Her only consolation was that that her mother had explained it all to her before leaving for a party one afternoon when Lisbeth Dryden had said, in a rare outburst of maternal affection, "Honey, Laurence is a fling. Your father was the one I wanted, but he left, you understand? And Laurence hasn't a dime, so you think I'd marry him? It a matter of why buy the cow, and so on... You understand don't you, babe? Soon it'll be just us, you'll see, so let me have a little fun, won't you? He is, you understand," Lisbeth Dryden had said, with her eyebrow tweezers pointed at Anna's chest, "beneath us. Beneath you. Beneath me, for that matter, and nothing."

Then, Lisbeth Dryden had laughed, spiritually bankrupt as Anna's father used to say, and, often, reflecting on her mother's cruelty, Annalise wondered if she would be the same. Besides, "The rich don't need God," her mother always said. "Except those Kennedies. They need all the help they can get."

Sometimes, Anna hated her mother so much, impossible love her at all. In the car, she stretched her arms above her head then replaced them on the wheel, hoping to find the store quickly. She felt calmer when Frank Sinatra came through the speakers, so turned up the radio and whispered to Mitz, "Do you think everything will be okay?"

Mitzi's sunburn, a red swath under her eyes, looked funny when she squinted, but Mitz said in her smooth, no-trouble voice, "It'll be fine."

"What?" Lacy boomed from between them. "What'll be fine?"

"Mind your own business," they said at once, then Mitzi flicked Lacy's nose, and Annalise kept driving.

The silence felt heavy as she pulled to the turning lane. She thought of the day in that pool two months ago, the taste of the chlorine, and way he had forgotten her name. She wanted to kill him for causing her this worry, for the days boxed off with the simple N.P. on her calendar, but "Do you think he noticed me?" Mitzi asked distractingly, referring to the lifeguard on duty at the beach when they left.

"What?" Anna asked.

"The lifeguard." Mitzi's intense look absorbed the side of Annalise's face, but Anna did not answer until Mitzi repeated, "Hey, Anna, did he?" to which she said only, "I don't know. I really don't know."

"Duh," said Lacy, piping up. "Totally!" and her outburst, in this instance, was welcome. Mitzi looked at Anna, then redirected her stare at Lacy.

"I know he noticed me, but do you think he really noticed me?"

"Yeah, um, I think so," Lacy said, uncertain since Mitzi's laser eyes had pinned her.

Anna stared at the road sign and yanked her mother's sunglasses from the rearview. "Look," she said loudly. "Do these make me look older?" A state trooper had rolled up beside them on the right, and she felt a pulse of fear as she saw his grim face, then asked the girls in a whisper, "Are you guys wearing seatbelts?"

"No," said Mitzi. "I forgot."

"No," said Lacy, "didn't even think of it," and her hand snaked down to grab the belt, but "Stop, you idiot!" Mitzi said then. "You'll make him notice us!"

"He's cute," Lacy said. "I hope so."

"Cute or not, he wouldn't go for you," Mitzi said. She glanced toward Annalise then back to Lacy. The light took forever to change, but finally the trooper sped ahead and Mitzi tapped Anna's thigh softly, saying, "Go, babe. Anna. Green light." Then Mitzi adjusted the straps of her bikini top and said, "We need to relax. We got through that, didn't we? We'll get through everything else," but worry was plain on her face, and this didn't help because Mitzi never worried. She had not worried when Anna had totaled Mitzi's mother's car, nor when Anna dyed her hair orange right before the Carlton Club dance, nor in any variety of nerve-wracking situations, but now, Mitzi's mouth made a grim line which sent a legion of butterflies jittering down to mambo in Anna's stomach— and that was worrisome.

Then Lacy blurted, "Why didn't you tell us we should put on our seatbelts when we first got in? I would have done it if you told me too!"

"Why don't you grow a brain and come back?" Mitzi said, and, "Hey Lace, did you know your village idiot is missing?"

"I don't have to be here," Lacy said. "I could be back at the beach relaxing. You two told me you wanted me to come, and then you act mean. Well, I don't have to take it."

"Good, get on a bus."

"I really don't have to deal with this," Lacy whined again.

"What are you going to do about it, Petula Pig?" Mitzi asked. "Walk off? Go ahead, walk back to the beach. You could use the exercise. Am I right, Anna?"

Annalise turned pale and felt her stomach flip-flop but commandeered all skills of haughty disregard to say, "Exactly, Mitz."

"Why'd you even ask me here if you didn't want me to come?" Lacy asked. "And why all your secret talk today. I don't even know why everyone's so nervy. I thought we were here for chips and soda."

"Shows what you know," Mitzi said, but "Please don't fight," Anna murmured then, pulling into the lot of the A & P and examining a blackhead in the rearview before saying sharply, "We're here. Do we know what to do? Let's review the plan."

She owed it to them to keep herself together, she thought, so stared at herself again in the mirror, looking into her own eyes and questioning her decisions. At least, they'd parked, and she hadn't hit anyone. That was good.

"Lacy can't speak. Rule one," Mitzi said.

"Agreed." Annalise said by rote, but thought only of herself. All day, she'd been fighting this drowning sensation, and now it claimed her, a rude, thought stealing void where everything came together and fell apart, so as Mitzi and Lacy duked it out beside her, insults piling up, she heard them argue, but only remotely. What she was listening to was the sound of water splashing against a tile in the pool when a head was under water—like the murmur in a seashell.

She was thinking of another N.P. and tracing back the days until that day, less than a month ago, which involved a man with golden hair exiting her pool, water dripping from his body; he was smiling. He gave her his eyes, and then they talked, just like adults do, while her mother was out at the club sucking down another Amaretto Sour, and Anna remembered him as beautiful then, the man, his body, the tailored joints of his muscles and bones, with his tan complexion and bright emerald shorts—beautiful down to the loose fit of his trunks, which revealed a honey colored-trail of hair beneath his belly.

She had wanted to kiss him there, kiss him then, with a hunger that surprised her, but he'd again looked away from her and sat down on the patio set, drinking his Smirnoffs, so she was angry. How could he talk to her so well, then abruptly turn her off? She walked over and plopped herself in front of him, her chin in her hands, saying, "Hey!"

"What you doin,' little girl?" he finally replied, glancing up to notice her—and whoever knew that "What you doin'?" would be a prelude to what would happen next.

It became a taunt in her head, then and later, but now, walking up to the store, thinking of it, she felt cold in her pink nubby one-piece, her arms riddled with goosebumps despite the heat of the day. Vaguely, she recalled that Mitzi had already told Lacy what to do, somewhere in the periphery of her awareness, so they all walked in, entering the dim of florescent lighting of the market as she stopped to take a glance around.

People stared at them—-the checkers, the baggers, everyone—so "Walk normal," she told Mitz. "Slow. Slower."

A flush rose to her cheeks, which she tried to ignore, as a housewife in curlers wheeled past, glaring at them. "Put some clothes on," was what the woman said. Then a little boy came up, a paper towel wrapped around his fist, and said, pumping his hand like a puppet, "Hi. My name is Malcolm."

"Oh!" Lacy said, "That's so cute! Look at that little boy!" laughing with her huge way, so Anna examined her cousin again, thinking: Can she know? Can I trust her? She looked at Lacy's fillings, apparent from her open mouth, ten too many from the metric tons of candy Lacy consumed as a child, but did not respond to Lacy or the boy. She watched him travel the aisles, saying the same thing to everyone.

It was dizzying. She looked down and the tiles were spinning, so, "Stay near me, Mitz," she said, clutching her best friend and pausing to stare at the racks, wondering: Where is it? Where is that package in this lousy place?

She was not aware that she'd said this out loud until Lacy said, "What? What are you looking for, Anna? Tell me!"

"We're here for cookies," Mitzi offered then, giving Lacy her saccharin grin. "So go look for them, okay?"

Lacy's face lit up until she realized the joke. She pushed in closer and said, "Why did we come here? Really, Anna? Tell me. I'm your cousin. I won't tell."

Anna didn't respond. The straps of her pinky one-piece had fallen, and she did not push them up. She had just begun to notice that one pimple-faced checker was watching them intensely—no, two—no, three checkers—as if they were shoplifters, so she drew her posture high, imitating her mother's regal walk, and said, "Shut up, Lacy," making her eyes cool.

Still the first checker would not take his eyes off her, so she wanted a wool sweater then, even in the heat, because he kept staring and would not stop. How she hated that! "Haven't you ever seen girls before?" she wanted to shout. "What are you? Some kind of freak?"

The green and cream tiles felt smooth under her feet as Mitzi whispered, "There it is, on aisle three. I see it," and pushed Anna forward.

Lacy had not budged from their sides, but then stated, "I will go look at the cookies, but only because I want to, and I'm sick of you both."

"Good then," said Mitzi, "Go," and dizzily, Annalise wove down the third aisle, taking in the sundries. Certain things amazed her like how they could have so many unrelated things on the same aisle. She'd even forgotten she had company until "What if the strip's pink?" Mitzi whispered. "What will you do then?"

Anna looked down at her flat stomach, then looked up. "It's not going to be."

"But, if it is?"

They regarded Lacy, visible near the cookies aisle, picking up one package then the next—Peanut Fingers, Oreos, Mint Milanos—and Annalise said, "My mother knows someone. He can fix this, and I—"

Lacy sped up with a vengeance. "Oh my God, you guys. You've made me so paranoid. Now I don't even know what cookies to get, so fine! Fine. I won't buy any. You want me to get thin, right? If I did that, would you like me more? Probably not—but anyway, I don't want to be touchy or anything, but—hey, what's with the silent treatment? Earth to Anna!"

Lacy had come up so quickly, they stood quietly, not knowing what to say. Shoppers rushed past, and the noise of the registers echoed loudly. "Go look again," Mitzi said, Lacy didn't move, and the checker boy kept staring, so Annalise wanted to fade into the tile as an electronic voice, which was attached to the store exit, kept muttering, "Ding Dong. Thank you. Come again," when a customer left.

And where the fuck was she anyway? Anna wondered. Why was she here? Oh. Yes. She returned to the pool in her mind, the way he'd used her, straddling her body on the concrete, tearing her insides, and then she remembered how he said, not long afterwards, "Lisbeth, hmmmm, that was —Oh god, Annalise! It's y—. What did—you can't—" and stopped in his tracks as if waking from a short and particular daydream. He walked away from her into her house and made coffee for himself, very strong coffee, as she trailed him like a puppy, then he finalized their conversation with, "This can't happen again. I am sorry, Anna. You're a big girl. Let's just forget it, okay?"

She did not say, "Okay." She didn't say anything, and half an hour later, she heard him call out from the shower, "What is this?" then, "Oh God! Blood? I swear I didn't—I couldn't," and "Oh, God. Oh, Jesus," but he said nothing more to her. Then her mother came home, staggering in the door, laughing to herself: "Hello, darling! Hello!"

"Anna," Mitzi said, shaking her shoulders. "Hello, Anna! Are we going to stand here all day? Get that thing. We have to get back before she looks for her car."

"Get what?" Lacy said as Anna realized her hand was out, wavering like a scale dial in a half moon radius of the desired item, but she looked again at the checker boy who was still staring, who was Laurence's young brother in another life perhaps, and she hated him then for watching her so closely—and hated Lacy, too, for her big bulgy eyes and free-wheeling tongue.

Her hand dropped toward the shelf and seized. Like a crane, it brought something back to her. Herring snacks? What in the hell was she doing with herring snacks? And Mitzi was beside her then, so why couldn't Mitzi grab the damn thing, get rid of Lacy, do something? Do. Fucking. Something. What was a best friend for?

"Okay," Mitzi said then, in her ear, in a dulcet tone, "you're right," as if Annalise had just made a stunningly correct decision. "We'll come back later." Mitzi looked at Lacy and announced, "This was what we wanted, Dumdum. Herring snacks. Satisfied?"

Annalise walked to the register, and they followed, but the only open checker was the boy whose eyes had glued themselves to her: to her body, to her breasts, to the place where her swimsuit dipped from the looseness of her straps.

She placed her purchase on the counter and said nothing. She thought for half a second that he looked at her sort of sweetly with his wide-gazing eyes—and what if he was the real kind of boy she should have lost "it" too, she briefly wondered, the right age, the right size, like Laurence but not like him—would he have been more tender? He watched as her fingers reached into the breast area of her suit, pulling out bills she'd hidden there, which were skin temperature, and looking up.

For an instant, Anna thought it was as if this was a private act between them, in a hotel room, far away. She saw lust in his eyes, and longing. For a moment, she felt it too. Not that she would have married him, no, never that, but she would have screwed him at a party. Definitely.

Mitzi's arm felt warm and comforting at her side. She looked away from the boy and the herring snacks, which were almost hers, as a manager came up to the register and stared them down—-some middle-class prig with talk of their beachy outfits. He gave lip-service to store policy, and Annalise wanted to shout, "Leave me alone. Stop it, you bastard!" but she could not. Ribbons of nerves like tightwire had constricted her throat. She blushed, and the boy seemed to empathize.

The manager looked down at her then, like a blazing tower, all prim and tight-assed, so she did the only thing she knew how to do, the only thing she did well, which was imitate her mother. She pulled up her posture, took the snacks regally, and walked to the exit like royalty. Mitzi and Lacy followed.

They heard the checker and his boss argue, but again, only dimly as the electric door whooshed open, "Ding Dong. Thank you. Come Again." The exterior glare then played havoc on her eyes as she heard the checker boy suddenly mutter, "I quit," though she had no idea why. This was the last of his words she could hear, and maybe it had nothing to do with her, maybe he and the manager had been long at odds, struggling over wages or stocking duties, but still, she could pretend.

Maybe, she thought, he was at that young age when a man cared enough to stick up for a girl rather than saying let's just forget this, let's ignore what happened, okay? But, maybe not. Maybe she just wanted this to be true. Walking out to the car, the asphalt again burned her feet, so she and the girls got back in and drove away. Inserting the keys in the ignition, Annalise then handed the herrings to Lacy and said, "You can eat one now, but please roll down the window. The smell makes me ill," and her stomach heaved again as Mitzi's hand clutched hers.

They zoomed into traffic, free, but the nauseating scent filled the car and the nasty smacking of Lacy's lips filled Anna's ears, regardless of the traffic noise. Still, she vowed to ignore it. They got back to the beach without a single mishap, even lucky enough to get the same parking spot twice.

It would be an invisible trip, Anna thought then, and when they sat on their towels in the sun, all three flipped open magazines as if they'd never left.

Mitzi didn't talk much, but Lacy kept saying, "Those herring snacks were so good, Annalise. It was so nice of you to give them to me, really. I knew we'd have a good trip this year," as if she'd just won some dumb sweepstakes.

Anna nodded. Mitzi stared out to the horizon, watching for the return of Lisbeth. Her lifeguard had changed shifts with some new girl, so "Did you eat them all?" Mitzi asked then, referring to the snacks.

"Yes," said Lacy, "and I threw away the jar."

Mitzi sighed, saying, "Of course, you did. Pig." She stared at Annalise, then said, "Let's walk to the water and wash our feet. Mine are dirty. Are yours?"

"Yes," Anna said. "Lets go."

"Can I come?" Lacy asked. "I want to come," but they walked off without her. Still, she pushed in, waddling behind them. When they got to the shore, whitewash breaking on their feet, Lacy spotted the swimmers they sought. "Look," she said, "they're coming. We made it just in time."

Annalise stepped forward. "There they are," she breathed. "Look." Laurence was so beautiful in that moment, so golden emerging from the surf, but he and her mother laughed privately, draped over each other like wet towels, both dripping with eyes only for each other.

Salt mist clung to their skin. They did not even see the girls until they were right on top of them, and then they laughed and kissed each other with their whole bodies pressed close.

"How R-rated," Mitzi said.

"They need a room," Lacy hissed, but, "N.P." was all Annalise stated, directly at Laurence, who heard her, who looked at her, briefly, then looked away. He and Lisbeth were almost at the blanket when she heard her mother ask, "What is N.P.? I never do know what those girls are talking about," and Laurence replied, "I have no idea," kissing Lisbeth Dryden's bony, high shoulders and returning his attention to the perfect half-moons of breasts above her suit.

He stared at Anna's mother as if she had carried the sun into the high atmosphere, and Lacy said, "He is so in love with her, and what a shame for us," as Anna started running to the water and Mitzi followed. Then Anna stopped, locked down to the shore in her watcher's position, listening to the waves. They roared and crashed.

Laurence could care less. He did not see her. She was not there for him. She felt another sort of void then as the waves beat against her feet and stole the sand from beneath them, hundreds of grains pulling out from between her toes, which left her stance unsteady. Everything felt unsteady as the water rinsed the asphalt away, scouring it gone, and then she turned to the sparkling sea and dove, but this was not a dive one would make into a pool, clean and neat, with her hands in an arrow above the head and a smooth, steady sluice into clear water, no, not so close to shore; it was the kind of dive that is actually half a run, half a crumple, where the spirit dives first as the body struggles to enter the water, and then both are walloped by a wall of ever-moving deep-end.

Morally bankrupt, she thought, echoing her father's murmur about her mother, but Anna shivered. She shook. She made a few, strong strokes, and then got out. Her mother and Laurence were nowhere in sight, but then there was Mitzi, handing her a towel. Its weave was rough, smelling of bleach. She looked up again at her mother's blanket and saw that she and Laurence were there, in it, after all, but writhing beneath the fabric like snakes. Watching them, the sand slipped from beneath her toes again, and she fell to the ground in a mass of seaweed until something scratched her face, sand fleas flew over her vision, and the cloudless sky spun counter-clockwise.

The next thing she saw was her mother's face, her mother's hands, with blue flashy nails, slapping her awake. "Oh, baby! I didn't see you looking ill. It must be the heat," Lisbeth Dryden said. "I think we should take her to the hospital."

Anna smiled wanly, both hoping and dreading the surprise, which may come to pass—and hoping it would come to all of them then, or simply fade past her awareness like his body had when he'd washed her blood away in his shower. saying: Oh. Blood. Oh, God. Oh, Jesus. Oh, God.

Laurence carried her to the car, but would soon plop her down in the backseat where she would disappear, like the trip to that dowdy little store had, so instantly, ten seconds after Lacy had eaten the last of those herrings.

Visible only by rear-view, Anna's mother had barely noticed her at all, talking of what they might do the next day and the next, and Laurence did not even look back once, as if his livelihood depended on keeping his stare forward to the glowing, sunlike radiance of her mother's open palm, beckoning, beckoning...

And this, too, was her legacy, this control, Anna thought, but Mitzi's legs twisted beneath her, making Anna's stomach turn and her skin stick to both of the girls flesh as Lacy opened her mouth but did not speak. Anna heaved, but did not puke. Then Mitzi pieced it together. She said, coolly, calmly, in her plain, all-weather voice, "So, Laurence, I hear you like young girls. How about it? Young girls like Anna? Then you forget them?"

A whisper could have been heard as Lisbeth Dryden pulled to the side of the road, turning her head to stare at the tangled girls. She looked confused.

The hospital glared brightly up ahead, and Laurence dropped his eyes between his feet, appeared to be making a prayer, but Lisbeth Dryden had a moment of understanding as she glared at Mitzi, who then glanced down at Anna.

Mitzi stroked her best friend's hand and murmured, "Shh," as Anna began to wail, but as Anna cried, Lisbeth Dryden slowly lifted her gaze to the passenger seat and said to Laurence, "Get out of my car, cabana boy," and so he did, still beautiful, still tanned, but walking away slow like a moving picture of a postcard.

Partly, Anna wanted to get out, to follow him, to call out, "Wait," but at the same time, she hated him so much she was glad for his comeuppance. Still, it pained her to watch him go as Lisbeth Dryden restarted the car and extended the blue talons of her right hand into the backseat and made a clutching motion for Anna's hand, looking back only once, with the faintest glimmer of moisture in her turquoise eyes. But it was the glare, Anna thought. Lisbeth did not cry. Oh no, her mother never cried, except about her father.

It was a vivid day, going on two p.m., and lighter and brighter than hell, so Lisbeth pulled out her cell phone and had a brief conversation as Annalise looked out her window and

Lacy said, "What's going on here? Why is Laurence leaving? Why won't anybody tell me what's going on?"

The trees lining the road flew past. "Shut up, Lacy," Lisbeth Dryden said, hanging up, then searched the front seat for her missing sunglasses, breathing jaggedly. A few streets down, Laurence receded to a dot on the afternoon sky, and when they next got out, more than an hour and a half later, they were miles away, but not a trace of upset could be seen on Lisbeth's face. Not a word had been said in the car.

Then Lisbeth opened the driver's side door with a set face and said, "We don't need a record of this, Annalise. I know someone here. Do you understand? If this is true—we need to take care of it, right now. If it's not, we go back to the beach, but Lacy will wait here, won't you honey? Someone has to watch the car."

"I want to go," Lacy said. "The car's hot."

Lisbeth rolled her eyes. "Can't you do something for me, dear? I take you here every summer, Goodman or not, all right? Lord knows your family can't afford it." She looked closer at Lacy until Lacy turned to the window. "I knew you would help like this," Lisbeth said. "Just watch the car, okay?" then "Come on, girls. Let's go."

When they were out of earshot, Lisbeth told Anna. "I made you an appointment, Anna. It wouldn't do for this to go on and on. Did you have a good time with him, baby? Good. Hold your head up. Walk straight. That's my girl."

Annalise walked on her trembling legs like a new gazelle, following her mother and matching pace with Mitzi while Lacy fumbled with the keys inside the car and turned on the radio. Then Lacy increased the volume as "Big Girls Don't Cry" blared from the tuner, and Anna looked back just once to see Lacy bopping her head and singing wild, fist-mike karaoke. Then Annalise lost glimpse of the outdoors and absorbed the powder-blue walls with faux art, wishing like hell she were back in the car or walking down the boardwalk, maybe even with the young boy from the store, or anyone in fact, even her father, though he was estranged, maybe even with Lacy, who she would be nicer too from now on, if only to get out of this.

Yes, even walking with Lacy would be better than this, but this would not go away until her mother was satisfied, so Anna looked at Mitzi then, standing so coolly beside Lisbeth, and then she looked at Lisbeth, too, having a quiet conversation with a middle-aged man in a white coat.

Her mother's gold rings flew through the still air, explaining, and Annalise felt the urge to run. So, she ran, but why she couldn't exactly explain. It was not tenderness for the possible baby but a larger-scale rejection of her mother. She had to be free of her, and the sky was blue and cloudless, a relief after those faded clean walls.

She gasped for breath as the hot air flooded her lungs, but she was at the car's window, beating on it, shouting, "Let me in, Lacy. Let me in right now!"

Lacy stared at her and unlocked the door. "Where were you guys? Did you come to wait with me?"

"Yes, I did," Annalise said. "I'm sure their business will be over soon." As she said this, Lisbeth Dryden and Mitzi scuttled from the entranceway. She saw her mother was furious, her arms swinging, her feet speed-walking, and Lisbeth spoke to Mitzi as if she were her close friend instead.

Mitzi kept a flat expression and used the one moment Lisbeth looked away to run her finger over her throat like "You're dead, Anna."

Annalise made the sign for blabbering, four fingers closing on her thumb very quickly like lips, then pointed to herself and then Lacy.

"Did I tell you I had sex last month, Lace," she asked. "With a boy?"

"No way? You did?"

"Yes. And he was Laurence. That's why he got out of the car. That's why he left."

"Ohmygod, Anna. Your mother will be mad."

"She already is," Anna said. "But I don't care." She was thinking of contacting Laurence, holding him again, maybe kissing and touching him.

"Annalise Dryden!" her mother called. "I hope you're happy with yourself! You need to march back in there right now. Right now! Dr. Killomanjo is waiting."

"And now Lacy," Anna said in a loud whisper, "my mother wants me to go back in that building to kill the little baby in my womb and send it away because, you see, I'm pregnant, but I don't want to go in there."

"Oh god, oh, ohmygod," Lacy said, clenching and releasing her palms.

Lisbeth mirrored her startled look. "So that's the secret you wanted to know at the store, and now you know it all," Anna said. "Happy?"

Lacy looked ready to pass out, shaking, and her mouth hung open as Lisbeth's face turned red as the swath of sunburn beneath Mitzi's eyes. Lisbeth tapped her foot then walked back into the building, and Mitzi gaped, her perfect orthadentured teeth neatly exposed in the summer air. "You really pissed her off now, Anna," she said.

"I do what I please," Anna replied.

"I won't tell anyone what you told me," Lacy said then. "I swear. I'll never tell a living soul."

"No," said Anna, "tell everyone, please. And tell my mother you plan on doing that if you really want to help." Then Anna put her arm around Lacy's shoulder because Lacy was blubbering and said one last thing, "Please, Lace. For me. Tell everyone. I mean it," and Lacy said, "I will. You're my cousin, and I love you. I swear," and then the three girl stood together for the first time ever, for the first time that summer but not the last, all three, waiting for Lisbeth Dryden's furious return.

"You know," Mitzi said then, "I could help you lose weight if you want to, Lace. We could even do your hair when we get back."

"And I could show you how to crimp it," Anna said. "We could have a sleepover. You want to?"

"Yes," Lacy said, and then they squinted in the glare, hands to their foreheads, as Lisbeth Dryden marched back. To their surprise, taupe eyeliner smeared a light, muddied path down her cheek, almost hidden beneath a newly applied layer of foundation.

To Lisbeth's right, a little boy and his mother rushed out, and Annalise watched the boy, obviously punished for something, his head down, his bottom lip hanging, as his mother's finger wagged and the sharp tone of her voice flew past. The boy had blue eyes and looked sad, so Anna wanted to raise her fist to make a talking head, say, maybe like a ventriloquist: "Hello, my name is Anna," but she did not. She watched her mother who breezed up, gesturing for her keys, with the white sarong she'd worn flapping around her black suit as her wooden beach clogs slapped the pavement, and "Get in the car, girls," Lisbeth said then, not looking at any of them. "Let's go."

It was then that Anna felt her action was foolish. All actions. Any action. She felt the unbearable shame of letting her family down, shame in her stomach, in her bones, in her blood—a queasy feeling, and she thought, really thought, about bringing a life into this world that half-belonged to Laurence. But there was nothing more to be done. They'd left the clinic, with her belly full and her mother hating her.

The road ahead of them was hot and hard—it would be separate from thereafter.

The Impossible Dripping Heap

Jeff Brewer

Nag resurfaces outside my window as I'm having a bad time of it. He tells me that what I'm going through is all in my head. He wants to help, if I'll let him help. I tell him I'm finished, nearly finished. He asks if I am spreading sawdust across the floor again. I tell him I'm also molding mounds of sand in certain tender spots. He tells me that no one in his right mind should go this far for a nebulous drop of muck that refuses to drip from a ceiling. I tell him how there is a world in that hanging drop—an always in between tauntingly stagnant pit, it's angry and thirsting for something but deflated and finished with it all.

He tells me that I should focus on something simple, something I can grasp. I tell him I'm waiting for something simple—it's right here—and he says what I need is a little give and take. I tell him it's out of my hands. He tells me I have lost it. I tell him it's right here. I'm merely waiting for it to drip. He tells me that I'm merely imagining it.

Then he hacks yellow mouth foam onto the ground, smears it with the tip of his shoe, and tells me that it's funny I should mention things dripping because he has had an aching case of it for sometime—it's ticking up my spine, it's burning and tickling, it's everywhere, he says. He stretches his mouth wide, asks if I can see it, and I ask him how he plans to help me and solve it. He says how he has never felt more alive, every orifice screams, he says, every time he goes to the bathroom he shivers from not being cold in as long as he can remember, you just have to learn to let go of it, he says.

I tell him that I just don't know, and he says that if I could only understand it than maybe I would understand. I tell him I probably wouldn't understand. He then says that if I help him through the window, he will help me understand it. He says I should have a taste of it. I tell him that I have decided to forgo the inevitable anguish of interactions, so when the drop finally drips, I say, I'm finished. How, I'm not sure. It is merely a matter of when. He then tells me to wait, to just wait—says if I can just hold off until he comes back than he'll help me learn how to handle a little give and take. I tell him that it's out of my grasp, and in the end, I have decided to let the drop decide when my end will arrive, and he says how he will hurry back.

The weight in the wait for the end aches—so I wait, sleep standing, crane-necked, at the foot of my bed—It's in the weight of waking under light bulbs long spent, of nearly drowning on my tongue severed in sleep, of blood clots long since spilled into my beard—It's in the weight of standing in darkness, of inducing a dream not dreamt through a tear-bursting tongue bite, of my tongue further severed, under the drop dripping onto my moist shoulder—it's everywhere—above the glow of a lit match under the above drop dripping and recoiling into a watermarked spiral stretching across the entire ceiling—it's everywhere—under the drop dripping into a stream running through my clotted beard, streaming into a blood puddle soaked into sawdust, rising above the sole of my shoe.

There is relief: a gentle toe tap in the blood slush before testing the give and take of the tightening noosed curtain around my throat. There is the agony of interruption: Nag resurfacing. He's pushing someone in a wheelchair. He sees me through the window, and he tells me to wait, and I tell him I have been waiting and the drop finally dripped. Now it's merely a matter of how. He says to un-loop my neck so I can meet the man in the wheelchair. His son. Nag tells me that he thinks about me as if I were also his son. He then tells me not to worry. The wet bloody rag that covers his son's face is not his son's rag. The blood on the rag is not his son's blood, either. The potted vine plant in his lap is his son's, though. He says that his son is taking care of something, and what I need is to nourish myself by taking care of something, a little give and take, he says. I wipe blood from my beard. I tell him that I need a proper hook, something sturdier than this shoddy curtain rod. His son's nervous legs twitch under a waterlogged blanket. Nag straightens the plant, says that the vine comes with a hook and a rope for the pot to hang from. His son mumbles in agony and confusion as he shivers or convulses from the chest down. I rest my cheek on the damp windowsill and watch Nag's ruined fingers straighten the plant, tuck a necklaced whistle into the collar of his son's damp dressing gown, adjust the soaked stocking cap that holds the bloody rag over his son's face as Nag says that the blood on the rag is the only thing neglected here.

I tell Nag they disgust me.

There's something dripping, something has happened, Nag's son says.

Something is happening, Nag says.

It's unbearable, I say.

Nag says that if he could leave his son in one of my closets for a while maybe his son would stop complaining long enough for Nag to put everything in order. I remind him that I am actually living in a closet and that my closets are nothing more than a run down industrial sized washer and drier set. Shortly before I moved in, a tenant tried to cremate a three-legged dog in the drier. The poor dead thing crashed around in there until its blood split through its stomach and splattered onto the circuits. Shorted it out. Burnt the room in half. Dog clumps still clog the lint filter. As for the washer, it's somehow hooked to a long since rotted septic tank. My most awful excrement would freshen the set.

Nag interrupts, says I would only have to wait for his son to whistle me. I tell him there's no room for his dripping heap of a son; I already have a near river leaking onto the foot of my bed. He says he needs to put things in order so that he can help me. Says his son will catch his death out here, you don't want that on your hands, he says. It's my time, I say. Nag's son says that something is dripping again. So I press my forehead against the windowsill and tell Nag that I have things to do, and that whether his son lives or dies is out of my hands. When I lift my head, I ask Nag where he is going, he says he will hurry back. His son, however, remains outside my window.

I decide to push Nag's son into my apartment after watching him cough and shake and moan for some time. He continues to complain that there's something dripping. I tell him that from where he's sitting it's raining and where we are heading, well, it's just awful. He repeats that there's something dripping, so I tell him that he wouldn't understand, that if he could understand than maybe he'd understand, and he tells me that something is happening. So I tell him that in a while he will be able to once again say that something has happened.

In my apartment, after sometime, Nag's son removes the bloody rag from his face. He is wearing dark glasses. He clears his throat onto the floor and asks if I'm curious to see his eyes; they have turned all white, he says. No, I say. Besides, I say, the light in here is terrible. He yawns, says that he wants to go bed then, and that he wants a fresh sheet. I tell him that I only have one sheet and right now it's hanging from the window. He asks what do I use to keep warm. The curtain, I say. I then tell him I have things to do.

He says that outside of my apartment is death, this, in here, is it. He then asks me for a painkiller. I look around my apartment for objects that would end me, and I tell him that it's time it ended and he confronts me about it. If it means misery, he says, take a look at me and talk about it. Then he asks why I don't kill him. I won't, I say. He asks me why not. I tell him I have only what it takes to finish myself. So he asks if I'll finish us. I tell him that I will finish myself, first. He says that my mere presence pollutes my apartment, and that he wants me to place him in front of the washer and drier, beside my bed. He says that he wants to be front and center when it begins. You mean when it ends, I say. Don't you know the end is in the beginning, he says, and why did you sludge up the floor, I'm sinking, he says. To soak up the stench, I say, when it ends. You mean when it begins, he says. Whenever it is that I'm finished, I say.

So he starts blowing his whistle, asks me when I'll get him a painkiller. Tells me there's some in the cupboard. I tell him I do not have a cupboard. Then I wheel him under the dripping spigot in the ceiling, tell him that the streaming drip needs to nourish his plant, it needs to give a little, I say. He says for me to be quiet, that there will be no more conversation, no more words spoken until he gets his painkiller. He then interrupts the silence, says how there's something dripping, always the same spot. Perhaps it's a heart in the pot. It's finished, nearly finished, he says.

Why don't you tell me a story, he says as I re-noose the curtain. I tell him that my dying light is projected on the ceiling. He says he sees some naked give and take. So I let go of the curtain and show him, in the shadow of a lit match, how each watermarked spiral on the ceiling bends and bubbles the paint. Under another lit match, I show him how something is happening, the spiral is webbing down the walls. Watery veins have bulged spores under the paint. He tells me to scratch at he wall, peel back the paint. See if the spores have bloomed; get it started, he says. I tell him that this is my story, and they'll bloom when they bloom. He says that I'm no fun, and what I need is a little initiative. So I tell him that soon, the pot will overflow. The vines will vein my mattress, creep up the walls and blend with the spores. My pillow will quickly dissolve into a feathery sludge. My single blanket will turn gooey. The sawdust and sand on the floor will turn to a soup and start to rise.

That will do, he says—do I smell a dog, he says, it is coming from there? He points motions over his shoulder, at the washer and drier. Open it. Let it out, he says. There here is no dog, I say. You probably don't need to open it, then, he says. There is nothing, I say. Then open it! He says. Have you opened it? He asks, yes, I say as I open the washer. He then blows his whistle again, something just crawled across my foot, hold my hand, he says. That's the plant overflowing, I say. The plant has a hook, he says, why don't you hang it in its rightful place and move me into the center of the room, I want to be in the right place when it begins.

I tell him I'll do so if he holds the curtain while I hang the hook. He asks me if it is time for his painkiller yet. Soon enough, I say. To my surprise he welcomes the bloody rag when I cover his face with it. Then I place the wound curtain on his head. He thanks me for the sheet. I stand on the arms of his wheelchair and screw the hook into the spot where the drip has been streaming. Do you know what it is, he asks. What is it? I ask. It always happens without me, he says as I string the noosed curtain to the wavering ceiling.

I awake at the foot of Nag's son, under a chunk of electrical wires and rusted water pipes that hang and shoot sparks and spray rust water onto the noosed curtain. Nag's son's shoe is floating in a pool of rust and blood-soaked sawdust. His toes are tapping in a wake of rising water cresting along the clotted tip of my beard. I strained my shoulder in the fall. Lost a tooth. Planting soil clods my hair, which is twined in vines. Nag's son says something has happened. I begin to ask him if the mold spores are blooming, but I'm distracted by a noise coming from either the washer or drier. A voice is echoing and something is scraping against something. Teeth grinding down to the gums. A sharp edge digging through a bone. Something is happening, move me to the center of the room, Nag's son says.

In between the washer and drier a shapeless shaded mass scrapes something against the drier. I ask it if it has come for me. When the shaking stops, a voice echoes from the drier and a foot creeps out of the shade and lights a match with its toes. A woman's wet face glows above the lit tip of a match. A tooth of hers spits toward me. At first, I think it's a match. How it doesn't singe onto the wet sawdust and how she tongues her gums under the flame of another lit match tells me otherwise. She sits, rain-drenched, her short sleeve shirt soaking her armless sockets. I ask her if she has come to finish me. She lights a cigarette with her toes, raises it to her lips, and continues tearing matches. I'm amazed that she can keep her cigarettes and matches dry. With an arched foot, she cups the flames. Then she flicks tiny bursts of fire toward me. Nag's son sits at the foot of the bed with his back facing her. He asks what's happening as she says something out the side of her mouth and blows smoke rings that lift through the room. How she pulses smoke rings. Each tight circle brims, vibrates, a floating target for another matched fireball to float through.

What is it, my pet? She says as she stands. She circles the drier, then climbs into the open washer and curls in.

Time for love? She asks as smoke rings circle out of the washer.

What's happening, Nag's son says.

I walk over and lift the lid of the drier. Nag has been in there for I don't know how long. He's laughing or crying. I close the lid on the drier. Nag's echoing voice asks the woman for a kiss. Laughter echoes from the washer and drier. Nag's son asks what's happening again. I tell him that something is taking its course—it must be nearly finished. It has to be nearly finished, I say as I close the lid on the washer.

He tells me not to speak anymore about it. It's time it ended. He lifts the bloody rag from his face and he tells me he'll help, if I'll let him help, just move me to center of the room, it's time it ended, he says. You mean it's time it began, I say.

Don't you know the beginning is in the end, he says.

FROM SEXUAL STEALING

Wendy Walker

Introduction

I wish to re-establish the tie between the genre of gothic and its early epithet "terrorist literature," as I believe this tells us something about its increasingly central position in American literature and current American foreign policy.

The roots of Gothic writing go deep in the United States, where it was planted from England. Of the four inventors of Gothic literature in English, two, William Beckford and Matthew "Monk" Lewis, were owners of major sugar plantations in Jamaica. Horace Walpole's father, Robert, as head of the government that sponsored the Royal African Company, oversaw the African Service whose officers staffed Cape Coast Castle on the Gold Coast, where slaves were brought for transshipment. As a child Ann Radcliffe lived with her uncle, partner of Josiah Wedgwood. Their pottery firm produced the medallion of a slave kneeling beneath the legend "Am I not a man and a brother?" which became an emblem of the anti-slavery movement.

"Sexual stealing," therefore, is a fundamental structural principle in gothic narratives. "Sexual stealing" may be defined as the illegal appropriation of a highly libidinized object: a person's land, liberty, sexual consent, virginity, life. The stealing is performed by the powerful and is unacknowledged as stealing, indeed proclaimed as legal and honorable. Then the victim rises up as daemon to avenge the outrage. This is the only narrative solution in a world where justice does not function to protect people, but the "justice" of the gothic novel is to suppress the daemon.

My *Sexual Stealing*, a work in progress, uses a constraint to reappropriate an account of chattel slavery by extracting the discourse of the plantation from within a gothic novel, Radcliffe's *The Mysteries of Udolpho.* Selecting one word from each printed line, I have kept them in the order in which found and added no others, but made line- and section-breaks to articulate the derived story. Where in my research I found passages or images apposite to the implications of my material, I have interpolated them; the images, unfortunately, could not be used in this version.

1

banks of the plantations
whose forms gleamed
sometimes tremendous
flocks herds and distance

the margin floated
pastoral portrait
delineated corrected
benevolence scenes

literature of deficiency
intrigues honour
a death amiable or necessary

sold to felicity
treasures attached
delight entrusted
obliterated circumstances   shade character
waves remembered   disengaged wishes

building beauty
a fabric remembered
building taste
conspicuous in manners
enriched modern grove
towards caught landscape
precipices scarce
among feast pursuits

little basket of scenes
abstract wandering enthusiast
of bosom
of repast
of rocks adjoining room
books exercised taste
made windows
and palm-trees

the climate of figure
adjusted to chateau
was excellent story
was tasteful
yet
sacrificed prospect
that wept
a plantation

palm-trees
a river
fine setting-sun
distant gray children
ever simplicity
tumultuous heart experienced
nothing moral
blessing
favourite hour   dark hour
often pastoral   often breathing

melancholy interruptions by consideration of truth
renders character anxious hereafter

uncommon benevolence advanced her object
congenial penetration dangerous to self-command
he instructed passions
with obliged indifference
occasioned her eyes
awakened her
"eye contagious"
her sciences
her might
early inclination against ever escape thinking
gratifications necessary
indolence beautiful
dissipation interest
was it

This morning Old Tom Williams called, and made his observations as usual; he once killed a Negro girl of his own that had got looseness, stopping her A – with a corn-stick. And one of the girls cleaning the hall when he thought it did not much want it he shit in it and told her there was something for her to clean. Frequently at home wears nothing but a shirt, and fans himself with the forelap before his daughter, &c. &c.

Douglas Hall, *In Miserable Slavery: Thomas Thistlewood in Jamaica 1750-86.*
Thistlewood's *Diary*, Thursday, March 19th, 1752

wild silence
impressed scenes faded
were woods of circumstances
her little glen
wound screened   eye shattered
by emerging vine-covered

gradually groves
tint favourite books

2

dusk of accents
from trembled excursions
lines

        sonnet to go
        steps all ah!
        sweet
light'ning portrait
all ah!
        conceal away!
        who would

lines to being   compelled

painful
she to presume
away thoughts exercise
indisposition fever
a recovery advanced
air provisions
no torturing

As Sally steals everything left in the cookroom, and eats it if eatable, Phibbah had her tied with her hands behind her naked for the mosquitoes to bite her tonight. She bawled out lustily, but before 9 o'clock in the evening broke loose and ran away. I got up, and all hands went to seek her. I catched her near the Rockholes, in ditto provision ground. Her hands were tied up so tight that the string hurt her very much. Brought her home and secured her for this night in the bilboes.
About 9 in the evening, *Cum* Sally *(mea) Sup. Terr.* in Rockhole provision ground.

Thistlewood's *Diary*, Tuesday, August 7, 1770.

botanizing gratitude gave Monsieur pleasure
confinement conceptions of every shade
the sensible romantic
with daughter degree
could himself forbear secretly
regret useless
to temper
to surprised instrument
her silence her person
timidity of whether

she entered faltering

to Madame her wherefore
only apprehensions
faint wainscot tremour
now added doubt
Monsieur of palm-trees
vallies inhaled
of delicacy   much detained
sails of unpleasing alas!
ever recollected

long loss
her resemblance
really became absence
informed   unreasonable
music
disappearance

Set all the blackies to scrape and clean all round the house, the lawn, &c. Treated them with beef and punch, and never was there a happier set of people than they appear to be. All day they have been singing odd songs, only interrupted by peals of laughter; and indeed I must say, they have reason to be content, for they have many comforts and enjoyments. I only wish the poor Irish were half as well off. Had a visit and a good long conversation with Mr. Ward today.

Lady Nugent's Journal of Her Residence in Jamaica from 1801 to 1805, January 23, 1802.

restrained determining
Monsieur musing
on Madame perplexed   about servants
having horses
perceived Paris way
purchased the relationship

intercourse aim
object attainment
not virtues of marriage
ambition consequence
desired also happiness

same Monsieur readily
expressed contempt
concealed resentment
restrained resentment
understood his heiress
woman determined not to display intelligence
listened for latter
permitted ostentation
a negotiating of class
importance not opinions
nor what Madame could   describing banquet   honour
with minuteness
fancy heightened to happiness

The carriages were sent to Port Henderson for some Navy men. We had twenty at breakfast and at dinner, in addition to our party.-- Much talk about peace; some pleased, some the reverse. I am of the contented party; and went to dress in great spirits for the grand ball, given me to-night by the Council, &c.: put on my smartest dress, with a gold tiara, and white feathers, and made myself look as magnificent as I could. At 8, was received at the entrance of the House of Records by the Members of Council, some of the Assembly, and some military. Was conducted to a sort of throne, covered with pink silk and draperies festooned with flowers. The decorations of the room were beautiful, and the supper was superb: one dish I shall never forget; it was a roasted peacock, placed before me, with all the feathers of the tail stuck in, and spread so naturally, that I expected every minute to see him strut out of the dish. Danced myself almost to death, to please both civil and military, Army and Navy, and stayed till 1 o'clock .

Lady Nugent's Journal of Her Residence in Jamaica from 1801 to 1805, November 25, 1801.

I sigh for the politics
or I exist
where conscious
I know improvements
I bring enquiry
should I number servants people
accommodated   improved
since living at chateau
cut the should side
hollow enthusiasm
use will
the mansion amidst heavy reading
landscape the leaves
speaking old-fashioned tree
believe chesnut poplar
a spiry pine
unquestionably gothic

sir   *a propos*
some possession improvements
I hear mentioned
difficulty
of deferred hope

In the morning a carpenter, from Spanish Town, applied to General N. to respite a slave, sentenced to be hanged to-morrow. The law of the land is, it seems, that three magistrates may condemn a slave to death. This case was, that two slaves, one, an old offender, the other, a boy of sixteen, robbed a man of his watch, &c. The old man shewed the boy how to get in at the window, and gave him all his instructions, while he remained on the outside, and received the things stolen. The old man has been condemned to hard labour, and the boy to be hanged. General N. made every exertion, but in vain, to save the life of the boy, and send him out of the country; but it appears that it could not be done, without exercising his prerogative very far, and giving great offense and alarm to the white population. -- This law of the three magistrates appears to me abominable, but I am too little versed in such matters to do more than feel for the poor sufferer.

Lady Nugent's Journal of Her Residence in Jamaica from 1801 to 1805, January 10, 1802.

separated alone
subject
much sorrow
enquire of that subject

Oh Saib! my heart once was gentle, once was good! But sorrows have broken it, insults have made it hard! I have been dragged from my native land, from a wife who was everything to me, to whom I was everything! Twenty years have elapsed since these Christians tore me away: they trampled on my heart, mocked my despair, and, when in frantic terms I raved of Samba, laughed, and wondered how a negro's soul could feel! In that moment when the last point of Africa faded from my view, when as I stood on the vessel's deck I felt that all I loved was lost to me forever, in that bitter moment did I banish humanity from my breast. I tore from my arm the bracelet of Samba's hair. I gave to the sea that precious token, and, while the high waves swift bore it from me, vowed aloud endless hatred to mankind. I have kept my oath, I will keep it!

Hassan in Monk Lewis's *The Castle Spectre*, 1796

days with dining Madame
prompted wish
liberty rational
no shackles
herself well
together walk
income large
not weekly grievances
smile returned

where throng various stories

gloom now beneficent pleasure
gloom enthusiasm
I listen
to tear
describe here   now
being
them gone sir

so come further
charm with   sir venture
repeat   venture
fancy spells
sir *not*
thought irregular

GLOW-WORM

how a glade swallows
the twilight   the heads   the trembling guides   the dance
the dying defend the shadowy
they not yet benighted

would bind the shapes   shout
terror elves
with string
round glade
plighted   lighted
free band
the will to foil
the slave
faithful of fade
cheerless
pale

    think that silence

    erroneous surfaces
    half-waving mountain-tops
    gleam uncertain

Notwithstanding the sensuality in which Vathek indulged, he experienced no abatement in the love of his people, who thought that a sovereign giving himself up to pleasure was as able to govern as one who declared himself an enemy to it.

William Beckford, *Vathek*, 1782

chateau languor
called suspended fever
disorder taken upon heavy anxiety
detained feelings visited
and concealed hopes
when disorder circumstances formed anxious sorrow of regretted manner

family approaching
prepared to induce affliction
teach physician abruptly
restrain affliction occasion first
mind mother   the disorder
suffering only always
her grief   much resignation
with effort affected
dry countenance
but never
so practiced pressure
for comfort

ODYSSEUS IN HELL

Zachary Mason

A man picks his way along a steel cable strung over a refulgent blue abyss, a ship's oar over his shoulders for balance. The cable groans and sighs in the infinitesimal breeze. It is so narrow that the man is, when he thinks of it, surprised that he is able to keep his footing. Miles in front of him the horizon is shrouded in bright clouds. It may well be the same behind him but he has never looked back. The cable sags, very slightly, just discernibly over the course of what may be hours, or days - he is descending.

Above him (he sees this out of his peripheral vision - to look up would be fatal) is an irregular dark massiveness suggesting mountains. There are iridescent patches that could be lakes or possibly cities. Below is open sky, gradations of deep featureless blue. Now weariness comes over him and he stops to rest, squatting and balancing the oar across his shoulders, gripping the cable with feet and hands, peering down into the void in which he finds a measure of comfort.

He has been walking and balancing for a long time and his mind wanders. For the most part his reflections are vacant or circular recapitulations of the conditions of his confinement in this limitless open air. When a thought crystallizes it is this: Somewhere a judgment is being made. Even now advocates are striding in flapping robes through bleak arcades toward the ante-rooms where they will make their case before a judge, whose name he almost knows - Minos, or possibly Yama. This stirs something in his arid, empty mind - he wants to argue the case himself.

He knows that if the judgment goes against him a wind will rise in the west, a white rushing mass devouring a hemisphere of sky, racing over him and scouring the cable clean. He considers tactics for such a situation - leaning into the wind and walking on the wind side of the cable or breaking into a dead run when he sees the storm rising, with every hasty step risking a sudden, final slip, though there is no end in view. He recognizes the futility of these plans but this does not permit him to stop formulating them.

The cable might be getting narrower. His legs might be weakening. He might feel the air stirring. Eyes closed, he hesitates and imagines the languor of falling. He sees himself snatching futilely at the cable, missing, how quickly it would dwindle as he kept his eyes and hand turned to it, his sole reference point, and how he would at last have the luxury of looking up at the world he was falling away from, secure in the knowledge that whatever else came the worst had happened. He steadies himself and takes another step.

Once a generation, the spring tide reaches the broken walls of Troy and it is granted him to recall that once he was Odysseus.

THE REAL, TRUE-LIFE STORY OF GODZILLA!

Curtis Smith

Billy Glenn grew up in a dusty map speck of a southern Iowa town. He hated the town for its smallness and isolation, hated its provincial ways, the communal thrill that accompanied the changing of the feature at the Bijou or the purchase of a new fire company engine. He hated himself for hating a town that loved him in return, the high school gym where his retired basketball jersey hung from the rafters, the Main Street diner where his favorite order, a cheeseburger with green peppers and onions, had been renamed the Billy Glenn Special. Most of all, he'd grown to hate the town's water tower, a red and white colossus that stood guard over the endless corn fields. The roads leading to town ran arrow straight, heat-glimmering stretches where tar sucked at his wheels and only gospel stations broke the radio static, and when Billy drove home from college for summer break, he'd catch sight of the water tower from as far away as Grantville, a rusting star on the distant horizon. Miles passed, and as the tower lifted ever so slightly into the blue sky, Billy's muscles tightened involuntarily, spasms so intense he sometimes had to pull onto the shoulder and catch his breath. Lying across the car's sticky-warm seat, hand clenched over his heaving chest, he imagined the news bulletin interrupting the stories of salvation -- Billy Glenn, starting forward at State, second all-time on the Iowa high school scoring list, found dead on a lonely farmland roadside, the circumstances mysterious, his body robbed of oxygen, an apparent drowning miles from the nearest body of water.

He left college after his junior year in 1959, military service avoided due to the knee operation he underwent near season's end. He tore the ligaments on an awkward landing after a practice lay-up, a motion he'd performed in drills since elementary school, only this time there was a different ending, a buckling in his joint, a pain that radiated down to his foot, and his first thoughts weren't of his team or his scholarship, not what his injury might mean to his chances to go pro. He thought of the water tower. The trainer's voice, the pull of athletic tape around a makeshift splint -- it all seemed miles away to Billy. Behind his shut eyes, he saw the tower's fat belly and long, skinny legs. And he saw himself gimping through town, the tower looming over him, its fading, painted letters forever reminding him of where he was and where he'd always be.

Wearing a skin-pinching brace, Billy Glenn hustled through countless tryouts, and in the course of three and a half years, he signed with four different semi-pro teams in the Midwest. Most of the teams were owned by local businessmen, carpet wholesalers or car lot owners, and the backs of their players' jerseys were festooned with advertising. *Buy your next car at Hartman's!* or *Big Al's, the Savings King!* They played in small, smoky gyms, and the spirit cheers Billy had grown accustomed to in high school and college were replaced by drunken curses, the angry plink of pennies hurled onto the court. Sometimes an owner visited the locker room, not to give a pep talk but to remind them of the bookies' latest line and of the stake he'd placed in the proper outcome. Deliberately missing a wide open jumper made Billy sick to his stomach, and after such games, he'd return to the cockroach flats his income allowed and guzzle cheap whiskey until he passed out.

Their circuit cut through the heart of the country. There were stops in Flint, Des Moines, Louisville, cities more or less the same in their size and gray drudgery. Inevitably they rolled through the college towns where Billy had once played, and framed in the bus's frosted windows were the great arenas, the bundled students hurrying to ivy-cloaked buildings. Billy saw these things and wondered where his life had gone so wrong. With a grimace, he gulped back more aspirin and closed his eyes until the cold, rattling bus was back on the highway. Into the ashy winter twilight they drove, passing farmhouses and cut fields, and eventually they'd near a town and Billy would spot another water tower, its ugly alien form rising above the snowy flatlands. He'd smile then and rub his aching knee, momentarily assured he'd made the best with the cards he'd been dealt.

Evansville was the last team to cut him. He still had his shot. He set his picks with rehearsed, mechanical skill, found his teammates with crisp passes, but his quickness, that initial, reactionary burst, was gone, and he knew it would never return. For two weeks he holed up in his apartment, hobbling up the fire escape to avoid the landlord. The metal steps rattled in time with the whiskey bottles he hid beneath his coat, and the slush that fell from his boots struck the trash cans below with loud, incriminating plops. He couldn't last like this much longer, the drinking and the debts, the bologna and peanut butter diet, but he vowed he'd scrape by hungry and broke before returning to the one place where everyone knew him. He feared a town populated by the ghosts of his past, the boy who shoveled snow from the schoolyard basketball court and practiced foul shots long into the dark, the type of early, unwavering focus that caused his teachers and most everyone else to say, "Keep an eye on that boy. He'll go far." Most people's dreams were carefully hidden, and the disappointment of not attaining them was limited to private regrets, but the entire town had cheered

Billy's pursuit, and by returning home, his failure would no longer be his alone. He'd be watched by the women of the United Methodists' sewing circle and by the men who pitched horseshoes behind the dry goods store, and in thoughts both expressed and not, they'd interpret his actions and moods, reading into them some sort of mythic, plain-hardened drama, the story of a young man whose desires had outstripped his talents. The strange truth was Billy Glenn had never given his town or its water tower a second thought until he'd gone to college and come up against players better than himself, and he'd gladly go back home tomorrow if only he could return as someone else, someone with a history as blank as a cloudless summer sky.

The call from Jim McSwain came on a snowy morning. The ringing startled Billy because he thought the phone company had already shut off his service.

"Billy, Jesus Christ, you're a son of a bitch to track down!" Wincing with a hangover's pain, Billy held the receiver away from his ear. Profane Jim McSwain, as his players called him, was the owner of the Gary Smokestacks, the second-to-last team to cut Billy. McSwain was a celebrity of sorts in Gary, the owner of a successful sporting goods chain, the star of his own TV commercials, hubris-filled outbursts in which his burly arms whipped baseball bats and hockey sticks like assaulting weapons, the rhinestone crown proclaiming him **King of Sports** teetering atop his square head.

"You need me for the Smokestacks?" Billy asked hopefully.

"Smokestacks are fine, Billy. What I got to offer you is something much fucking bigger."

McSwain went on, but a hinge-rattling knock at the door distracted Billy. "Phone company!" called a grumbling voice.

"I'm listening, Jim," Billy said, "but make it quick."

"We're going to play fucking ball again, Billy." Over the

staticy line, Billy heard the click and puff of McSwain lighting one of his trademark cigars. "In fucking Japan."

As the phone man disconnected his line, Billy packed his duffel bag and lit down the fire escape. His size fourteen footprints crossed the snowy yard, and he turned once at the sound of his landlord's threat to call the cops before he broke into a run. He didn't stop until he reached the Western Union office a half mile away where the wire Jim McSwain had promised him soon arrived. The telegram accompanying the money outlined his itinerary -- take a bus to Chicago, then hop the first train to San Francisco where he'd meet McSwain and the rest of the team in three days' time at an airport bar called The Flight Deck Lounge.

During the cross-country trek, Jim McSwain's words twisted in Billy's head, how the Japanese loved all things American and why not basketball, too? Hadn't McSwain gotten to know the Japanese mindset during his service stint with the occupation force? McSwain boasted they'd be the ambassadors of the game, celebrities, that it was only a matter of time before the whole damn country was at their feet. With the snow capped mountains gliding past his window, Billy realized he didn't care a lick about an entire country falling in love with him. In fact, love was the farthest thing from his mind.

Duffel bag slung over his shoulder, Billy stepped into the dimly lit Flight Deck Lounge. The stink of his own clothes repulsed him. Less than fifty cents jangled in his pocket, and the rough stubble of his chin itched like mad. He recognized a number of the faces huddled near the bar fish tank. Stan Shapiro and Big Dale Brown were ex-teammates from the Smokestacks. The redhead who tapped the aquarium glass and made puckered faces at the fish was Derek Reeves, a shameless gunner from Ohio State Billy had played against in college. Casey Poe, a worn covered Bible in his massive hands, had been released from the Globetrotters for "undisclosed reasons," which everyone knew meant too much booze. Speedy Luther Berry dealt a hand of black jack to Swoop Nixon, the one time Celtic who'd silenced the Garden two years before with an Achilles rupture so loud half the crowd ducked for cover, thinking they'd heard a gunshot.

"Stop right there, you mother fucker!" Pushing his way through the gin-sipping businessmen, a smoldering cigar between his ringed fingers, McSwain approached his player with opened arms. McSwain had lost a little more hair since Billy had seen him last, the wrinkles around his quicksilver eyes etched a bit deeper. "The last piece of the puzzle!" McSwain bellowed. He embraced Billy in a bruising hug and shoved a ticket into his shirt pocket. "Jesus, kid, you look like shit." McSwain yelled back to the bar. "OK ladies, let's get this goddamn circus on the road!"

Far above the dark Pacific, Jim McSwain outlined the mission of the Tokyo Gladiators. The game had been introduced by GIs like himself during the occupation, and when he'd visited Japan last year, McSwain had discovered that amateur leagues had sprung up in a number of the major cities. The first part of McSwain's scheme had already been set in motion, and each of these leagues had agreed to select its best players into a type of local all-star team. For the first year, the Tokyo Gladiators would criss-cross the mainland playing exhibitions, and the following season, they'd ride the crest of their own buzz all across Asia, playing before standing-room-only crowds in Taipei and Saigon, Seoul and Singapore. McSwain poured champagne into plastic airline cups.

"When they write the history of this league," McSwain said, "yours will be the fucking picture on the first page." He raised his plastic cup over his head, but a sudden burp of turbulence sloshed the champagne from his glass, a fizzing cascade that wet the hair and cheeks of a suddenly anxious looking Casey Poe.

McSwain went on, lecturing them on the peculiarities of Japanese customs and giving quick, Midwestern-accented lessons in basic phrases. Next to Billy, Luther Berry shuffled and cut his deck of cards, grinning each time he upturned an ace or face. Billy gulped down his champagne and rested his head against the tiny window. What a desperate crew they were, all of them either egotistical or fragile, out of luck or, like him, running from their pasts. His eyes closed, he allowed himself to drift into sleep. The rise and fall of McSwain's voice reminded him of the tent revival preacher who passed through their town every summer, and Billy grinned at the idea of Profane Jim McSwain as a man of the cloth. Perhaps McSwain couldn't offer him salvation, only a reprieve, but for Billy, a reprieve was salvation enough.

Red eyed from champagne and jet lag, the Gladiators played their first game less than sixteen hours after landing in Tokyo. Already Japan was proving itself a vexing place, its eerily clean streets and suffocating subway cars, the bedless shoebox apartments McSwain had arranged for them. Whispers and giggles rippled behind their backs, and their approach to the gym doors was met with open stares, an occasional bow. Inside, the thunder of beating drums echoed beneath the ceiling's exposed girders. Screaming fans waved fluttering banners written in indecipherable Japanese.

"Un-fucking-believable," McSwain said. With an expert flexing of jaw muscles, he transferred his cigar to the opposite corner of his mouth. "This, gentlemen, is ground zero for something big."

The locker room was being sprayed for silverfish, and they were forced to change in a dank hallway. The gym ruckus intensified. "Sounds like a goddamn war in there," Stan Shapiro said. The new uniforms scratched Billy's chest. He looked down at the tank top's design, a snarling samurai warrior, one hand brandishing a sword, the other dribbling a basketball. Samurai . . . Gladiator, Billy guessed they were close enough as he and his teammates started their shoot around. Their skills were rusty at first, but soon they rediscovered their touch and the net shivered with repeated cottony whispers. For a moment, the display seemed to quiet the crowd. Then the home team jogged onto the court, and Billy flinched under the renewed avalanche of drums and whistles, foot-stomping chants.

"You've got to be shitting me," Big Dale Brown said.

The rest of the Gladiators stopped their shooting and gathered at midcourt to witness the disheartening spectacle. Clad in old Gary Smokestacks uniforms, the Japanese performed a two-line lay-up drill. Half shrimps, half stork-legged glandular cases, they dribbled with slapping ferocity, their downward focus broken only when they stepped into the paint and flung up shots that more often than not clanked wildly off the rim. Their infrequent goals were met with standing ovations, furious drum beats. As each player joined the end of the line, they paused to bow to the drop-jawed Americans.

"This ain't going to be pretty," Speedy Luther Berry muttered. "For either of us."

Jim McSwain huddled with his players at the foul line. "This whole thing is new to these backwards fucks, remember that. Now I want you to put on a good show, but don't fucking embarrass them. No bullshit, no cheap shit, no yucking it up, got it? The Japanese ain't keen on humiliation."

Big Dale Brown won the opening tip and Stan Shapiro flew down the court for an uncontested two. Derek Reeves stole the ensuing inbound and snapped a behind-the-back pass to Billy, who sunk it from the top of the key.

"Take it fucking easy!" yelled McSwain.

Billy and the others backpedaled, glancing toward the refs who seemed oblivious to travels and double dribbles. The twig-limbed Japanese center heaved a shot that barely nicked the backboard. A collective "ahhhh!" rose from the bleachers.

The Gladiators did their best to keep the Japanese team in the game. Big Dale Brown, wanting to see if he might be ambidextrous, launched only left handed hook shots. Billy stuck to jumpers that tested the absolute limit of his range. Shapiro made dramatic defensive swipes only to pull his hand back at the last moment, a gesture that reminded Billy of the stage slaps his theater major roommate had practiced in college.

Despite their lack of effort, the score started to pile up, and as Billy deliberately short-armed his first shot, what little joy that lingered within him died. At the other end of the court he simply stepped back, hands raised in a defensive charade that left lanes wide enough to drive a Buick to the hoop. Derek Reeves threw an errant, lazy pass, and not one of them gave chase to the Japanese fast break that required three successive beneath-the-rim put-backs to score. That's when Billy noticed the change in the crowd, the ebbing silence that seeped into the din, the cheers softer, shorter, lifeless.

"Try harder!" McSwain snapped during a time out.

"Try harder to lose?" Swoop Nixon asked.

"Yes, goddamn it!"

But it was too late. They'd crossed some cultural boundary of shame or honor or simple bad manners, and no amount of playacting could bring them back. By the second half the fans started filing out, lugging their silent drums and ripped banners, some even crossing the floor as the game limped on.

The following weeks proved no better. In long, sweaty practices before each game, McSwain and his players tried to coach their opponents. McSwain ground his chalk into white nubs as he set up plays that should have guaranteed a modicum of success, but the Japanese, while keen on drill, lacked the skills to execute. The crowds dwindled. Soon the Gladiators found themselves participating in bizarre promotional gimmicks orchestrated by the increasingly agitated McSwain. Big Dale Brown wrenched his back wrestling a sumo-in-training in Yokohama. In Kobe, they ran half-time suicide sprints against bike riding monkeys. When the handful of spectators cheered for the monkeys, Casey Poe broke down and cried like a child.

McSwain lugged his gloomy troop across the mainland, their lanky American frames no match for the dollhouse proportions of Japanese trains, and one by one, his recruits bailed. They lost Shapiro in Kyoto, Reeves and Swoop Nixon in Osaka. Before an exhibition held in the parking lot of a Matsumoto dog show, McSwain himself disappeared, taking with him the last shreds of his players' faith and the promise of overdue paychecks.

The rush hour bedlam of the Matsumoto train station had separated Billy from the others, and he arrived alone in Tokyo to discover he and his teammates weren't the only ones McSwain had stiffed. The doors to their apartments had been padlocked, and amidst the alley's fly-buzzing stink, Billy picked through cans of foul garbage for his few remaining possessions. He unearthed a pair of jeans, a single sneaker and his aspirin bottle, the alarm clock that had seen him through college, all of it coated with a slimy residue and speckled with fishbone shards. In a disgusted rage, he smashed the alarm clock against a cinder block wall. The glass face shattered. The casing broke open, and the springs and cogs and knobs scattered over the macadam. He overturned the trash cans and then kicked his way through his teammates' shoes and empty liquor bottles, their razors and jockstraps and letters from home. Overlapping dog barks echoed up the narrow alley. Angry faces leaned from opened windows, cursing him in an unknown language.

Billy cursed them back, but when a voice answered with what he thought might be a threat to call the police, he fled the scene. The alley dogs hurled themselves against their fences, the chain link shaking, their jaws snapping at his scent. He was running again, just as he'd done from his Evansville landlord, as he'd done for the past four years. He ran for the sake of running, ran only not to be still, for it was then that he sensed the hopelessness of his situation. His knee clicking, he sprinted down one block, then another, jostling startled pedestrians, hurdling the broom of a shopkeeper sweeping his sidewalk. Cars honked as he zigzagged across a busy street.

He glanced over his shoulder, scared he was being chased by cops or the people he'd bumped into, by the alley's howling dogs, by the whole basketball-hating nation.

Looking back, he didn't see the frantically waving boy on the bicycle pedaling toward him. When the bike struck Billy's side, he tumbled headfirst, his world in a strangely peaceful free-fall until he landed with a thud on the sidewalk. His pants ripped, exposing the long, white scar on his knee. The bike skidded until it collided with a newspaper box. The bike's rider, a small boy in gray shorts and a baseball cap, struggled to his feet.

"Mr. Glenn," the boy said breathlessly. "I sorry. I saw you. I came riding to catch you."

Billy recognized the boy as Hiro, the Gladiator's towel boy, one of a half dozen locals he knew in a city of millions. By now, a curious knot of strangers had gathered around them. "Jesus, kid, are you OK?" He picked up Hiro's bike.

"I came to see if any player was left, but no one was at apartment." The boy studied his scraped elbow. "Then I saw you running. I took short cut to catch. Team is gone?"

"Gone." Billy straightened Hiro's jacket and dusted it off. "You sure you're OK, kid?"

"You need job, huh? You need money. I get you job." Hiro clamped onto Billy's wrist. "Four blocks. Good job. You see."

Billy insisted on pushing Hiro's bike. This arrangement seemed to please the boy, and he grew more animated, and in fractured, percolating English, he explained that his uncle worked in a place called Toho Studios. A tall concrete wall hid the grounds from the street. He led Billy past the guard at the studio gate and into a concrete plain of warehouses, barracks and weaving trams. A man in army fatigues passed, another in a tux and long tails, a cave woman with a bleached bone twisted in her black hair. Running the other way was a circus lion tamer followed by a trio of clown-faced midgets. "Here, here," Hiro chirped.

They entered a cavernous warehouse. Billy blinked until his eyes adjusted to the shadows. "You fit, Mr. Glenn," Hiro said proudly. "You fit good."

He ushered Billy into a circle of white-shirted men. Hiro addressed the men in rapid Japanese, gesturing proudly toward Billy. The men looked Billy over from his freshly ripped pants to his unwashed hair, and then blossomed into a single smile. One sprinted off and breathlessly returned with what appeared to be a giant, green animal hide.

"See? See?" Hiro said. "You fit good. You big like Godzilla."

At first Billy balked, hands waving in what he hoped was a gesture of polite refusal. The white-shirted men nodded and grinned through Billy's objections, and then offered him the suit again.

"Too big," Hiro explained. Kneeling on the concrete floor, he unlaced Billy's sneaker. "No one fit. Big trouble around here. But with you it good. Everything good now."

Under their urgings, Billy stripped down to his underwear and socks. The white shirted men smiled. Two of them held the costume, and with the hesitancy of a wedding-day bride, Billy shyly guided himself into the rubbery suit. His hands and feet disappeared into the dark holes. The zipper hissed behind him, and for a moment, his world went dark. He hadn't anticipated the weight of the suit, the smothering effect of isolation and the moist, curling warmth of his trapped breath. He was cocooned, adrift in a black world, even his sense of touch robbed. Standing perfectly still, he listened to the rhythm of his nervous heart and wondered what pathetic turn his life had just taken.

With a twist from behind, a pair of tiny slits appeared before his eyes. A narrowed perspective opened where his new, nameless friends bowed toward him like happy pistons. One of them guided Billy's lumbering steps toward a full-length mirror where he beheld himself reborn as a buffoonish walking lizard.

"Godzilla very good!" one of the white-shirted men said.

The fact that Billy had never heard of Godzilla disheartened the producers who'd hurried down to see their new star. They spent the afternoon in an executive's five-row theater watching reels from the first two Godzilla movies. Every so often one of the producers would rise onto the little stage, sputtering mostly nonsensical English phrases while helpfully acting out the flailings of the angry lizard. Their compact shadows fell hard and crisp over the screen, and the projector light glistened on their glasses. Sitting in the dark, absently nodding to the producers' gibberish, Billy began to empathize with the monster, the two of them foreigners washed up on this crazy island, oversized castaways who seemed destined to suffer one beating after another.

He slept that night on a backbreaking cot in the director's office. The director rousted him at six, imploring Billy to join him in his grunting morning calisthenics before feeding him a breakfast of orange slices, a hard-boiled egg and tepid tea. On the set, the tech crew watched unemotionally as Billy struggled into his costume. The eyeholes had been cut into the neck, and the monster's head sat atop his like an awkward, weighty hat. The director communicated with charades, wild arm swings punctuated with guttural impersonations of explosions and destruction.

The first shots called for Billy's clawed feet to stamp across a desert island set. Off camera, the director and his assistants gestured for Billy to react like the primordial beast he was. The tech crew yanked his tail with a system of fishing wire and pulleys, and their arrhythmic jerks caused Billy to stagger like a drunken frat boy. His neck muscles ached, but the one time he tried to remove the costume's head, he was roundly scolded. Between the baking studio lights and the suit's thick rubber, Billy began to feel woozy. Sweat rolled down his back, soaking his underwear and socks. His head spun from breathing stale air, and as he raised a balloon boulder over his head for the thirteenth take, he lost consciousness. The crew revived him with cheek slaps and smelling salts. When Billy's blurred vision came back into focus, they gave him a healthy thumbs up and promptly plunged the monster's head back over his own.

Before lunch the next day, Billy had gagged on the smoke of a spewing volcano, turned his ankle stomping a miniature village. A spark from a crushed power line defied all laws of probability and flew into his eyehole. Twice he failed to sidestep the swooping Mothra, his chest absorbing the brunt of the creature's blow, unscripted topplings that thrilled the director but infuriated the set manager, who was forced to rebuild half a fishing village and a canvas mountainside.

Near day's end, Billy peeled himself out of his costume. Headachy, exhausted, he collapsed on a bench outside the set. He'd raced bike-pedaling monkeys and now he'd become a mutated lizard, and he wondered how much farther down the evolutionary chain he'd sink before accepting defeat and heading home. Little birds hopped around his sneakers, and their pointed beaks chirped a trilling tune he'd never heard before. At that moment, with the sun beating down upon his neck and his slumped shadow stretching before him, he understood how a man could miss something as inconsequential as the sounds of familiar birdcalls and recognizable voices. He kicked at the birds, but civilized creatures that they were, they only scattered a few feet before returning to peck for crumbs in his shadow. Their twittering warbles grew, high-pitched scales that jabbed at Billy's skull. He covered his ears, and when he heard muffled words of English entwining their incessant songs, he thought he'd finally cracked, the border crossed between simple foolishness and full blown, Dr. Dolittle insanity.

"Excuse me," repeated the gentle bird voice. "Mr. Glenn?"

Billy brushed the stinging salt from his eyes. Before him

stood a young woman, noticeably tall by Japanese standards even though she wore flat-soled shoes. Black, bluntly cut hair framed her delicate face.

"Mr. Glenn, I am Masago Hideyoshi." She bowed. "I am here to assist you."

In precise yet slightly hesitant English, she informed Billy she'd been sent from the studio's central office to help establish communication with their American monster. She'd perfected her English during her two years at Penn before returning home to work in Toho's overseas distribution office.

"They realize I'm not an actor, don't they?" Billy asked.

Masago covered her smiling mouth. "An actor is not needed to play a monster. You have heard there was some confusion with the costume design. They were going to go back to the old one before they met you. Now they like the taller Godzilla. He is more . . . imposing. And they like you."

"Please, don't snow me."

"Snow?" she asked seriously.

"I've done nothing but mess up since I got here."

"Oh no, Mr. Glenn." Billy noticed her habit of leaning forward slightly when she spoke, and he wondered if this was tied to the custom of bowing or if it was some self-conscious reaction to her height. "The studio is very enthusiastic about yesterday's rushes, Mr. Glenn. They believe you bring a certain . . ." her downcast eyes seemed to study the crumb-searching birds, " . . . a certain athleticism to the role."

"Obviously they haven't seen me play ball recently."

Masago smiled, bowed. "Very good, Mr. Glenn."

The following morning Masago was waiting when Billy arrived on the set. She wore the same outfit she did the day before, a white blouse and a black skirt that fell below her knees. No rings adorned her slender fingers, no necklace for her throat. A clipboard clasped over her small chest, she listened to the director's instructions, then hurried to Billy with clipped, expedient strides.

"He says to tell you Godzilla is angry. Very angry." She glanced back toward the director. "Yet I believe in this scene Godzilla must be played with a touch of sympathy. He is a monster, yes, but that is not of his own doing. He is . . . he is like a storm, harmless over the ocean, yet deadly upon landfall. He would rather abandon this world of men and be left alone, but peace is not his to have."

"Sounds like you have this guy figured out," Billy said, his voice muffled by the suit's covering.

"Monsters and men, sometimes there's little difference between the two, Mr. Glenn."

With Masago's help, Billy's work on the set came easier. She intervened on his behalf, persuading the director to grant Billy hourly breaks where she'd sit by his side, ready with salt tablets, water and tiny cucumber sandwiches from the studio commissary. With her help, he found an apartment in her downtown high-rise, and together, they braved the rush hours, Billy staying close to her side as Masago fearlessly led the charge through the city's subway stampede, a swirling odyssey of shoving and transfers that magically deposited them at the studio gates. Back in costume, his perspective narrowed to the width of rubbery slits, Billy sought her out among the off-camera crowd. With an arch of an eyebrow or an encouraging nod or a sour-faced wince, she gave him subtle clues whether to play violent or hurt, bewildered or contemplative. The director shouted his approval.

After particularly difficult days, they treated themselves to a cab. Caught in downtown traffic, they talked of the States and basketball, Godzilla and the tribulations of living a foreigner's life. One night they decided to stop at a restaurant, and over sake and rice, she peeled back the petals of her life, the father she knew only from a stern military photo, the young mother who'd died in a bombing raid less than a month before the war's end. Her face in the flickering candlelight reminded him of moonshine on a lake, and he leaned closer to hear her soft words amid the boisterous, singing din of drunken businessmen. They were the same age, yet he wondered if two lives could be more different. An orphan, she'd scoured for her existence in the rubble and humiliation of post-war Japan, while he had grown up in the geographic insulation of Middle America, a stranger to typhoons and earthquakes, incendiary bombs and the high altitude whine of B-29s. She told him she did not believe in fate or God, only in the dignity of each moment, and as they crowded beneath her umbrella on the rainy walk home, stepping over puddles electric with neon and oil, he couldn't help but feel ashamed when he compared this quiet strength to his own cowardly habits.

Less than two weeks into shooting an electrical fire gutted a portion of the set. Miniature Tokyo lay destroyed, the forest-green uniforms of the Japanese military gone, Mothra's wings burnt to their skeletal wiring. Masago and Billy stood in the smoky aftermath. Water dripped from broken pipes, the rhythmic plops joined by the harsh scraping of shovels scooping up charred debris. Thin, gurgling rivers snaked their way toward the floor drains. Above them, the sun burrowed a brilliant shaft through a section of destroyed ceiling.

"What now?" Billy asked.

"I go back to work." Masago stooped, picked a tiny railroad car from a puddle. "And you can have a vacation if that is agreeable to you. Come to my apartment tonight. I'll tell you what I can about the shooting schedule."

At seven that evening, Billy rode the elevator to Masago's apartment. Near midnight, she cracked her door and discretely removed his shoes from the hallway. Women were still very much a mystery to Billy. There was the girl from his hometown, the one who cried softly after they had sex in the back seat of her father's Ford. In college there were the basketball girls, the cheerleaders or statisticians or regular hangers-on who circulated among the team, girls either too possessive or too clinging or too anxious to break his heart. In his semi-pro days the older players had introduced him to prostitutes, the sad and hard women who counted his money twice and then stared into the room's dark corners as he fumbled away on top of them.

Sitting close on the couch of her sparse, modern apartment, they kissed, their movements daring them closer, a meeting as inevitable as the joining of two streams. Before the moment their lips met, Billy hadn't thought of her sexually. She wasn't particularly beautiful, a bit flat-chested and pigeon-toed. More importantly, she was his guidebook, his compass, his sole link to this peculiar land. Yet in a heartbeat, they were naked, their clothes in soft piles by their feet. Her dark-eyed focus unnerved him for she'd rarely looked him in the eye before. The other women he'd known in this way would look him in the eye during every moment but this one. They stumbled kissing and groping into her bedroom. She whispered words he'd never heard, and he wondered if she'd forgotten his lack of comprehension or if she felt free because of it. Shade-slitted bands of blue neon stretched across the ceiling, and everywhere else there lingered a watery mix of darkness and smog-filtered moonshine, a light in which his hands appeared even darker and rougher against her milky skin.

Red pen in hand, Masago settled herself on the couch and looked over the script. Billy watched her, amused by the way her lips moved, as if she were digesting the pages word by word.

"What are the odds?" Billy said. He'd been turning through the channels when he came upon a Godzilla movie. "Be honest. Which do you like more, old Godzilla or new?"

"New, definitely." She touched her pen to her flat nose. "Although I am not Godzilla's biggest fan."

"I'm crushed."

"Look at it," she said. On the tiny black and white screen,

a hysterical mob stampeded between the cavernous walls of Tokyo's high-rises. Behind them, a fire breathing Godzilla blocked out the sun. Busses were crushed, buildings destroyed. Destruction rained down upon the unfortunate. "The world must laugh at how empty our country is, how we have this need to fill ourselves up with such fanatical nonsense. Our fathers filled themselves with thoughts of empire. Now we fill ourselves with fads and dreams of better dish detergent. The wonders of a new car. And monsters."

Billy rubbed her neck. "You think that's unique to your country? You should have seen the crew I came here with. Talk about meaningless dreams." He watched as Godzilla swatted back attacking jets. "Maybe filling empty spaces is the one, true international language."

Masago nestled against his side, her eyes fixed on the set. "I don't know if that makes me happy or sad."

Some days Billy accompanied Masago to the studio. He pitched in where he could on the set, running errands, nailing backdrops. Most days, however, he remained behind. Half asleep as Masago kissed him good-bye, he woke only when the sunlight claimed its midmorning spot over the bed. He enjoyed his time there alone. Draped in one of her bright, silky robes, he sipped his morning tea and snooped in a polite, respectful way. The mismatched scraps in his apartment could have belonged to anyone, but her things, while few, seemed essential, important, each a tiny mirror that reflected another facet of who she was. He ran his fingers over her sugar bowl and candle holders, smelled the collars of her shirts. At night, she taught him Japanese, and soon, he'd mastered enough to venture out on his own. He visited the hushed Shinto shrines, strolled around the Tokyo University campus. Before Masago returned, he'd go to the grocery where more often than not, he left with what he thought he'd ordered. They'd eat to the tinny strains of her kitchen radio, and after, she smoked his cigarettes, her long body relaxing in poses worlds removed from the stiff-spined postures she assumed at work. Then they'd retreat to her room of watery light where the hard mat of her bed became a raft just large enough for their two clinging shapes.

One night, as they lay sweaty and naked, she softly kissed each of his fingertips. "Billy -- isn't that considered a boy's name? Do they call grown men 'Billy'?"

"If you wanted to be formal, I guess you could go with William."

"How about Bill? Do you like Bill?"

"Everyone's always called me Billy, but I could live with Bill, sure." He listened to the sound of it, short and to the point. "Bill," he repeated, trying to align images of himself with the truncated word.

"They're almost finished rebuilding the set," Masago said.

"You don't sound too excited about it."

"I like coming home and finding you here," she paused, then added, "Bill."

"Not much we can do about it, is there?"

She lay with her head on his chest, and he felt the muscles of her face gather into a smile. "I could start another fire."

He grinned. "When we flew here, the guy who ran the team gave us this long talk on Japanese women. Obviously he never met you."

For a minute or more, she said nothing. Billy assumed she'd gone to sleep, and when she did speak, her words jerked him from his own blissful drifting. "After my mother died, I imagined myself as a dot. A tiny dot. Meaningless. When I saw girls my age on the street, a parent holding each hand, I saw them as sentences without beginnings or ends, each with a history infinitely deeper than mine. And I was just a dot. A period. A speck on the breeze." She kissed his chest. "All those things your friend told you about Japanese women stem from the notion of tradition, and tradition means much less when there's no eye for you to see your reflection in."

"Does that upset you?"

"If I hadn't been a speck on the breeze, I wouldn't have met you, would I? In that way we are much the same."

"Maybe so," Billy said.

When filming resumed, Billy happily stepped back into his monster's skin. His smile masked by painted rubber, he stomped modern skyscrapers, withstood the piddling attacks of missiles and tanks. No longer did he recoil at the flash powder stink of volcanoes and bombs for he knew that once the smoke cleared, he would see Masago standing dutifully in the director's shadow.

The pace of their work quickened, fourteen-hour days, pre-dawn shoots. The fire had sent them over budget, and tensions on the set ran high. A sound engineer punched an extra who'd stumbled over his cords. The assistant director suffered a mild heart attack while arguing with the producer over the price of catered lunches. Some days were pure chaos, sets erected minutes before the cameras rolled, yet Billy remained calm amid the storm. No tragedies real or cinematic mattered because behind Masago's locked bedroom door, he'd discovered a place he didn't want to escape from. There, they'd sit half-naked on her floor, eating peanut cookies and unagi, feeding each other cut pear sections, barely noticing the building summer heat, the constant street serenade of honking cars, passing fire engines. As she slept in his arms, he whispered *I love you* just to hear how it sounded.

"I'm pregnant," she said softly. Her head was bowed, and it was impossible to see her face. They sat on her couch, and the kitchen light shimmered on her dark hair. "I didn't mean --"

"Shh," Billy said.

"I'm sorry for --"

He scooped her into his arms. His scarred knee momentarily buckled as he rose to his feet. Her tears wet his neck. Without a word, he carried her into her bedroom and shut the door behind them.

The final days of filming were saved for water shots. Billy spent hours in the frigid tank, Godzilla emerging from the deep, stirred by atomic radiation, wounded Godzilla retreating to the safety of the sea. As he waited for the cameramen to load new film, he stood shivering, his eyes just above the water's surface. He moved his hand, watching the ripples he made. From beneath the camouflage of his costume, he studied the faces of the crew and imagined the hidden layers of life, the secrets people kept, the unguessed at worlds hidden behind locked doors. Masago stood by the director's side. She raised her eyebrows, silently asking if everything was all right. With the cameras reloaded, the director motioned for Billy to submerge. Billy held his breath and the water seeped into the eyeholes, an icy trickling that collected in puddles around his feet. He thought of the succinct sound of 'Bill.' He thought of the child growing in the watery world of Masago's womb, the mass of cells probably no bigger than his thumb. He'd seen the pictures in a college text, the fetus's alien appearance, the sea horse body and the miniature, vein-throbbing head. Muffled by the water, the director's megaphone order for action sounded like a monster's call, but Billy didn't respond. His heart drummed, and for a moment, he feared he was drowning in a five-foot pool, paralyzed by his own thoughts and dragged down by a waterlogged suit. The director called again, and one of the tech crew knocked on the tank's side. With an air-sucking gasp, Billy reared out of the pool, hands clawing the air. The sprays of water that flew from his scales wet the director's glasses and shorted out a row of lights.

Billy told Masago he'd pay for the procedure. He had the money, having signed a contract for two more films during the wrap party. He'd call McSwain for the number of the doctor who'd helped Swoop Nixon out of a similar jam. They were young, Billy told her. There'd be time for children later. For now they should just relax and not cancel the post-shooting vacation she'd planned for them at the Shuzenji hot springs.

Masago said little that night as she lay next to him. The next morning she called from the office. The ringing woke Billy from a dream of singing carp. She said she'd been asked to help proof a script for an English dubbing project and that she'd take the next train to Shuzenji. She wanted him to go ahead and secure their room, and she'd meet him that evening. The carps' song echoing in his ears, Billy agreed and promptly went back to sleep.

The train was hot and crowded. The engine lurched from the station and slowly settled into a peaceful, clicking rhythm. The city's glass towers gave way to lower buildings, tiny houses that blurred with the train's increasing speed. An elderly woman in a traditional robe glanced at him once and then stared down at her sandaled feet. Billy wondered what she thought of him. Did she see him as a monster, no different that the other monsters who'd left a trail of corpses and smoldering stones across her country? Was he just another man? Could he be both in the same breath?

A young family crammed into the seat opposite him, and their black haired daughter gawked openly at the towering American. Billy waved, and the girl buried her face in her mother's lap. By the time the tiny houses faded into farmland green, the girl was asleep, her mouth opened wide, her head pitching thoughtlessly with the hurtling motion of the car.

He'd been an only child, and rare, the times he'd actually seen a child sleep like this, oblivious, peaceful, secure in the protective love of her mother. Ever since he'd left Iowa, he'd been on the run, either chasing a dream that wasn't meant to be or running from the knowledge that without that dream he couldn't really say who he was. Basketball player or monster. Billy or Bill. Years of running. And now, lulled by the rock-a-bye motion of the train and the image of a sleeping child, he became inexplicably tired. If he could only sleep like that child, lay his head on Masago's cool shoulder and sleep.

He called her from the train station the moment he arrived, and when there was no answer, he became excited. She was already on her way, perhaps boarding the train, and when she stepped onto this platform, he'd be waiting. He'd hold her, kiss her, Japanese customs be damned. He'd tell her he wanted this child, tell her he wanted her.

In town he paid for their room, then hurried back to the station, but she wasn't on the next train. Or the one after that. He waited on a hard wooden bench, and after a policeman's stick nudged him awake the next morning, he walked stiffly to the phone and called the studio. Harsh morning sun streamed through the windows, assaulting his eyes. On the other end of the line, the phone was passed among the secretaries until one was found who could relay the information that Masago had cleaned out her office yesterday.

Billy bought a ticket for the next Tokyo train. He seethed the entire way, kicking himself for mistaking the local line for the express. He hailed a cab at the station and smacked the seat like horseflesh in his urgings for the driver to go faster. Three blocks from their apartment, traffic snarled. Billy threw fluttering yen notes into the front seat and took off on foot. His knee throbbing, he ran the shadowed sidewalks. The elevator was out again in their building, so he charged the steps, taking two and three at a time until he reached the seventh floor. Doubled over, gasping, he hobbled to her door only to find it locked, his old basketball sneakers set neatly in the hallway. He pounded the door until it shook on its hinges, his assault answered by the perplexed, mop-wielding landlord who was busy cleaning the space for the next tenant.

In the years that followed Billy and Godzilla battled the likes of Baragon and Ghidorah, Rodan and Oodako and Ebirah. A new interpreter was sent, a jittery man half Billy's size, but by his third feature, Billy's grasp of the language had improved to the point where he no longer needed his help.

Billy tried to find Masago those first few months after her disappearance. He haunted the stores where she'd shopped, questioned the studio secretaries. He even got hold of a Tokyo phonebook printed in English and made halting, bumbling calls to every *M. Hideyoshi* listed. A year passed, two, and in time, he abandoned his hopes of reuniting with her.

It was 1969. Billy was in costume, a department store opening, a chain partly owned by the studio. Vibrant blossoms hung from the cherry trees, and a cool spring breeze kept Billy from getting too hot in his suit during the ceremonies. There were speeches, raffles. A band played covers of the latest radio hits. Children fidgeted in nervous anticipation as they waited for their parents to take a snapshot of them with Godzilla.

When the time came for the ribbon cutting, Billy lumbered over to the throng of identically dressed businessmen. A row of photographers lined up before them, and beyond them, a small crowd. Daydreaming, Billy scanned the on-lookers. At the crowd's edge stood a tall, thin woman with a little girl by her side.

"Masago?" Billy said, a muffled exclamation from beneath his disguise.

His heart racing, he stepped toward her, breaking flanks with the businessmen. It was her. It had to be her. She had been looking at him, and he was sure she knew it was him. The studio head cut the breeze-fluttering yellow ribbon. In the same instant, the reporters snapped their pictures, so many flashbulbs exploding that their starshine blinded Billy. The businessmen applauded enthusiastically. The band struck up a feedback-laden tune. Hands raised, Billy tried to shield his eyes. He waved away the photographers who only laughed and snapped more pictures at his antics. Popping afterimages dancing before him, Billy waded into the crowd, where all he found were laughing children who tugged at his lizard's tail.

GO NINJA GO NINJA GO

Crispin Best

Leonardo

Leonardo is reading an article about prisoners' last meals before they are executed.
Leonardo tries to think something smart about the article. He doesn't know what to think right now.
He reads a list of prisoners' last meals.
It would feel bad to eat a last meal.
Lots of the prisoners chose cheeseburgers.
Lots of the prisoners chose ice cream.
Lots of the prisoners chose French fries.
A few of them chose 'okra'. Leonardo doesn't know what this is.
Most prisoners ordered a lot of food.
One prisoner ordered two dozen scrambled eggs and a bunch of other things.
One prisoner ordered a fried chicken, a fried catfish, onion rings and carrots.
One prisoner's final meal was 'Mexican lunch'.
One prisoner just had a pack of Jolly Ranchers.
One prisoner just had a jar of pickles.
One prisoner wasn't allowed bubble gum.
One prisoner just had yogurt.

Some prisoners just had a Coke.
Some prisoners just had fruit.
Some prisoners declined a final meal.
Leonardo finishes reading the article and feels stupid and quiet and the wrong way round.

Donatello

Donatello has an iPhone. He is holding it and touching the screen with his fingers. He can turn it and the image on the screen turns also.
Donatello is on a bus. It is full and quiet.
At the back of the bus, there are two young boys talking to each other loudly.
One of them says,
- But if the tits are that good, it's just… then the pussy can be anything.
The other boy laughs through his nose. He says,
- Exactly. But then like if the pussy's that good… the tits can be anything too.
And the first boy laughs,
- Yeah.
And the second boy laughs.
Donatello is holding his iPhone in his lap and looking at it. He has an application on his iPhone that makes the screen look like a glass of beer, and when you tilt the iPhone by your mouth it looks like you are drinking the beer. He pours the beer into his lap. And again. And again.

Raphael

Raphael is eating a plate of spaghetti. He is using two forks. He feels smart and good about his two forks. He is looking out of the window. Raphael can see three trampolines, in different gardens. They are not being used. It is raining gently.

Raphael wants a dog to climb onto one of the trampolines and stand there. He wants the dog to do a poo. Then he wants to look down at the poo sitting quietly on the trampoline for a while. And then later he wants to watch the children find the poo on the trampoline.

The spaghetti is so good. Raphael feels so good.

Michelangelo

Michelangelo is hungover.

He is watching the movie *Renaissance Man* starring Danny DeVito.

He does not want to move from the sofa.

The movie is not good.

Before this he watched *What Women Want* starring Mel Gibson.

While he was looking at Mel Gibson he was thinking about Jesus.

Michelangelo thinks there should be a TV channel over Easter that shows what Jesus would have been up to at that point, in real time.

Whenever you wanted you could just switch to that channel and there Jesus would be eating some last supper, or sad up on the cross, or there'd be a shot of the cave and some sky and a bit of wind.

Michelangelo thinks people would watch that.

He feels definite.

He is going to write up a proposal before next Easter.

The proposal will be double-spaced on 8 ½ x 11 paper.

Michelangelo is going to be incredibly famous.

He is watching Danny DeVito doing acting on the TV.
Michelangelo is going to be incredibly famous.

Splinter

Splinter is cold in bed.
There is an electric heater next to his bed.
He turns the heater up.
He is still cold.
He gets out of bed.
He puts on his red robe.
He gets back into bed.
He is still cold.
He gets out of bed.
He puts on a pair of gloves, ear muffs, his knee brace.
He gets back into bed.
He is warm now.

April O'Neil

April O'Neil is doing sit-ups on the floor of her living room. She is wearing a yellow sweatsuit.
There is a soap opera on the TV.
A boy is kissing a girl on the TV.
April stops doing sit-ups and watches
The boy on the TV looks very serious and says,
- Happy zero anniversary.
April laughs.
April does some more sit-ups.
A girl on the TV is getting kidnapped now.
A lady on the TV is really drunk now.
A man on the TV is crying and shouting now.

Krang

Krang used to date a girl.
She is sort of famous.

She did all the recordings that play on the number 11 tram, the ones that say the name of the next stop.
That is her voice.
She broke up with Krang because she wanted to have sex with her drama teacher.

Most days Krang buys a ticket and just rides around on the number 11 tram.
Krang listens to her voice saying the names of the stops and sits there and tries to be calm.
He listens to her voice and scrolls through old text messages on his phone.
He listens and after a while he looks up and looks at his hand pressing the red button that says 'Stop'.

Shredder

Working in the office is part of Shredder's community service after he was found guilty of a string of mail frauds.
Every day the Fat Man says,
- Tina, I need you to dispose of these delicate documents.
And Tina takes them through to the copyroom.
Shredder is in there, sitting up on the surface next to the trimmer, looking at his knees.
Shredder is wearing chrome body armour with spikes on his shoulders and forearms. Metal blades are attached to his knuckles, a helmet covers most of his face. He wears a cape made of chain mail.
Tina walks forward, looking away, shaking. She holds out the documents in front of her. Shredder grabs them, rips them in half, then in half again. He throws the scraps in the air and shouts,
- Ta-dah!
And Tina runs away, weeping.
And this happens every day.

Bebop and Rocksteady

Bebop and Rocksteady are playing Xbox.
Bebop rattles a box of Oreos.
Bebop says,
- It's your turn to buy the Oreos.
Rocksteady says,
- Get fucked.

WHAT YOU SHOULD HAVE KNOWN ABOUT ABBA

Erin FitzGerald

Forming the Group

There was a blonde one, and a brunette one. They grew up in houses next door to each other. These two houses were identical except for the color of the front doors. When the blonde one and the brunette one were old enough to leave their families, they moved to a tastefully decorated cottage in the city of Stockholm. The city of Stockholm is made up of thirty-eight islands, and their cottage was located on one of the six islands that floats in the air.

Despite this inconvenience, they maintained the cheerful confidence they'd had as children. The blonde one met the short guy, and the brunette one met the tall guy. They fell in love over coffee at Edgar's Cafe on 84th Street. They got married, and thus became ABBA. The ceremony was unremarkable in most ways, but only two of their mothers cried.

Breakthrough

At first, married life was everything ABBA had hoped for. But after a few months of having fondue parties, drinking homemade beer and playing doubles tennis poorly, ABBA began to feel old. On a Sunday in April at 4 a.m. Central European Time, ABBA found itself staring through the shower stall door in the bathroom of its tastefully decorated cottage in Stockholm, realizing it had miscalculated what the world had to offer. Perhaps more important, ABBA was afraid to guess to what degree it had done so.

By 8 a.m. Central European Time, ABBA decided to spend the weekend recording a pop song using a metaphor from eighteenth century European history. That song[1] catapulted ABBA to fame. More important, it brought potential for legend that, even covered with shampoo in the shower on gray mornings in the previously referenced Stockholm cottage, ABBA had not dared to imagine was possible.

Superstardom

ABBA's next single explored the reveries of a foot soldier in the early twentieth century Mexican Revolution, and the fervor of the fans rose to a fever pitch. The United Nations declared ABBA to be a Star Student of the Planet[2]. This allowed ABBA to wear a prominent glittered sticker on its shirt that smelled like chocolate when it was scratched. It also allowed ABBA to go to the head of all queues, including those at restrooms.

Within 36 hours of the release of an ABBA song that was constructed upon a repeated onomatopoeia, every single person

1. Over the years, "Waterloo" would become the greatest European song of all time. A video performance of "Waterloo," aired by the BBC in May 1981, singlehandedly dismantled assassination attempts on Margaret Thatcher and Leonid Brezhnev. As of January 1, 2007, reciting the song's lyrics replaced the Schengen visa in twenty-two countries (exclusions: Poland and Malta)

2. Six years later, it would be determined via an unearthed series of text messages that the Bee Gees privately harbored resentment regarding this resolution. It is now believed that this discovery was the chief impetus behind the Disco Sucks Initiative of 1980.

on Facebook, no matter their language of origin, wished ABBA a happy birthday. It was not ABBA's birthday.

All of this success also closed many doors. ABBA could not grouse about the costs of gourmet cheese, fringed vests or carefully feathered hairstyles. ABBA would no longer brush the snow off of its own car, much less cars belonging to others. It did not get its own coffee, and it never thought about law school again.

Final Album and Performances

As ABBA walked and ruled with a gentle soprano/mezzo-soprano voice, the world was not content to enjoy the past. There must always be something to which one can look forward. Unable to circumvent this tenet of modern society, and wishing to push back the uneasiness which had never quite left after that last fondue party, ABBA created a series of .mp3 files -- commonly referred to at the time as a mix tape album.

The songs on this mix tape album covered a wide range of topics, including but not limited to: persecution of dissidents in the Soviet Union, endless minor responsibilities that accompany a rise in social status, entrusting small children to an anonymous public transportation system, pursuit of sexual congress with a consenting adult daughter, chronic insomnia, appreciation for current and former military personnel, and molar-shattering sadness.

The mix tape album was a critical success, but the subsequent world tour performances were a commercial flop. Audiences watched closely as ABBA made plans for the weekend and canceled them for no reason. They raised eyebrows when ABBA told them that someone needed to grow up. They yawned when ABBA agreed to have lunch and then spent the consumption of an iceberg wedge outlining the trivial flaws of others, and how much time it had already sacrificed to accommodate these flaws.

Finally, audiences told ABBA that they too had to cope with less than ideal day- to- day living... but you didn't see them recording multiplatinun songs about it.The audiences stood up from a chair at an indoor cafe on an autumn afternoon, leaving enough money to pay the bill. ABBA watched the audiences stride off and eventually disappear around the corner. ABBA scratched its chocolate-scented United Nations Star Student of the Planet sticker. A little piece of glitter came away in its fingernail.

Breaking Up

The Stockholm cottage had been abandoned in favor of a mansion with a regularly blacktopped driveway and marble kitchen counter tops, but it had never been sold. When ABBA arrived on the floating island and slipped around to the cottage's back door, it discovered that the house key was long gone from the keyring. ABBA took off its brown suede jacket, rolled the sleeve around its fist, and punched a hole in the glass panel closest to the doorknob.

The inside of the cottage had a musty smell. ABBA had expected that. ABBA had been less sure about the water and electricity[3]. To its relief, both worked. Less miraculously, there were also towels in the linen closet and a tube of overly aromatic body shampoo hanging from a small plastic hook in the shower stall. Before disrobing and stepping into the shower, ABBA

3. The cottage had been a subject of ten minutes' discussion amongst a sub-subdivision of ABBA's management team several years previous. One of the sub-subdivision's managers had grown up in St. Paul, Minnesota. While this manager was more slightly more familiar with Norwegian life than Swedish life due to her Minnesotan cultural heritage, she was profoundly aware of the dangers of leaving a home completely unheated in a harsh winter climate. As the rest of her coworkers looked on, she used the Internet to locate a housekeeping service in Stockholm. After some frantic hand gestures and searching of sticky notes on an absent coworker's desk calendar, the cottage was saved from a water pipe burst that, in all fairness, should have happened years before.

took one last glance out the window to make sure the sky was appropriately gray.

ABBA turned the dial on the wall to 4 a.m. Central European Time. The pipes shuddered, and the hot water soon arrived. ABBA didn't know what to expect as it began to dissolve. Would it become four again? Two? Three? Those were the outcomes, in order of likelihood.

There was one outcome that ABBA hadn't considered, and that was the one which occurred. As the hot water dribbled along its weary skull, ABBA dissolved into sections, then clumps, then blobs, then specks, then molecules. Each ABBA molecule had a slight negative charge from recent events, and bonded with the positive charge in the oxygen of a water molecule. The resulting solution proceeded down the shower drain and into nearby Lake Malaren. From there, it continued into the Baltic Sea and subsequently northeastern Europe, in defiance of several diplomatic accords.

Eighteen years later, ABBA can be found in nearly all of the world's aqueous solutions. This includes surface water, polar ice caps, and artesian aquifers. Unlike salt, however, ABBA cannot be removed from water by reverse osmosis.

After ABBA

He got her email the day before he started the trip. He thought about ignoring it and pretending that he didn't receive it until he came home again. But 4 a.m. Central European Time comes to everyone, and by 8 a.m. Central European Time he had written back: Sure, that sounds great. How about Edgar's on 84th? Is that still there?

It was, and he arrived first. Not out of anticipation, but an interest in getting this overdue reunion over with quickly. He hadn't spoken to her much since reconnecting on a creaking electronic branch, but he knew what to expect. A little professional jealousy, a lot of complaining, and that unpleasant post-snack maneuver where she would cram a napkin to her lips to stifle the inevitable burp.

She arrived ten minutes late, and she was lovely. Her hair was well maintained, and her clothes fit perfectly. She smiled when she saw him and her smile was genuine, but it was also polite. He stood up and she hugged him, just as a truly appreciative pop star might hug a fan wearing a button bearing her name. She smelled wonderful, like air that curled around the capital of a distant Scandinavian nation.

After they ordered coffees, he realized that he had already caught up with her on the mundane details of elapsed time. In accordance with the tenets of modern society, they were now left with small talk.

"Did you see the movie?" she asked, after she'd finished her biscotti. "I never did see the musical, so I thought I should."

"I did."

"It was well done, but I couldn't get into the story. Pierce Brosnan singing that song. It means something completely different to me." She looked down into her coffee cup. It was the only moment that entire hour when she seemed at all vulnerable, and he didn't recognize it until much, much later.

After he paid for their coffees, he walked her to the corner of 84th and Eighth. He watched her go, with a surge of that well-known sadness. There was no hurry anymore.

He used to love the blond one. But on the plane home, he loves the brunette one most of all.

SO COLD AND FAR AWAY

Kathleen Rooney & Lily Hoang

Ruth props herself on her elbows, her body a diagonal platform. Just as quickly, she collapses.

Above her, there is exactly half a moon, a penny cut in two on railroad tracks. Even though she knows it won't look anything like it does now, she takes a photograph anyways. Caption, she mumbles, so cold and far away.

Ruth has an entire collection of photographs captioned so cold and far away, but she doesn't let anyone see them. She puts them in plastic frames with engraved placards taped to their backs. She stows them in a locked drawer, lest Naomi comes snooping around—as she inevitably does—and finds them.

Ruth first began this collection of photographs the night she slept at the feet of Boaz. After she'd removed his shoes, just as Naomi had instructed her to do, she examined his toes. She said to herself, So cold and far away, which she'd intended more as a desire than a description, and snapped a quick shot before he woke.

This is not to say Ruth did not like Boaz. She liked him as much as any widow could like her dead husband's next of kin. Which is to say that she loved him enough to marry him.

It was unbearably bright the day of their wedding, despite the heaps of snow surrounding them. They couldn't dig their way out to get to the church, but they married each other anyways. That night, Ruth fled her bedchamber to steal a glimpse of the stars. Instead, she saw Naomi's silhouette slinking slowly towards Boaz.

Ruth doesn't blame Naomi, but at times, she is resentful.

Ruth doesn't blame Naomi because as long as she is married to Boaz, she is free to do as she wishes, as long as she maintains the guise of marriage. To Ruth, this is the best part of married life: the parties, the dinners, the reasons to don pearls and sapphires. They are simple people, but that does not mean they never indulge in small decadences.

And Boaz is a kind husband. He gives her private quarters. Although hers is a small house, more befitting servants or mothers-in-law, Ruth does not complain. It is an attempt at privacy, but she is unsure whose privacy Boaz is trying to protect more.

Theirs is a complicated love, one that is entirely unfair to judge from exterior walls, and they are a private family, one whose walls extend deep into the night sky.

Ruth doesn't blame Naomi because this was, after all, Naomi's clever scheme. Although Naomi is a woman at the height of middle age, her body and beauty have not waned. In fact, Naomi is perhaps more radiant now than when she was

Ruth's age. Her skin is buoyant, her breasts resilient. Her eyes are magnets. But it would not look right, a woman of Naomi's age—much less one burdened with her dead son's wife—to be on the market, unless of course, her dead son's wife were to be married off. And so it was Naomi who suggested that Ruth go out dancing, take some French lessons, start working out, and it was Naomi who first knew Boaz, who first guided his hand towards Ruth's thigh. It was misleading, certainly, because Naomi wanted Boaz for herself. By then, surely, Ruth was devastatingly in love, but she was indebted to Naomi.

The day Boaz proposed, he indulged Ruth in unquantifiable ways: a quick trip to Paris for the most lavish dress, brunch with the Queen of England, a private concert by the Berlin Philharmonic, and of course, a spa treatment. Even then, she was surprised when she found a diamond ring at the bottom of her champagne glass. He thought it was original. Ruth used her hands to cover her smile. It was not that long ago that Naomi's son had used the very same tactic on her. She had found it cliché then, as she does now, but Naomi's son is dead and Ruth is a widow, and by any measure, Boaz is a fine man with fair wealth, and Ruth is not such a fool as to ignore any of these truths.

The night Boaz proposed, he demanded sex, but Ruth, being cunning, demanded that he again indulge her in unquantifiable ways, and once sated, she would give him sex. And so for hours, Boaz pleasured Ruth. For hours, Ruth sighed and hummed, until finally, exhausted from anticipation, she screamed. Then, she used the browned skin of her belly to clean off his face and called in Naomi to return his favor.

That night, Ruth went into the night and looked at the moon. It was large and distorted, more oval than round, a penny smashed by a train. She had never felt so invigorated and disgusted. She wanted to call Naomi a whore. She pursed her lips to squeeze out the sound but could not. Of course, she'd known Naomi was lingering outside their door all night. She knew Naomi was waiting for Boaz. She knew Naomi had been fucking him for months, and so only out of spite, she would not give Boaz what he was already getting from her mother-in-law.

There were lines, Ruth thought, between a wife and a mistress, and if a mistress provides a husband with a certain service, the wife should feel no obligation to provide that same service. Otherwise, there would be no necessity for the mistress.

No, Boaz would not get the same goods from both women, and for that reason alone, Ruth would be her husband's greatest conquest.

And so it was for years and years. Boaz would enter Ruth's quarters early in the evening, when the moon was close enough to touch, and he would pleasure her for hours. Some nights, the enticement of her body would be so keen that he would orgasm without being touched. Because she would not allow traditional penetration, Boaz would attempt to impregnate his wife by aiming his ejaculate as close to her as possible.

What Boaz did not know was that despite Ruth's shields and pride, it was out of fear that she would not allow penetration. Her first husband—Naomi's son—had died before they had consummated their marriage. Ruth was, in fact, a virgin.

The nights Boaz came and went from Ruth's quarters, she would lie in bed and listen for Naomi. Every time, Boaz would call out not Naomi but Ruth's name. Every time, as her mother-in-law fucked her husband, she would take a photograph when he called her name. On their backs, she inscribed, So cold and far away. They are a random assortment of photographs, most of them blurred and dark.

But Ruth loved those photographs as she loved Boaz.

During the day, Ruth had no obligations. She wandered around town, buying this and that. Then, she would return home and read or nap. All that was expected of her was that she dine exclusively with Boaz. It was not too much—he said—to ask of his own wife. And so for breakfast, lunch, tea, and dinner, Ruth would trek to the main house, where Boaz and Naomi lived, to eat with her husband. During those meals, Boaz would tell her about his day, his business ventures, his unconditional love. During those meals, Boaz would explain to Ruth how Naomi was not his wife. Surely, he could recognize his luck in having two beautiful women but what he wanted most was Ruth.

Ruth would listen and occasionally clarify her plans for the day if they conflicted with his.

Naomi was never invited to dine with them. Instead, her meals were brought up to her room, which although it was in the main house, was in a separate wing. Boaz insisted that his room should be shared by no one but his own wife.

Yes, of course, Naomi was jealous. And she did not know how to moderate her jealousy.

There were days when Naomi was so enraged that she would wedge herself into the china closet, just to spy on the married couple's mundane conversation. There were days when Naomi would ravage Ruth's room, looking for proof of infidelity or foul play. There were days when Naomi would gather strands of the married couple's discarded hair and stroke them against her face and stomach. She thought, Even their hair in better than mine. Then, there were nights when she would not lie with Boaz, arguing that she is at once his in-law's in-law and his mistress, and although she has at times been content with that, she can no longer tolerate it. Those nights, she would give Boaz an ultimatum, but before she could finish speaking, he would tell her he chooses Ruth.

Those nights, Naomi would laugh at him and say, Ruth! She'll never be the wife you want! She was my son's wife, and during that time, not once did she touch him. Not even an embrace!

Those nights, Boaz would laugh back and say, There is more to love than desire, Naomi. Perhaps that is why I don't love you.

Somehow, those nights would end in fucking.

Every morning, Boaz goes for long walks in his garden. He carries a pair of shears with him so that he can collect flowers for Ruth. Even in the winter, even when snow erases any semblance of color, Boaz brings Ruth a bouquet of fresh flowers. It is a small gesture of affection that a husband shows his wife.

Ruth is not without kindness. Although she offers Boaz neither flowers nor jewels, after dinner, she cleans his feet with warm soapy water and rubs them with lavender oil. It is a small gesture of affection. For them, this is more intimate than anything that could happen behind locked bedroom doors.

Ruth takes scores of photographs, many of which cannot be aptly labeled, So cold and far away. These photographs litter the walls of the main house. Boaz has each one professionally matted and framed. Even when Naomi wants to escape, these photographs stand as reminders that Ruth will always be first.

For their one month anniversary, Boaz gave Ruth a tripod.

For their one year anniversary, Boaz built Ruth a dark room.

Each day of the month that marks the day of their marriage, Boaz gives Ruth a gift relating to photography. Sometimes, it is something small—a new memory card, a new strap for her camera. Other times, his gifts are more extravagant.

The truth of it is that Ruth does love Boaz. She often thinks her love for him could literally kill her. And that is why she refuses to show it.

This is not say that Boaz has given nothing to Naomi, nor that she does not expect sumptuous gifts. But Boaz makes sure whatever gift he gives Ruth, he gives one of at least one-third the value to Naomi. He came upon this formula rather arbitrarily, and he rarely speaks of it.

Still, all the craftsmen and jewelers know Boaz and his preferences. As such, whenever he goes shopping, everyone knows to offer him selections in mismatched pairs: diamonds and topaz, necklaces and a pair of earrings. Everyone knows that Boaz will give Ruth the better selection, which she will only reluctantly accept, shyly, as if she were not even his wife, and he will give Naomi the lesser present, which she will wear with pride, as if she were not his wife's mother-in-law and his lowly mistress.

Although Ruth followed her mother-in-law across many lands when her husband died and although Ruth was given the choice—and let the record reflect that she was encouraged to go back to her family rather than stay with Naomi—she did not hesitate.

So long ago, ages ago, Ruth had said, For wherever you go, I will go; And wherever you lodge, I will lodge; Your people shall be my people, and your God, my God. Where you die, I will die, and there will I be buried.

She would come to regret this decision almost immediately, but at that moment, Ruth understood that Naomi was a lonely woman, one whose husband and sons had died, one who was left with neither money nor family. So when Ruth told Naomi she would follow her anywhere and be the faithful daughter she'd never had, she'd had no idea what to expect, but this arrangement, this was beyond any reasonable expectation for a faithful daughter.

Then came the day Ruth learned she was with child. That day, she locked herself in her closet and refused to emerge. She pulled her sweaters, hats, and scarves down to the ground and built a barricade around herself. There, she softly sang songs of mourning and death to herself and to her child. Even then, she knew it was impossible. Although her own mother had never taught her, Ruth knew where babies came from, and she had never done the necessary deeds to make a baby.

More importantly, however, Ruth understood that Boaz would never believe her fidelity. He would never trust that this child was his. He would call her a whore, as she'd wanted to call Naomi so many times, and banish her from his home, and Ruth would have nowhere to go. Worst of all, Ruth understood this baby, this child, would restore all authority to Naomi.

But perhaps even worse than the previous worst, Ruth thought, was the essential truth that she was faithful to Boaz, that she loved him immensely, and even worse than all that was that she could never say any of these things to him.

For three days, Ruth stayed in her closet, and those were the first times since their marriage that Ruth did not eat breakfast, lunch, and dinner with Boaz.

The first morning, Boaz waited patiently, unwilling to touch his eggs Benedict until Ruth arrived. The eggs eventually became so cold that when the maid came to remove the dish, the yolk had fully solidified.

For the first time in his entire life, Boaz missed breakfast.

More hurt than concerned, Boaz went about his day. Then came lunch.

Boaz sat at the table, his fingers drumming the hard wood of his chair. He was hungry. He was angry. But he refused to eat.

Then, finally, Boaz realized, almost by epiphany, that something must be wrong. He is a quick one, this Boaz.

That first day that Ruth stayed hidden in her closet, Boaz personally went to the kitchen. In many ways, he was surprised he even knew where it was. Boaz asked his cooks and his servants to prepare the most delicious meal for two and deliver it to Ruth's home. He told his butlers to enter quietly and set up a table and chairs, candlelight, the finest silver. He arranged for a cellist to serenade them.

But when they arrived in Ruth's house, they found no one there. Still, they set the table and chairs, the candles, the finest silver. They arranged the meal so that no servants would be necessary and Boaz could have complete privacy with Ruth. Even the cellist was instructed to perform in the main house and speakers were set up at the foot of the table, so to provide mood without being obtrusive. It was perfect. Boaz had not forgotten even the smallest detail. Except, of course, Ruth.

When Boaz arrived, he did not knock. He simply entered, as though expected. Boaz was surprised that Ruth was not there, not eager and anxious to see him, ready to wet his face with kisses. He walked through the house many times, which was not difficult because the house was rather compact. Boaz was angry. For Ruth, he'd endured many blows to the ego, but this, this was unforgivable.

But then, again, almost by epiphany, he searched the closets, and there, he found Ruth, sleeping under a pile of sweaters, her hand clenching a large stack of photographs.

Boaz was the first and only person, other than Ruth, to see these photographs, each with an engraved placard taped to its back that read, So Cold and Far Away. Although Boaz could not quite make out what many of the photographs were, others were recognizable.

And then he knew Ruth loved him, even if she could not say it herself.

Of all of this, Naomi knew nothing. That morning, Boaz had handed her a wad of cash and told her to visit the ocean for a few days of relaxation and pampering. He had not specified which ocean, which gave Naomi free reign. For months, she'd been feeling a steady suffocation. She wanted to run away. She was tired of Ruth and her antics. She was tired of being treated like some cheap whore, and even though Boaz would never treat a woman this way, Naomi often found herself wondering whether he thought of her more as mother or mistress.

To Ruth, she was a perpetual mother. To Boaz, she was a mistress on demand. It had grown so hard for her to play chameleon constantly.

So Naomi, that morning that Ruth locked herself in her closet, packed her bags and had the chauffeur take her as far away from land as he could. She knew nothing. That morning, Naomi unfettered.

Because Ruth would not come out, Boaz brought food to her, and together, in the closet, they picnicked over sweaters and scarves. In those dark, tight confines, Ruth talked constantly, openly, about everything except the reason why she refused to re-enter the world.

For three days, the married couple stayed hidden in Ruth's closet. The servants came and went with food, water, wine, fresh clothes. Only occasionally, Boaz would have to take a business call of the utmost importance, but Ruth remained nuzzled at his side so he could not consider it work. Hidden in

Ruth's closet, Boaz believed that he was truly the luckiest man in the world.

But soon, they would have to emerge. Both Ruth and Boaz understood this.

After three days, Ruth opened the closet door, crawled out, and stretched her legs and spine several times before standing. Boaz, with sleep still sealing his eyes, motioned for her return. Then, Ruth said, Boaz, I am with child. It is your child. I have not been unfaithful. I am your wife, and I will be the mother to your child.

Later, Boaz would come to understand what an occasion this was, but right then, he merely responded, I love you.

Of course, Ruth was disgusted by this cliché, but she whispered, lightly, into his ear, I love you too, Boaz.

Then, she divested herself and offered Boaz her virginity.

She took a picture of the spots of blood on her sheets, and her husband engraved the placard. Together, they taped it to the back of the plastic frame and kept it hidden in a locked drawer, lest Naomi came snooping, which she inevitably would.

The day Naomi returned from her visit to the ocean, she was no longer mistress. That day, she learned of all she had missed. That day, she sighed to herself, Grandmother.

Because she can no longer be mistress or mother, Naomi asked to name the child.

Ruth had been partial to the name Bernard. Boaz had preferred Pauline or Harold.

But the day Ruth gave birth to a healthy baby boy, they held up the child to Naomi who clearly and articulately said, Obed.

And so Ruth begat Obed, who begat Jesse, who begat David—David who would become the greatest of kings.

OUR RETELLERS...

MATT BELL is the author of *How They Were Found* (Keyhole Press), as well as three chapbooks, *Wolf Parts* (Keyhole Press), *The Collectors* (Caketrain Press), and *How the Broken Lead the Blind* (Willows Wept Press). His fiction has appeared in *Conjunctions, Hayden's Ferry Review, Willow Springs, Unsaid,* and *American Short Fiction,* and has been selected for inclusion in anthologies such as *Best American Mystery Stories 2010* and *Best American Fantasy 2.*

CRISPIN BEST is putting together a collection of short stories dedicated to every year since 1400. He lives in London, next door to the house he grew up in. His fiction has appeared in many journals, including *Dogzplot, Killauthor, Pequin, Wigleaf, Yankee Pot Roast.*

J. BRADLEY is the author of *Dodging Traffic* (Ampersand Books) and the author of the flash fiction chapbook *The Serial Rapist Sitting Behind You Is A Robot* (Safety Third Enterprises). He is the Interview Editor of *PANK Magazine* and lives at iheartfailure.net.

JEFF BREWER is from Portland. He now lives in New York. He is curiously bipolar. His writing has appeared in *Oregon Literary Review, The Portland Review, Promethean,* and is forthcoming in *The Ampersand Review.*

BLAKE BUTLER is the author of the novella *Ever* and the novel-in-stories *Scorch Atlas,* named Novel of the Year by *3:AM Magazine.* His novel *This Is No Year* is forthcoming from Harper Perennial. He edits *HTML Giant,* "The internet literature magazine blog of the future," as well as two journals of innovative text, *Lamination Colony* and *No Colony.* His writing has appeared in *The Believer, Unsaid, Fence,* and Dzanc's *Best of the Web 2009,* and has been shortlisted in *Best American Nonrequired Reading* and widely online and in print.

TERESA BUZZARD has a smile that sank a thousand ships. Once, she smiled at a polar bear picture and the ice caps began to melt. Her smile is a team of abductors waiting to kidnap your boyfriend's heart and, without extra equipment, that of your girlfriend as well. Her smile escaped from a maximum security penitentiary, to be found later tattooed into the wrists of Bohemian artists and their lovers. Teresa's smile can cut diamonds. She is fond of beauty and chases it relentlessly.

PETER CONNERS is author of the memoir, *Growing Up Dead: The Hallucinated Confessions of a Teenage Deadhead* (Da Capo Press). His new book, *White Hand Society: The Psychedelic Partnership of Timothy Leary & Allen Ginsberg*, was recently published by City Lights. His other books include the prose poetry collection *Of Whiskey and Winter* and the novella *Emily Ate the Wind.* His next poetry collection, *The Crows Were Laughing in their Trees*, is forthcoming from White Pine Press in spring 2011. He is also editor of *PP/FF: An Anthology*, which was published by Starcherone Book. His writing appears regularly in such journals as *Poetry International, Mississippi Review, Brooklyn Rail, Fiction International, Salt Hill, Hotel Amerika, Mid-American Review, The Bitter Oleander,* and *Beloit Fiction Journal.*

DARCIE DENNIGAN'S first book, *Corinna A-Maying the Apocalypse*, won the Poets Out Loud prize and was published by Fordham University Press. Her poems and other writing have appeared in *180 More: Extraordinary Poems for Every Day, Atlantic Monthly, The Believer, Tin House*, and elsewhere. She is a recipient of a "Discovery"/*The Nation* award and a Bread Loaf Writers' Conference fellowship. She is currently Writer in Residence at University of Connecticut.

ERIN FITZGERALD'S stories have appeared in fine publications such as *PANK, Hobart, Word Riot, Monkeybicycle,* and *Necessary Fiction.* She writes, teaches, and lives in western Connecticut.

HEATHER FOWLER is the author of *Suspended Heart* (Aqueous Books). Her work has appeared in many journals, including *Necessary Fiction, Dark Sky Magazine, Word Riot, Exquisite Corpse,* and *Mississippi Review.* She is an editor at *Corium Magazine.*

TIMOTHY GAGER is the author of eight books of short fiction and poetry. The most recent being *Treating a Sick Animal: Flash and Micro Fictions* (Cervena Barva Press). He hosts the Dire Literary Series in

Cambridge, Massachusetts, and is the co-founder of the Somerville News Writers Festival. He has published over 200 works of fiction and poetry, of which eight have been nominated for the Pushcart Prize. He is the current Fiction Editor of *The Wilderness House Literary Review* and the founding co-editor of *The Heat City Literary Review.*

MOLLY GAUDRY is the author of the verse novel *We Take Me Apart* (Mud Luscious), and the editor of *Tell: An Anthology of Expository Narrative* (Flatmancrooked) She is the founding editor of the environmental literature journal *Willows Wept Review*, co-founding editor of *Twelve Stories*, and interviews editor for *Keyhole Magazine.* She runs Cow Heavy Books, a chapbook publishing company, and she is a regular contributor to the arts and culture site Big Other.

ROXANE GAY has appeared in *Artifice, Annalemma, Mid-American Review, Mud Luscious, Monkeybicycle, McSweeney's Internet Tendency*, and many other journals. She is an associate editor of *PANK* and a frequent contributor to HTML Giant.

ALICIA GIFFORD'S short fiction has been widely published in journals and anthologies online and in print. She divides her time between the Los Angeles area and Mammoth Lakes, California. She has watched a lot of *I Love Lucy* episodes.

DANIEL GRANDBOIS' writing has been described as "Dr. Seuss for adults," "avant-garde standup," and "between Brautigan's and Basho's." He is the author of *Unlucky Lucky Days* (a Believer Book Award Reader Survey Selection, an ABA Indie Next Notable Book, and a CCLaP Best Experimental Book) and of *The Hermaphrodite: An Hallucinated Memoir*, an art novel with forty original woodcuts by renowned Argentine artist Alfredo Benavidez Bedoya. His writing appears in many journals and anthologies, including *Conjunctions, Boulevard, Mississippi Review*, and *Fiction.* Also a musician, Grandbois plays in three of the pioneering bands of "The Denver Sound": Slim Cessna's Auto Club, Tarantella, and Munly.

STEVE HIMMER'S stories have appeared in various journals and anthologies. He edits the web journal *Necessary Fiction*, and teaches at Emerson College in Boston. His novel *The Bee-Loud Glad* is forthcoming from Atticus Books.

LILY HOANG'S first book, *Parabola*, won the Chiasmus Press Un-Doing the Novel Contest. She is also the author of the novels *Changling*

(Fairy Tale Review Press) and *The Evolutionary Revolution* (Les Figues Press). She is currently a Visiting Assistant Professor of English & Women's Studies at Saint Mary's College in Indiana.

SAMANTHA HUNT is the author of *The Invention of Everything Else* (Houghton Mifflin) and *The Seas* (Picador). Her short fiction has appeared in *The New Yorker* and *McSweeneys* and on *This American Life.*

HENRY JENKINS is the Provost's Professor of Communication, Journalism, and Cinematic Arts at the University of Southern California. He is the author and/or editor of twelve books on various aspects of media and popular culture, including *Textual Poachers: Television Fans and Participatory Culture, Hop on Pop: The Politics and Pleasures of Popular Culture* and *From Barbie to Mortal Kombat: Gender and Computer Games.* His newest books include *Convergence Culture: Where Old and New Media Collide* and *Fans, Bloggers and Gamers: Exploring Participatory Culture.* He is currently co-authoring a book on "spreadable media" with Sam Ford and Joshua Green. He has written for *Technology Review, Computer Games, Salon,* and *The Huffington Post.*

TIM JONES-YELVINGTON lives and writes in Chicago. His work has appeared or is forthcoming in *Annalemma, Keyhole, Monkeybicycle, PANK, Ampersand Review, Smokelong Quarterly, Storyglossia* and others. He edited *Flushed,* a chapbook of fiction by women about menopause, available from Bannock Street Books.

MICHAEL KIMBALL'S third novel, *Dear Everybody* is now in paperback in the US, UK, and Canada. *The Believer* calls it "a curatorial masterpiece." *Time Out New York* calls the writing "stunning." And the *Los Angeles Times* says the book is "funny and warm and sad and heartbreaking." His first two novels are *The Way the Family Got Away* (2000) and *How Much of Us There Was* (2005). His work has been featured on NPR's *All Things Considered* and in *Vice,* as well as *The Guardian, Prairie Schooner, Post Road, Open City, Unsaid,* and *New York Tyrant.* He is also responsible for *Michael Kimball Writes Your Life Story (on a postcard)*—and two documentary films, *I Will Smash You* (2009) and *60 Writers/60 Places* (2010).

TOM LA FARGE published three books of fiction with Sun & Moon: the novel *The Crimson Bears* and its second part *A Hundred Doors,* and a book of fablels, *Terror of Earth.* Green Integer published his second novel,

Zuntig, in 2001. Tom is now at work on a manual of constrained (Oulipian) writing, *13 Writhing Machines*, a series of pamphlets being published by Proteotypes, the press where he is managing editor. *Administrative Assemblages*, the first, came out in 2008, the second, *Homomorphic Converters*, in 2009, and the third, *Echo Alternators*, in 2010. His chapbook, *Life and Conversation of Animals*, a set of cut-up assemblages from G. White's *The Natural History of Selborne*, appeared in August, 2010. "Wood Well" is part of a play, *Night & Silence.*

JOSH MADAY has been published or has work forthcoming in *New York Tyrant, elimae, Phoebe, Apostrophe Cast, Keyhole Magazine, Lamination Colony, Action Yes, Word Riot, Barrelhouse, Opium*, and elsewhere. He co-edited, with Jeff Vande Zande, *On the Clock: Contemporary Shorts Stories of Work* (Bottom Dog Press). He reviews books and literary magazines and is a member of the National Book Critics Circle.

MICHAEL MARTONE is the author of twelve books of fiction and non-fiction, including *Unconventions: Attempting the Art of Craft and the Craft of Art* and *Double-Wide: Collected Fiction of Michael Martone.* His work has been recognized with two NEA Fellowships and the AWP Book Award for Non-Fiction. He teaches in the program for Creative Writing at the University of Alabama.

ZACHARY MASON is the author of *The Lost Books of the Odyssey* (Starcherone Books/Farrar, Straus and Giroux).

COREY MESLER has published in numerous journals and anthologies. He has published four novels, a book of short stories, numerous chapbooks and one full-length poetry collection. He has been nominated for a Pushcart numerous times, and two of his poems have been chosen for Garrison Keillor's Writer's Almanac. He runs a bookstore in Memphis.

PEDRO PONCE is the author of two fiction chapbooks, *Superstitions of Apartment Life* (Burnside Review Press) and *Alien Autopsy* (Willows Wept Press). His fiction has appeared in *Ploughshares, The Beacon Best of 2001, Double Room, Minima, Gargoyle, Alaska Quarterly Review* and *Quick Fiction.* He teaches at St. Lawrence University.

JOSEPH RIIPPI is the author of the novel *Do Something! Do Something! Do Something!* (Ampersand Books). Recent writing appears in *The Brooklyn Rail, PANK, Everyday Genius, elimae, Emprise Review, Epiphany, The Bitter*

Oleander, and *Salamander*. His latest book, *The Orange Suitcase*, is coming in 2011 from Ampersand. He lives in New York.

KATHLEEN ROONEY is a founding editor of Rose Metal Press and the author, most recently, of the memoir *Live Nude Girl: My Life as an Object* and the essay collection *For You, For You I Am Trilling These Songs.* Her first book of poetry, *Oneiromance (an epithalamion)* was released by the feminist publisher Switchback Books.

JIM RULAND is the author *Big Lonesome* (Gorsky Press). His fiction and nonfiction have appeared in *The Barcelona Review, The Believer, Black Warrior Review, Esquire, Hobart, L.A. Weekly, Los Angeles Times, McSweeney's, Opium, Oxford American, Village Voice*, and *Razorcake.* He is the recipient of numerous awards, including a fellowship from the National Endowment for the Arts. He hosts Vermin on the Mount, an irreverent reading series in the heart of L.A.'s Chinatown.

SHYA SCANLON is the author of the poetry collection *In This Alone Impulse* (Noemi Press), and the novel *Forecast* (Flatmancrooked). He received his MFA from Brown University, where he was awarded the John Hawkes Prize in Fiction.

CURTIS SMITH is the author of the novels *Sound and Noise* and *Truth or Something Like It* (both from Casperian Press) and the story collections *The Species Crown* and *Bad Monkey* (both from Press 53). Sunnyoutside Press will soon release his essay collection *The Agnostic's Prayer.* His stories and essays have appeared in over sixty literary journal and have been cited by *The Best American Short Stories, The Best American Mystery Stories*, and *The Best American Spiritual Writing.*

WENDY WALKER'S most recent books are *Hysterical Operators: The Inspector of Factories Visits the Lover of Melodrama*, and *Blue Fire*, both from Proteotypes. She is a core collaborator at Proteus Gowanus, an interdisciplinary gallery/reading room in Brooklyn, where (with Tom La Farge) she runs The Writhing Society, a salon for the practice and invention of constrained writing techniques. Her other books include *The Secret Service, The Sea-Rabbit, or, The Artist of Life and Stories Out of Omarie*c (Sun & Moon) and *Knots* (Aqueduct Press.)